THE ULTIMATE BETRAYAL

By Gráinne Farrell

Copyright © Gráinne Farrell 2021

Contents

PROLOGUE

My dearest Bill,

I'm sorry I didn't wake you, but you looked much too peaceful to disturb. I have a busy day ahead and know you're going home later to your mouse. Thanks for an amazing weekend; it was a great way to celebrate my birthday. You are just as desirable now as the first night we were together. Like, what's it now? Must be a year at least! Well my darling, enough for now, I must run. Au revoir.

R

Xxx

CHAPTER 1

A crow swooped down flapping its dark grey wings with an air of authority and succeeded in dislodging the little robin from its perch. Laura watched from the upstairs window as the robin flew down to the ground, settling on a large stone along the flower bed, warily watching its aggressor. A shiver ran down her spine and Laura shook herself. The scene was not unlike one she had endured before.

The curtains began to move slightly which caused her to frown. There must be a draught coming in somewhere, as both windows of the double glazed were shut tightly. She would have to get Bill to look at it. Although chance might be a fine thing considering he was hardly ever home anymore.

'MAM,' shouted her firstborn Jessica, startling Laura. 'MAM,' came the bellow from the kitchen.

'Why on earth are you shouting like that? For god's sake, the neighbours will be wondering what's going on,' scowled Laura at her fifteen-year-old daughter as she came down the stairs, though she was inwardly smiling.

She strolled into the kitchen pleased to see Jessica tidying up after her breakfast, wiping down the large island top in the kitchen. It looked as though she had spilled some orange juice and it was beginning to drip onto the floor. Laura walked across the kitchen, passed the large window over the sink looking out to the back of the house. The utility room was quite small and just about fitted the washing machine and dryer, along with the mop and bucket. Moving back to the spillage, she started to clean the floor. Jessica looked up at her with the same dark brown eyes as her husband Bill had done so many times.

'I'm sorry Mam. I just sort of knew you'd be lost in thought, so I shouted to get your attention. What do you think of this top I'm wearing? Does my tummy look big in it?'

Her daughter had inherited her paternal grandmother's hair colour, with a lovely long golden-brown mane. Thank god that's all she had inherited from her.

'Jessica, darling, everything you put on looks good on you. You have a fantastic figure'.

Her daughter frowned crossly at her in response.

'Mam don't call me Jessica, it's Jess! How many times do I have to tell you? Even Dad has the hang of it now, and that's surprising since he's never here.'

Laura's eyes lowered and she sucked in a breath. Crossing the kitchen, she sat down at the table at the far end. There were magazines and newspapers thrown across it, with several pens and pencils. She made a mental note to go through it all later and clear it up.

Turning to her daughter, she replied, 'Don't say that sweetheart, your dad works hard to keep a roof over our heads and…'

Jess stood abruptly now, hands in the air, and interrupted her.

'Ye, ye, ye heard it all before, and to put food on the table and clothes on our backs. I just think he should spend a bit more time with you. I don't like you being alone; you should have gone with him.'

Laura's heart contracted and she began to blink rapidly. She stood up now herself and started to tidy the mess on the table. Taking a deep breath, she said, 'Jess, pet, I like having some time to myself, it gives me a chance to catch up with the girls and that.'

Well, this was partly true; she was meeting the girls that weekend as Bill was away in Brussels on business. Laura would have liked to have gone with him, but he didn't think this was a good idea. He had a lot of work to do and she would be bored. Laura had been disappointed, but at the same time knew her husband had a point.

Although she was beginning to wonder lately where the fun had gone between them. They never found time to do anything together anymore. Even just to walk the dog. Something they used to do all the time. It gave them a great chance in their otherwise busy lives to have a good catch-up and general banter. Laura loved their walks. Bill would always have her laughing like a schoolgirl, pointing out people and making funny comments.

He would pick her up and twirl her around on the footpath. Or sometimes he would pretend he was blind and get Laura to hold his arm. Oh god, that was terrible when she thought about it now. Mocking is catching and all that. But they did have great times. One day on the promenade just down from the beach, there was a woman walking in front of them. Her skirt had been torn at the back and you could see her underwear. They couldn't stop laughing. She and Bill really acted like two kids that day. It didn't help that the woman's knickers were bright pink with polka dots. Laura had a pain in her arm trying to restrain Bill from running up to the woman and saying something.

She tried to resume these walks occasionally, but her husband was always doing something, or going somewhere, or had work to catch up on. 'Oh, stop overthinking things,' she scolded herself.

'Jesus, Mam. What on earth can you be thinking about?' cried Jess as she broke into Laura's thoughts. Her daughter was tying her shoelaces using a stool for support.

'If you were in my class, you'd be in trouble all the time. You have the attention span of a goldfish,' she teased her mother.

Laura's eyes twinkled as she replied, 'Don't be so cheeky young girl, I have a lot on my mind. You wouldn't hear Amy Dawson speaking to her mum like that,' she scolded, waiting on her daughter's inevitable reaction. Amy Dawson was Jessica's best friend since they were young kids and very pleasant.

'Yeah, right, she even swears at her mam. I heard her just last week when I was staying over. Her dad sent her to her room and so the two of us had nothing to do all evening. I'd never swear at you though, Mam. I'm sorry for being cheeky,' Jess said, looking at the floor.

God give me patience, thought Laura, as she stood up from the table and walked over towards her daughter.

'That's okay, now that top is fine. Go and brush your hair, Amy will be here soon.

'Okay Mam, thanks, you're not that bad!' shouted Jess as she ran from the kitchen.

'Not that bad,' Laura repeated the words quietly. She didn't know what to make of that. Coming from a fifteen-year-old girl, she supposed it was nice.

She knew before the doorbell rang that Amy was here as Barney, the three-year-old mongrel, was barking and yelping in delight. He had been having a nap over beside the stove in the kitchen. Although the fire was not actually on, it was still lukewarm from the night before. He had a little bed beside it, which Laura had bought for him in the local pet store a couple of years before. It was a bit ragged now from its monthly wash.

She should buy him a new one, now that she thought about it. Barney continued to yelp in delight, waiting impatiently to greet whoever was coming up the path. Honestly, she thought, if a burglar tried to break in Barney would welcome them licking their faces and thumping his tail in delight.

Laura opened the front door just as Amy arrived on the front step. She was dressed similarly to her daughter and blinked a few times as she looked up at Laura, pushing back one of her black curls from her face.

She was a pretty girl with a striking petite figure.

'Hi, Amy, Jessica's on her way,' Laura said as she waved out at Amy's mother Paula, who was letting down the window of her open top BMW.

'Hi Laura,' she called in a loud piercing voice. 'I'm dropping the girls into town. I was going to bring the jeep, but it was low on diesel, so I had to take my baby instead,' she boasted, a wide smile on her face.

Never heard of a petrol station you stuck-up plastic bitch? Laura had to stop herself from saying. She found it difficult to listen to Amy's mother. Amy might have inherited her mother's hair and looks, but she got her good nature from her father. Laura braced herself and replied, 'Oh it's lovely.' She turned as her daughter came out of the front door and passed her.

'Have a great time love, and you too Amy, I'll see you later.' She went to go back into the house as she could not stomach any more boasting from Miss Perfect. Before she was inside, her daughter suddenly grabbed her and wrapped her two arms around her mother.

'You sure you're OK, Mam? I won't go if you'd rather I stayed?' Laura's heart tightened. A massive lump formed in her throat, and she swallowed a couple of times before managing to say, 'Don't be so silly, get out and enjoy yourself, sure your brother will be home in an hour or so. Go on, I'm sick looking at you anyway,' she joked hoping that Jess wouldn't notice the shake in her voice. It seemed she hadn't, as she replied, 'OK, Mam, see you later,' and with that bounded down the step into the classy sports car. Jessica took after her mother when it came to her height, with her slight build and long legs, they both had an athletic appearance. But Jessica's bust seemed to be from other genes, as they were bigger than her mother's already. Laura blushed to herself at this thought.

She walked back into the kitchen, pottering around making a mental list of things to be done, a frequent habit of hers. Messages to be looked at and jobs to be sorted around the house. She was trying to block out the persistent black cloud that was forming in her mind. She didn't want to think about it.

Putting the kettle on, she decided to relax for half an hour before Ben came home. She smiled now when she thought of her son. He was such a pleasant child, always trying to please her and his dad. He had a real happy-go-lucky attitude. Nothing fazed him. With his mousy brown hair, and a small cluster of freckles around his nose, it was all Laura could do not to squeeze him in a big hug each time she saw him. No doubt his clothes would be in a state after his rugby match that morning. He was playing locally today; the pitch was just a five minutes' drive away. Laura usually went to his games, but this morning she had wanted to make a dent in the housework.

It was early November, and the kids were off school for a few days. Something to do with a teacher strike. Laura couldn't keep up; she felt there was always something keeping the children out of school. Teacher meetings, opening days, heating breaking down, Teacher off sick, and the list went on.

The local rugby coaches had taken advantage of the strike and arranged a game which suited Laura just fine. The thought of Christmas made her feel depressed. It wasn't that she didn't like Christmas; it was the fact that she would have to cook for Bill's mother this year. Pauline Murphy was a force to be reckoned with. AKA, a bossy old cow.

Laura sat back suddenly as Barney interrupted her thoughts, jumping up putting his paws on her knees and prodding her with his head. He had his lead in his mouth and she felt pangs of guilt for not taking him out for his morning walk. She could ask Ben to do it when he came home, but he would probably be sore and tired from the rugby.

'Ahh,' Laura sighed aloud. 'Come on Barney, I would say we'll just about fit a walk in before your other master arrives home.'

Two days later the familiar song blasting from Jessica's mobile phone, made Laura drag herself out of bed to answer it. After shouting several times but to no avail she got out of her warm comfortable bed. Storming across the landing, she went into Jessica's bedroom, to find she wasn't there. Laura picked up the phone at the same time realising her daughter was gone to her Saturday job in the local shop.

'Hello,' she sighed, fully expecting one of Jess's friends to start yapping down the line.

'Jess love, how are you?' came her husband's voice. She sat down on Jessica's bed and was somewhat taken aback.

'It's me, Laura.' She spoke very quickly. 'Is everything OK?' Her heart was hammering in her chest.

'Oh, eh, I was just ringing to see how Jess was,' he volunteered. Bill didn't sound like himself... Something wasn't quite right.

'Oh, how come you didn't call me first? You said you'd ring last night but you didn't. Is something up?' she stammered. She was rubbing down the duvet with her hand and making a mental note to hoover Jess's room later. It was like she was trying to fill her head with subjects other than her husband.

'No, no, don't be such a worrier. I'm sorry I didn't phone last night, I got held up in a meeting. I was calling Jess first because this is her break time in work, and then I was going to ring you honey,' Bill explained. She supposed that made sense. But wasn't sure why he sounded so off if that really was the case. Ah, well. Maybe she would give him the benefit of the doubt. After all, all he had done was call her daughter instead of her. It was just out of character for him.

'Ah OK,' she replied in a cheery voice. 'So, how are you getting on there? What time will I pick you up at from the airport?' she asked noticing at the same time that Jessica's posters had been removed and replaced with collages of photos of her and her friends.

'I have been very busy all weekend; it's been crazy. I won't need you to collect me. I'm not sure what time I'll be back at. I'll get a taxi firm at the airport rather than having you on standby all day. That wouldn't be fair,' he replied.

'No, honestly Bill, I'm looking forward to seeing you and so are the kids. I'll pick you up. Just give me a buzz. The airport is only twenty minutes from here,' Laura spoke very fast, which she realised, was becoming a habit.

'No, no, I know you mean well Laura, but it wouldn't be fair on you. Look honey, I got to go, I'll see you tomorrow, OK, bye. I love you,' her husband replied in a rushed tone. Laura pleaded with him to allow her to collect him, but her pleas were in vain as he was gone.

CHAPTER 2

Laura descended the stairs, her shoulders low and her heart heavy. The phone in the hall began to ring. She ran to it, thinking and hoping it might be Bill. She stopped beside it, taking a breath and telling herself not to sound so needy. To her disappointment it wasn't him. 'Hiya, hun, you all ready for tonight?' Her friend sounded full of the joys. Laura took a minute to respond.

'Hello, are you there?' Sharon asked.

'Oh yes, sorry, Shaz, Yes, of course I'm ready. Looking forward to seeing everyone. It's been a while since I saw the rest of the girls.' Laura tried her best to sound in good spirits and keep her worries from her friend.

But Sharon knew her better than anyone and her tone suddenly changed.

'Is everything all right; you don't sound yourself?'

Was she OK, Laura wondered to herself now? She felt fine, she wasn't sick or anything. But there was something bothering her, she didn't know what exactly. Something to do with Bill. And his behavior the past while. She had been blocking it out, making excuses. But she wasn't sure she could do it much longer.

Laura wanted to clear the air with him. Get answers for some of the things that weren't adding up lately. But she wasn't ready to confide in her friend.

'Don't be silly, I'm grand.' Pausing for a moment she continued, 'So, what are you wearing tonight? Shall we go extra sexy or sophisticated?' She could hear Sharon laugh at this and she came back with, 'Neither, it's got to be smart casual. We're going to some place in the middle of nowhere in the mountains outside Dublin! Gabby said it's meant to do fantastic food and they have a band at 9.30. It's supposed to draw a good crowd at weekends. Or so she said.'

Mmmmmmm… Laura thought to herself. She wasn't sure how she felt about being dragged to some dump in the middle of the country.

It wasn't her idea of a good night out. Sounded more for couples. But she was looking forward to seeing the others. And they did always have a good time no matter where they went. 'OK, let's take Gabby's word for it. So what time are we heading off at? We're hardly getting a taxi all the way down there?'

'No, are you crazy? That would cost us a fortune. Gabby has organized a small minibus; the driver is a friend of her husband Dick. There are five of us, so it suits brilliantly, as taxis nowadays only take four. Not like the old days when there would be seven or eight of us hanging out of the windows and doors,' reminisced Shaz. 'Oh ye. And if any of us get sick in the bus we probably won't have to pay the fine with him being a mate of Dick's and that.'

Laura wasn't shocked at this outburst. She was used to Sharon's way. But she still said, 'For god's sake, you are unreal. I think I might organize my own taxi if that's the way you're thinking.'

Laura didn't want to have a lot to drink tonight and then end up with a hangover the next day. Especially as she wanted to spend some time with Bill, see if something was wrong.

'Ah relax Laura; you know I'm only joking with you. Right so, I better go, I must collect Rob from the football and pretend I care whether they won or lost. You know how it is,' Shaz sighed.

'Yes, I do indeed. OK, Sharon, I'll see you later then, is it still 7.30?' asked Laura.

'Yep, sure is, make sure you're ready, we don't want to be hanging around in that mini bus for long because by the sounds of it the bus is a bit old and skittery. That wouldn't do for the folk in Clontarf now, would it. The neighbours will start a protest to get you out of the neighbourhood! Ha! Right, I'm going now. I'll talk to you later, byyeee.'

Sharon didn't even wait for Laura to reply as she ended the call. She was getting used to that lately. Sharon was Laura's best friend since school. They had always been together, primary school, secondary and then to college where they both studied Business Management. Her friend's mane of blonde hair and vivacious personality making her the more outgoing of the two. Not that Laura minded. She was happy for Sharon to take the reins in their friendship, being much more the laid-back one.

Laura began to make a mental list of what she needed to do before her night out. Jess and Ben were staying at her parents. They lived in Castleknock, about a thirty-minute drive, depending on traffic. Thankfully, her dad was in the city doing some errands, so he had collected them on the way home. Laura was very close to her mother and the rest of her family at that. Her mam Gilly had a huge heart and always on hand if needed. Her father was cut from the same cloth too. He had always been there for them. They were a close family and got on well with all the neighbours and always joined in the local community events.

When Laura's brother Shane had got married, they welcomed his wife Emma into the family as one of their own. Shane and Laura moved to London after Shane got a new job over there. It was sad in a way, as Laura didn't get to see them much. She missed her little chats with her younger brother, and the friendly banter they used to engage in. Shane loved to tease Laura about the boy bands she used to follow. She had tons of posters all over her bedroom.

Her parents used to laugh, saying they needn't have bought any wallpaper for the room, as there wasn't an inch of it you could see. Laura teased Shane about his crush on Sharon. He was like her little shadow, following her around all over the house when she stayed over. Laura smiled at her memories. Then she shuddered as she remembered what had triggered her thoughts. Pauline Murphy – her beloved mother-in-law. Not.

Laura made the huge mistake of believing that all mothers and families were close.

No, no, not in Pauline Murphy's books (or the poisonous dwarf as Laura had secretly renamed her). Bill's mother honestly thought butter wouldn't melt in his mouth. Forget about her Laura, enjoy tonight, she scolded herself.

Jess had been a bit annoyed at not being treated as an adult. She was at the stage where she didn't need a babysitter, or so she thought. However, the kids loved their grandparents, so she knew her daughter would be fine. Laura had tried on three different outfits by now and still didn't know what to wear, or what *smart casual* was for a pub in the middle of nowhere for that matter!

She ended up wearing a pair of skinny blue jeans, a black fitted blouse and her black boots. She looked in the mirror and as her reflection glanced back at her she decided that she'd do. Her hair fell nicely on her shoulders, and she would have easily passed for thirty (well, thirty -five maybe). She sprayed some Chanel Mademoiselle on her neck, chest and hair, an excellent tip she received a few years ago as the smell lingers better, and then fumbled round for a suitable jacket. The doorbell startled her.

She was used to Barney going crazy before anyone had the chance to get near the door. However, he had gone with the kids to her parents. She didn't like leaving Barney on his own in the house, so she tried to avoid it as much as she could. Her father was very fond of the dog he had bought for her. Laura grabbed her denim blue jacket and bounded down the stairs, feeling her mood lift and excitement build about meeting the girls, despite her earlier misgivings. She still ached for Bill to come home. But she was going to enjoy herself tonight and put him to the back of her mind for now. Tomorrow was another day.

And maybe she and Bill would spend a romantic night together. That's what they needed. It had been four weeks since she had last made love to Bill. Maybe tomorrow night if he was lucky. Or if she was lucky, for that matter.

Sharon had been right. The mini bus was ridiculous. She was also right about the neighbours. They would be ashamed. A lot of them were stuck-up and fitted right in with Paula Dawson. Just as well she didn't really mix with them. Laura could see some curtains twitching and her face began to burn in embarrassment. Bill would have a good laugh at this if he were here. Although she doubted, he'd dare get into it.

The door roared back, paint falling of it as it rolled.

'Hiya Laura,' screeched Carol. 'Great to see you again, you're looking well.'

Damn, damn, damn, thought Laura. So much for trying to be discreet. With Carol shouting out her name they were sure to know

Laura knew them. She felt shallow for thinking this about her closest friends, but she couldn't help it. Some of her neighbours were such snobs she hated them sneering at her or giving them something to talk about.

'Hi girlies, how are we all?' Laura tried to sound enthusiastic. For the next forty-five minutes the girls chattered away as if they saw each other every day, and not six months ago. It was always the same with them. They could go such long periods without speaking to each other, but once they did manage to catch up, nothing changed between them. Carol, Becky and Gabby were good friends and they had all spent a lot of time together in their much younger carefree years. But as they got older, life had got in the way as it does, and Laura didn't see as much of them anymore. She still saw a lot of Sharon though, and thanked god they were still very close. Becky and Gabby were the two loudest in the group, always up to mischief and creating havoc. But they were good girls. Carol was quieter, more level-headed, although she had a very witty nature and would have them in stiches at times. Her overall quiet-natured, grounded appearance added to her funny stories and comments. Sharon and herself, Laura thought, were a mixture of the three. They had their moments, she supposed; although Sharon was more boisterous than herself, Laura liked to think.

Luckily there was not much traffic and so their journey was shorter than they had all anticipated.

'Drop us off round the corner, we don't want people seeing us getting out of this thing,' Becky cried.

Thank god, thought Laura, someone feels the same as me.

But she was glad she hadn't voiced her thoughts aloud, as an angry response came.

'Don't be so ungrateful. Jamie has put himself out to bring us all down here for free and all you can do is moan about people seeing you,' Gabby shouted.

Becky lowered her gaze, looking a bit shame-faced, as did Laura. 'Suppose,' mumbled Becky, but not before Laura caught a hint of a smile in her response. Laura tried but failed to keep a straight face and then they all burst out laughing. Ah, it felt good to be with the girls again.

'OK, Jamie, you can leave us here, it will be easier for you to turn. Could you pick us up after midnight, around half past please?' Gabby asked the driver. Jamie looked relieved to have the first leg of the journey over. His head must surely be fried with all the giggling and screeching from them. 'No problem,' he replied with an exaggerated grin.

It being November, it was a cold and dark night. Just as well there was a footpath. The sight of the pub gave Laura a pleasant surprise. It was lit up by several decorative lamps. Two bay windows showed people inside both eating and drinking. It looked very welcoming. Smoke bellowed from three different spouts which signaled that three fires were roaring inside.

The smell of food was delicious, and her tummy rumbled violently as if in protest for not receiving any food for eight hours. She was saving herself for tonight and by the look and smell of things she had done the right thing. Carol opened the door and they all scrambled into the warmth; pushing and shoving each other, as well as teasing and joking. It was quite embarrassing when they realised they had come in the side door which left them directly in the middle of the restaurant. It wasn't even an official door but an emergency exit that had been open. Everyone stopped to stare at the loud newcomers in disapproval.

Laura found it very amusing, it wasn't as if she knew any of them. The restaurant seemed to be made up of different areas; it wasn't just one big room. There were little corners here and there and Laura counted three parts that made an L-turn off to the sides, tables laid out the whole way. It was obviously quite large, but in a cozy, intimate way. There were large wooden beams across the roof, and Laura could see two large stoves burning ferociously. A lady dressed in a black and white uniform came over. They all awaited a scolding. However, the woman turned out to be very pleasant and smiled from one girl to the other. 'Happens a lot in here, our own fault for not keeping the door closed,' she smiled. 'Your table isn't quite ready yet; would you like to go into the back lounge? It's usually quieter in there than the bar, and the fire is on.'

'That's great, thanks a lot, we'll do just that.' Sharon took over. Gabby was still getting over the embarrassment of barging into the restaurant as she had seen a man that worked with her at *Nationphone*, the mobile phone company.

'I think I'll go to the bathroom first,' said Laura.

'Me too,' piped up Becky.

'OK, we'll see you in there, we'll get the drinks in,' Gabby said. In the bathroom, Laura and Becky were brushing their hair when a woman stropped in wearing high heels, the shortest skirt Laura had ever seen and a top that shouted expensive boutique.

As Laura's eyes travelled up the woman's body and reached her face, she nearly dropped onto the floor. Her throat went dry, and her heart pounded as it always did when she was in this woman's presence.

'Are you OK, Laura?' Becky asked, worried about her friend who had gone the colour of a ghost. 'Laura, Laura,' she pleaded as she shook her. 'I'm OK, I'm OK. Shhhs, stop bloody shouting for fuck sake, I don't think she saw us,'

Laura said. 'Who? What are you on about?' Becky was now even more worried that her friend was losing it.

The bitch Rita Johnson, the one that had made her life hell, had just strode into the toilet looking a million dollars. Thankfully, she had gone straight to a cubicle and didn't see Laura. Although not before she had given herself an admiring glance in the mirror as she passed. Laura's hands were shaking. She dragged a protesting and bewildered Becky out of the toilets.

'That was Bitch Johnson.' Laura took a minute to catch her breath, and then continued as she watched Becky's eye grow wide in recognition.

'The one who sailed in looking like Julia Roberts in *Pretty Woman*!' Laura's voice quivered.

'What, no way, you got to be joking. No way, that absolute bullying bitch!!' roared Becky who knew all too well of the mental torture Laura had suffered at the hands of this vile creature. Laura winced.

'Will you for god's sake keep your voice down. Come on, let's go out to the others. I couldn't bear the thought of that psycho pretending to be pleased to see me.'

Laura grabbed Becky by the hand and dragged her down the hall in the direction of the signs for the back lounge. As they entered, it was as Laura suspected, oozing cosiness with a log fire and intimate seating. Not that it mattered now. Laura felt as cold as stone. Although the place was crowded, looking around, she quickly spotted the others and darted over with Becky in tow. No sooner had they put their bottoms to the chair than Becky had bellowed out the whole story. The next five minutes were full of 'fuck, bitch, tramp, bully', and other names that Laura had never heard before. Her friends were a good supportive bunch. She wasn't really listening to them now, though. She was just sitting there, not knowing what to do. Should she leave? No, Laura had grown strong since then. Why should she leave? Damn her. She wasn't leaving. Things had changed. Years ago, she wouldn't have had the courage. When Laura worked for 'Miss' Johnson she had lost all self-confidence. The constant put-downs from her boss made herself believe that she was worth nothing.

Johnson had been jealous of Laura because she was very popular, and her future looked bright. Johnson was the opposite. No female friends and certainly no husband. She was a stunning-looking woman and used her looks to get promoted and whatever else she wanted.

She had purposely changed the notes in Laura's folder before presentations which confused her and made her look a fool in front of important people, putting her job on the line the whole time.

Johnson constantly told lies about what time meetings were at and what information would be needed. This led to her either being late for meetings or missing them entirely or if she did make it, she would have the wrong details. Of course, the management wouldn't hear a bad word about Johnson, so any complaints would have been made in vain. Not that she would have dared say anything, as towards the end she could only keep quiet in her presence, not being able to contribute one word.

Laura's job as a gossip columnist had boosted her self-confidence immensely. Even now when the paper accepted another article, her heart soared. Well, enough was enough; if she did meet her, she would face up to her and let her know that she wasn't afraid of her. After all,

Laura was here with four friends. Who was she with? Some man no doubt.

More than likely some poor woman's husband. Johnson had several affairs with the senior managers when Laura worked for her. Laura had felt so guilty as she would have to cover for her sometimes. She'd think of the wives at home or at work, and that Bitch Johnson shagging their husbands. She had them all wrapped round her finger. She was fairly rattled the day Bill confronted her about her treatment of Laura. Johnson was used to men falling at her feet.

Yet Bill had shouted at her and called her all the names under the sun. He had also threatened her and insisted Laura got an excellent reference. That was the only occasion she had seen Johnson at a loss for words. Bill had then practically dragged Laura out of the building, as she had been too shocked to move. She'd never forget that day. Her life had picked up again and Laura sure as hell wasn't going to let that bitch shatter it all again.

She suddenly realised a silence had fallen over the girls, and as she looked up in the direction, they were all staring at, she could see why.

Johnson was on her way back from the toilets. Damn, she would be having a drink in here. All five girls twisted their necks to see where she was heading, or even to whom. She sat down to the right behind the jukebox and although the girls could see her companion was a male, they could not see who it was. They were sitting along a bay window, on two high stools.

'My god,' said Sharon, 'She reminds me of the devil, you'd swear the room went cold when she strolled in.'

'Your right, she certainly gives me the shivers, I can see now why you were so scared of her, Laura,' Gabby mouthed.

'Ouch,' screamed Gabby after Shaz had kicked her. 'I'm sorry Laura, that wasn't called for,' Gabby said. I didn't mean to offend you.' Laura shook her head.

'It's OK, you're right. I don't know myself why I let her push me around. Thank god for Bill. Only for him I might have still been there, trembling every time she breathed.' Laura sighed.

'Yeah, you're lucky, Bill's great, although I doubt you would still be there, I think you would have plucked up the courage to leave eventually,' said Carol supportively. Suddenly, Gabby sat up straight and whispered frantically 'Look, quick, there he is, he's going to the bar. She's going with him. God, how sad! Is she afraid he'll go off with someone else for the whole two minutes he is up there?'

Becky joined in: 'The woman would make you sick, look at her, feeling his ass and kissing his neck like she was a love-struck teenager! Ridiculous!'

The man suddenly turned around coming back to put the drinks on the table. 'Oh... my God, shit!' whispered Carol and, as she turned around in horror to the others, both Laura and Sharon had already disappeared.

CHAPTER 3

Sharon woke on Sunday morning with a pounding headache. Sitting up quickly, she sighed gratefully to be in her own bed. It wouldn't have surprised her if she had gone back to one of the girl's houses for a nightcap and crashed there. Regretful of sitting up so sharply, she lay down slowly as a black cloud descended on her. Sharon thought for just a minute that she was just badly hungover, but then she remembered the events that had occurred the night before. She let out a long sigh.

'Rough night then sweetheart?' came her boyfriend Rob's sleepy voice. Shit. Should she say anything to him? Sharon toyed with the idea of telling him the whole story, but she had promised her friend she would say nothing for the moment. She just hoped the other three would keep their mouths shut too.

'Yeah, it was all right, had a few too many,' replied Sharon.

Rob rolled over and pulled her to him.

'I'm not surprised, you weren't in till four this morning, I thought you said you would be home by latest half one,' scolded Rob. Sharon loved him so much. With his jet-black hair, winning smile and muscular body, she was as head over heels in love with him as she had always been. Maybe even more so now. And she knew she could confide in him and he wouldn't say a thing to anyone. But she still held back for now. It was too raw yet for her to talk about with him.

So, she laughed out loud and said, 'I know yeah, the mini bus broke down on the way, so it was near half two before he collected us, what a bloody nightmare!'

Sharon felt guilty keeping the truth from him, but she wanted to protect her friend. Sharon herself was still in shock over the whole thing, so she could only imagine how her poor best buddy was managing. She had always thought Bill and Laura were made for each other. He was a good bloke, a good husband and a great father. Thinking about it now though, he was hardly ever there lately when Sharon called over to her friend. He was always at a meeting or working late. And when he was there, he didn't seem his usual outgoing self. It was a wonder Sharon didn't notice this before. Or even Laura didn't, for that matter.

She had asked Laura last night if she had any inkling that her husband had been having an affair. However, she couldn't make out the answer, as Laura was too devastated to make any type of understandable conversation.

Sharon had recognised Bill shortly after he had stood up at the bar, and obviously so had Laura. Sharon had quickly dragged Laura from the pub before the others had time to realise themselves. Outside she had to put Laura sitting down on a garden chair; she had been very worried about her friend. If Bill had been having an affair with some strange woman no one knew, Laura might have reacted in some way. But the fact that he was screwing the woman that had made Laura's life hell for three years was just too much for her.

Sharon didn't know what to say but she did know she had to get Laura out of there. Typical. Stuck in the bloody middle of nowhere at a time like this.

'Are you two OK?' a gentle voice had enquired. It was the woman from the restaurant earlier. Sharon felt like hitting her. If she hadn't recommended the stupid back lounge this would never have happened. Although, she thought to herself, would that have been a good thing? Well, by the looks of Laura it certainly would have been. She was swaying back and forth like someone from an asylum.

'Yes, fine,' Sharon said tightly. Then she thought that the lady might know more about Bill and Bitch Johnson, so she took her aside and asked quietly to ensure Laura could not hear her.

'There was a couple in the back lounge, a tall dark-haired man in a black leather jacket and an even taller woman with long black hair and a short skirt,' Sharon said. 'Do you know these people?'

The woman was slightly hesitant, then she replied.

'Well look, you didn't hear it from me; we don't pride ourselves on telling tales down here, what people do is their own business, but that woman is Rita Johnson. Some big wig business woman. That's her boyfriend. He's a nice man. Too nice for her.' The woman paused, knowing she shouldn't be discussing this with customers. Sharon encouraged her.

'Please, it's just it will save us a lot of time if we already know the situation.' It seemed to work.

'They've been coming here regularly for over a year now. Often spend the night in one of our rooms. Sometimes they head back into town though. They don't give too much information about themselves.

'Like, keep themselves to themselves. At first, I just thought it was a fling as they were all over each other, but it's been going on so long now, I think they are serious. Why? Was your friend seeing him?' asked the woman with a concerned look on her face.

Sharon decided it was better to pretend this was the case.

'Unfortunately, yes she was. It was early days, but she thought he might be the one,' lied Sharon. Fecking hell, the absolute shit. Over a year!! What was he thinking? How?? Men. She'd never understand them.

They were lucky enough to intercept a taxi dropping off a young couple and got him to agree to take them home. The journey was long and would cost a bit, but on this occasion, Sharon didn't care about the cost. She would have paid anything to get her friend out of there and home safely.

'Ouch,' she cried coming back to the present, as Rob's sharp kick interrupted her thoughts.

'Sorry,' he laughed, but I couldn't get your attention, you were in another world, dreaming about some toyboy you met last night maybe?' he teased.

'Yes, I was actually. And a fine thing he was!' Sharon joked. She squealed as he started to tickle her and kiss her neck. God, she thought, what would I do if Rob ever cheated on me? He was perfect, and she loved every bone in his body. Things couldn't be better. Well, she thought: apart from that other thing. But then, no relationship was perfect. The one thing they couldn't agree on, and which caused huge problems whenever it was mentioned. A child. Sharon would have liked kids or even one. But Rob had never wanted any. And he had made this clear from the start. Sharon had tried umpteen times to persuade him, but her pleas were in vain.

He'd say, 'You knew what you were getting into at the start, if you want kids, you may go elsewhere.'

She used to be so hurt when he said this. He would go out in a strop and she would cry for hours. Sharon couldn't understand why he didn't want kids. Rob would be a fantastic father. He was so kind and loving. She just didn't get it. And Sharon was by no means stupid. She liked to think that she had a good head on her shoulders. That's what infuriated her.

What was it that made him dislike kids so much? Even when he was around them, he would back off. As if he was frightened. She couldn't explain it. Ah, well, she sighed quietly, she loved him to bits and so she was willing to sacrifice a life with kids to be with him. Rob was worth it! They lived in a large two bedroomed apartment, with a spacious living/dining area and a separate decent-sized kitchen. There was a communal garden they could use if they wished, shared with the other residents in the block, but they never did. They had a small balcony off the living area that had room for a small table and two chairs and it looked out on to a park area which was nice. They often had breakfast or dinner out there when the sun was warm enough. Which in Ireland wasn't a whole lot of the time. Oh, how nice it would be to live somewhere with a great climate, she thought. Sharon loved the sun. But good old Ireland would have to do.

Sharon was in the shower when the phone rang in her bedroom. Normally she would have left it, but she thought it might be Laura. She stepped out of the shower unit carefully and grabbed a towel before running to the bedroom.

'Hello.' she managed out of breath. God, she thought, I need to get fit.

'Hello Sharon,' came the voice of her boss across the line. 'I know it's a Sunday morning, and I'm very sorry to bother you. However, I just read in the paper that there's a conference concerning a new rival product *Elegant Stuff* that will be in direct competition with our *Classy Scent,* and it is taking place in London next weekend.'

Sharon felt her heart drop. Oh, no. The last thing she wanted right now was a work trip somewhere. She needed to be here for Laura.

'Eh, OK,' was all she managed. Sensing her reluctance, her boss pressed on.

'Since you are managing the marketing and the launch of *Classy Scent* I think it is important that you are there. Listen in and take notes, so as we can make changes to our marketing if we need to. We have to ensure that they don't have the competencies we have or that they haven't recognised our unique selling point. Otherwise, it could be very damaging for us.'

Sharon knew he was right. But this was all she needed. What could she do? She couldn't really say no on the phone, couldn't think of a good enough excuse on the spot.

'Sure, I understand,' replied Sharon, inwardly groaning. She hoped she didn't have to reinvent all the marketing plans after so much time and effort had gone into it. Michael White had been her boss now for five years. He was a good sort and recognised hard work and rewarded it too. She didn't like to turn him down as he was good to her and had been responsible for all her promotions in the past.

'OK Mick, it has to be done I suppose, not that I'm looking forward to it. What date is next Saturday,' she asked. Sharon was beginning to realise she wasn't going to get out of this one. She could send her assistant Orla, who was very competent, but she knew Mick would not be happy if she did so.

'Sorry, Sharon, I'm not quite sure. Look, I'll talk to you tomorrow about it. I just wanted to let you know straight away in case you had plans. I'll see you tomorrow and sorry again for disturbing you on a Sunday.'

Sharon tried to be cheery and pretend she didn't mind her plans being disrupted like this.

'No that's OK, don't worry about it. OK, see you tomorrow Mick, thanks.' She sighed deeply as she hung up the phone. She didn't relish the thought of going to London. She would probably have to stay overnight too. She wondered would Rob come with her. Yes, she thought to herself feeling happier about it; we can make a romantic weekend out of it! Sharon strolled over to her locker and took out her diary. She wanted to make a note of the meeting and find out the dates.

As she flipped through the pages, she noticed that she was due a doctor's appointment last Thursday for a renewal prescription of her contraceptive pill.

'Oh, fuck,' she thought, I totally forgot. The clinic won't be too happy with me. Suddenly, her heart began to pound. Sharon went to the doctor every six months to renew her prescription and on every visit for the last ten years she had left it to the last minute each time. She would start her new prescription within a few days after her period stopped. Most of her friends went two months in advance to ensure they were stocked up. Just as well Rob was out for his morning jog. Fuck, she thought, this can't be happening.

Sharon realised with a jolt that for the first time ever, she was most certainly late. She knew that she should work out by how many days, but she just couldn't bring herself to do it. She sat there, her head busting, hundreds of thoughts flying through her mind. Looking at the digital alarm clock on her bedside locker, Sharon realised only ten minutes had passed. She pulled herself together and opened her diary once again. She should have got her period on Wednesday the 8th of November. It was now Sunday the 12th!

'Oh bollox!' she cried. Sharon racked her brains thinking how, how, how. Then it occurred to her. She had been on antibiotics a few weeks ago. She hadn't had sex during their consumption, but she was told to wait seven days before having sex again.

Sharon often was on antibiotics or had got sick or had a bad dose of diarrhea. She always claimed to herself that doctors only said seven days to fully cover themselves. She thought five days was plenty. A friend of hers who was a nurse had once told her so too. So how could she be pregnant? How? She had been covered. No, no, she was being silly. She was under a lot of stress lately and that's what had stalled it. She'd go to the bathroom now and probably find she has it. But after checking, Sharon hadn't gotten her period.

'How didn't I realise?' she wailed aloud. 'How, how?' She had been so busy last week it had never occurred to her. Rob would throw her out. Or leave her. He wouldn't want this baby. No way. She couldn't lose him. Not after all these years, she thought. She ran over to her locker, opening the drawer in a hurry, frantically looking for the 'positive options' number, the agency that claimed to help woman in situations just like this. She had a leaflet somewhere from ages ago. She ended up ringing the operator and was put through to the helpline. A woman with a very gentle voice who claimed she was a doctor told her to calm down and asked her to explain. When Sharon had finished pouring out her story, her heart soared as the doctor told her that more than likely the reason she was late was due to the antibiotics she taken.

However, the doctor advised her to take a pregnancy test to be sure. Sharon promised she would and hung up the phone in delight. She was such an idiot. Pregnant, her? She was more careful than that.

Laura awoke with a jump. For a minute she didn't know where she was. Then she recognised the bay window of her sitting room. The window was one of the reasons she loved the house so much. She remembered when she first came to view the house, stepping into the sitting room, and the sun shining through the beautiful window. The whole room flooded in an uplifting brightness. It had given Laura a warm feeling at the time and she felt it was a sign that this was the house for them.

The room was large with an open fireplace which Laura and Bill had replaced with a huge stove. There was an expensive rug in the middle of the room, with an even more expensive dark wooden coffee table sitting on it. The forty-two-inch TV sat in the corner in a purpose-built unit surrounded by family photos. Laura had found herself sprawled on one of the couches they had only purchased the year before. A large, deep sofa that screamed comfort. She realised she had the remains of a bottle of vodka in her hand. Her head pounded like thunder raging through a storm. And then with utter devastation, Laura remembered the events of the night before. Her husband had cheated on her. And with none other than that bitch Johnson. She closed her eyes shut and fell back onto the couch, head in her hands. She was breathing very quickly and began to wonder if this was what a panic attack was like.

Or if she was about to have one. She couldn't think about Bill. Laura began to tell herself to breathe slowly. She took on a breathing routine she had learned in a yoga class from a few years before. After about five minutes she sat up again. She realised she couldn't bury her head in the sand. This had happened. Thinking back to last night, she had told herself that she wouldn't have minded if Bill had had an affair with some stranger. Laura would have maybe tried to forgive him. Or hear him out. But bitch Johnson? No. No way. Laura's stomach clenched, and she ran from the couch out into the hall and down to the bathroom, just managing to hold it in until she got to the toilet and heaved her guts up.

Sitting on the floor, wiping her mouth, she looked over at the huge shower area they had put in, with high pressure jets and multiple shower heads. It brought back memories of her encounters with Bill in the earlier years. They had such fun in that shower. Her stomach heaved again, and she leaned back up over the toilet and began to throw up once again.

She didn't know whether it was the vodka she had drunk or the thought of them two together had made her sick. Both, she supposed. Last night came back to her again. Sharon had been fantastic. God only knew where she would have ended up. Sharon had brought her home, made her a hot whiskey and comforted her repeatedly, saying that she was ten times the woman Johnson was.

Sharon had also phoned the other three and apologised for abandoning them but due to the circumstances they understood. The girls also promised to keep their discovery to themselves. Laura didn't know what she was supposed to do. Was there a book out there called 'What to do when you find your husband is shagging your worst enemy'? or even, 'How to commit a murder and not get caught.'? She wouldn't mind getting caught killing Johnson, but it was her children that made her realise she couldn't do time.

What was she to do? Confront Bill? How? What did she say? She had insisted Sharon went home last night even though her friend wanted to stay. She knew she meant well but the pity in Sharon's eyes when she looked at Laura was unbearable. To think Laura had once felt sorry for those other women whose husbands were shagging Johnson? How the tables turn. Now there was bound to be women out there who were feeling sorry for her as no doubt Bill's secretary had covered many times. She was a nice girl, but she had obviously been put in the same situation as Laura had been all those years ago. 'Ohhhhh, Lord,' sighed Laura, 'Please help me.' What a mess, she thought to herself, as she crumpled to the floor, overcome with tears once again.

Laura opened her eyes, realisation dawning on her, and looked at her watch, 11.30a.m, Oh, fuck. She had fallen asleep on the floor of the bathroom. Pure exhaustion. Although she was sure the amount of alcohol she consumed didn't help. Damn, she noticed her wedding and engagement rings were missing. She must have taken them off last night. Laura couldn't really remember. She had vague recollections of throwing them somewhere, and maybe Sharon running after them. Or did she? She wasn't sure. Nor did she care. Other than upsetting the kids of course. Ah well. She'd have to think of something for now anyway. She would have liked nothing better than to crawl up into a ball and spend the day crying. Laura did not realise that it was possible to hurt so much. She had always believed that it was better to have loved and lost than never to have loved before. However, she was now changing her tune. If she knew that this much pain could be inflicted on one's heart, she doubted she would have ever married Bill at all. She got up off the bathroom floor and stared at herself in the mirror. My god, she was a wreck. Black mascara trailed down her face, with smudges all over. Her lipstick was mostly gone, but there were traces of it on her chin. Her hair resembled a bird's nest gone very wrong. There was also evidence of dry tearstains, as well as the fresh ones beginning to fall. Laura fell to the floor again and wailed like a zombie. She thumped the ground hard and cursed herself for not realising something was wrong.

Bill had been acting a bit distant the past few months, year even, if she was honest, and was working more than normal. But then, he had such a busy work schedule, as Managing Director in Lyrics Computer Software. He was away every third weekend - Brussels, Paris, London, she had lost count of the different places he had been.

At the start she had gone along on some of them. The laughs they had together, Laura would laze in the room while Bill was at his meetings, he would come back at lunch for some bedroom fun, have a quick shower and head back to the meetings. Laura would then shower herself, get dressed and go sightseeing for the afternoon, meeting Bill for dinner then in the evenings if he couldn't join her before that.

But then life got in the way. Laura had got the job with the paper; she hadn't found the time she used to. So, her suggestion to go with Bill this time to Brussels had been her first offer in over two years. Laura had been hoping he would be delighted. But he had told her he would be too busy. He had really taken her for a mug. Why did he have to go elsewhere? They were happy. The fun between her and Bill was what had made them stick together. It was what attracted them to each other. Their ability to make each other laugh.

Laura hadn't lost her good humour, and her ability to throw out witty comments had only increased over the years. It was one of the things Bill said had first attracted him to her. Her dry sense of humour. Bill had overheard a comment she had made on the football field at a time when they didn't know each other. Oh, they had seen each other around school alright. Laura always thought he seemed a bit full of himself. One of the best players on the football team, the joker in class, extremely good-looking and so not her type. Always had a pretty girl hanging out of his arm. One afternoon Laura and her friends had been watching the boys' football team in the National School Finals. There had been a mother of one of the boys on the team, screaming from the sideline; shouting at the ref that her son had been fouled.

This woman was a repeat sideline offender. Her poor son wasn't the best player, but that didn't stop his mother believing he was. And when his opponent came towards him and scoped the ball cleanly from him, while continuing pounding down the pitch, the force of the action had landed the poor lad on his butt with a bang.

'*Ref, Ref are you blind?– Did you not see that? – It was a foul,*' his mother had screeched. To which Laura replied for her friends' benefit.

'Ehh, I think it's you that's blind – your son couldn't kick snow off a rope – he's worse than useless.' But she had heard a couple of sniggers and looked up realising two of the lads on the football field were positioned right in front of her. One of them being Bill.

He looked at her and a huge grin spread across his face. With dark brown hair, tall frame, and muscular build, she felt an electric bolt shoot through her. Laura had thought that she would never be interested in his type, but she was hooked from that moment. And it seemed, he was too. As after the game, he made a beeline for her joking about the comments she had made and asking her and her friend to meet the guys at the local diner afterwards. It seemed she had made an impression. A lasting one she thought. Obviously not.

Even Jess realised something was amiss. The thought of Jessica made her wonder about the kids.

'Fuck,' she cried aloud again. For someone who almost never swore, Laura realised this must be a side effect to what was happening.

'Please God help me, I need you now more than I ever did before, please help me through this.'

The sound of the house phone startled her. She debated whether to answer it or not but decided she better in case there was something wrong with one of the children. She pulled herself off the floor and ran up the hall to the telephone. Clearing her throat, she lifted the receiver.

'Hello.'

'Hi honey,' came her husband's cheery voice.

CHAPTER 4

'Hello,' she mumbled again, barely audible, drawing back in horror. Oh, no. I can't handle this, she thought to herself.

Hiya love, what's wrong, you sound sick?' came Bill's concerned voice.

What will I do? thought Laura. Will I hang up, pretend I got cut off? No, no. She had to deal with this. What had he said? Was she sick? Yes, she thought. Sick in the head. Because that's what she felt like now. How could she speak to him? She knew she'd have to wait till he came home to confront him. Otherwise, he would have time to make up a story. Pulling herself together, and with all her strength, she managed to reply.

'I'm fine. What do you want?'

She knew he would realise she sounded odd, but she didn't care.

'That's some way to speak to your darling husband. My flight's coming in early, so I'll be home in time for dinner. Around 1pm. Just thought I'd let you know,' he informed her.

How Laura didn't scream her head off there and then she didn't know. Lying bastard. She spoke again.

'Fine, see you then.' and promptly hung up the phone. She had no intention of being here when he arrived home. She needed more time. Her parents were expecting her at 1 o'clock to pick up Jessica and Ben, so it suited her.

Laura was on auto drive. She quickly showered and made herself look somewhat presentable. She arrived at her parent's house fifteen minutes early.

'Hi pet, how are you? Good night out?' called her dad from the garden as she slumped from the car.

The house was a small two story, with pretty front windows on the ground floor, thanks to her mam's hanging baskets and her father's painting skills. There was cheerful garden furniture surrounding the path leading up to the house. There were four bedrooms; three upstairs and one down. There was a kitchen-cum-sitting room to the right when you walked into the hall. It was a large room with the kitchen part to the back and the couch, TV, and fireplace to the front.

Years ago, when Laura had been a child, these were two separate rooms, but in Laura's late teens her parents had decided to knock down the wall to create one large space as everyone had a habit of lingering in the kitchen and there hadn't been much room the way it was. It was a warm, cozy house. Laura always felt secure here. But then she supposed most people felt that going back to their family home.

Coming back to reality and realising her father was waiting on a response, Laura replied.

'Yeah Dad, I had a great time, thanks, was good to catch-up with the girls,' she managed to say. 'How were the kids?' she asked.

Her father turned around and resumed his rubbing down of one of the garden gnomes.

'Huh, they're hardly kids anymore, but they're fine. Jessica stayed up late with me watching a film. Ben spent most of the night on the PlayStation. I bought him a new game yesterday, the new FIFA one'.

Laura smiled to herself. Her parents were forever spoiling them.

'You'll ruin them if you're not careful,' she scolded.

'That's what grandchildren are for,' he laughed.

The front door opened and out bounded Barney to greet her with such powerful force that he nearly knocked her down.

'Barney, get down darling, yes how are you sweetheart, were you a good dog?' she asked him.

Barney yelped in delight.

'Come on love, just in time for tea,' her mother called from the hall. Laura strolled in followed by both Barney and her father, seemingly now satisfied the gnome was as clean as it could be. Laura followed her mam down to the kitchen where Jessica was sitting reading a magazine at the table.

'Hey, Mam, tough night on the tiles?' she teased her mother after giving her the once over.

Laura squirmed inwardly.

'No actually, I just had one or two, but it was a great night,' she replied.

'One or two?' Jess exclaimed' To look at you, you would think you hadn't been to bed, you must have been hammered!'

Oh shit, thought Laura. How will I handle this? Deflect the situation. Laura looked at her daughter.

'Hammered? Where do you hear such words, Jessica?' Thinking to herself, she hadn't heard the word *hammered* in years. Another term for very drunk!

'Now where's your brother?' she asked.

'Ben,' screamed Jess. Her piercing voice went right through Laura's head.

But her son came scrambling into the kitchen and ran over to Laura, 'Hi, Mam,' he said as he kissed her. 'You look tired.'

Great, that's all she needed. Her twelve-year-old boy even noticed the state she was in.

'Ha,' said Jess.' Even Ben noticed!'

'Be quiet Jessica, now Ben, did you have a good time?' she asked him.

'Yeah, brilliant, Granddad bought me a new game, it's fantastic. I'll have to give you a go,' he exclaimed excitedly.

Jesus, that was the last thing she needed. Her mother put a cup of tea on front of her and told the kids to go on outside and leave their mam in peace.

Laura's dad accompanied them, recognising that his wife wanted to talk to their daughter in confidence. As soon as they were out the door, her mother started.

'OK love, either you have a very bad hangover, or something is seriously wrong. What is it?' her mother probed gently. Laura wondered should she spill the beans. She could do with the support, but she wasn't sure she could hold it together. Laura would like to confide in her mother but couldn't bring herself to do it at the minute. She knew once the floodgates open, she would have a hard time closing them. So, she decided to say keep it to herself for now.

'Nothing Mam, I'm fine. A bad hangover. Although I didn't drink that much. I think I might have got a bad pint,' lied Laura. Her mother didn't buy it though.

'Pint? Laura, you don't even drink pints,' she stated.

'Well, I did last night for a change. Honestly. So, how are you Mam?' she asked, changing the topic of conversation.

Nearly an hour later and after putting on an epic performance, Laura decided she better go home. She gathered the kids together and hugged her mam and dad, thanking them for looking after Jess and Ben.

'Anytime pet, you know we love having them,' said her mother.

Putting on her seat belt, Laura looked at her watch; it was coming up to 2pm as they pulled out of her parents' drive. Bill would be wondering where they were. She had purposely left her mobile at home. As if reading her thoughts, her daughter piped up:

'Hey Mam, I forgot to tell you, Dad rang when you were in the house. He wanted to know where we all were. I told him we'd be home soon.' Laura shook inwardly. She was beginning to fall apart. She mentally told herself to just get the children home safely. And then worry about things. She had to focus on her driving.

'No Problem love, thanks,' was all she could manage. Her heart was pounding. She still didn't know what to do. What to say to him? She couldn't confront him in front of the kids. Fuck, fuck, it hurt. As she pulled up in the drive, she nearly fainted. She couldn't handle it. No way. Not yet.

'Look kids, go into your father, tell him I'll be home soon that I have an errand to do,' she informed them

'You OK Mam? You're very pale?' enquired Jess.

'I'm fine love, go on, I won't be long.'

Seeing the children safely into the house, Laura pulled back out of the drive and drove in the direction of the seaside. It was only a few minutes' drive away and she pulled into the car park at the beach. Fresh air. I need fresh air, she thought to herself. Putting on her coat, she grabbed an old scarf she kept in the car and wrapped it around her neck. A walk on the beach should help her to think straighter. The wind was picking up and the waves began to crash violently along the shore. She was alone on the beach as it was such a rotten day. In the summertime the car pack would be rammed, with people having to park on the road. And even in the winter, it would usually be busy enough, with people enjoying their beach walks. But today was unusual. Not one person around. Not even a dog walker. The strand was about only around three kilometers long before it was met by a tall wall of rocks.

But it was a nice long walk out to them and back again. Usually took about an hour. There was no shelter around, and the wind was much stronger than she had realised. But Laura didn't care. Nor did she feel the cold, or the wind, or the rain that began to pound down on top of her; she felt nothing. She thought of Sharon suddenly, her friend would be worried about her. Laura couldn't help but smile. They were so different. Sharon was very bubbly and outgoing, always the first to start a conversation or share a joke. Laura had always been much quieter. In fact, if it hadn't been for the fact that there were only four girls in their primary school class, she and Sharon may never have become so close.

The other two kids were neighbours and close friends before they started school, so it left Sharon and Laura together with eight boys. It wasn't long until Sharon delightfully recognised that once out of her shell Laura could be very funny. She had been so quiet since the start. But as time went on, and she began to trust Sharon a little more, Laura began to feel at ease and be herself. Although quite innocent back then, funny little comments about the boys or the teachers, would have the two of them giggling at the back of the class. More than once they had been banished to the 'Bold Corner'. And after the first year together, the friendship was cemented. Although not normally two you would put together, circumstances intervened, and they remained close throughout their lives, understanding each other more and more as time went on.

She stopped suddenly and turned to stare out above the waves. She stood for a long time, just looking out and thinking, and eventually wondered should she walk in as far as she could go. Laura now knew how it felt to be at rock bottom. She didn't want to go on anymore. She had loved Bill with such intensity.

How could he do this to her? No, maybe she should end it all now. The kids had their dad, and despite him being a cheating rotten asshole, he was still a good father. But it was the thought of the bitch Johnson becoming a mother figure to her children that stopped her. Laura couldn't let Johnson have the last laugh. Not again. No way. She sat down on the wet sand oblivious to the weather that was howling around her, and for how long she sat there, she didn't know. She closed her eyes and stayed like that for a while. She felt strange. And very tired suddenly. She decided to lie down for five minutes, to rest. Her hangover must be kicking in again. She closed her eyes and felt strangely comfortable despite the weather. She must have fallen asleep. As when Laura opened her eyes again, she was lying in a hospital bed, with Bill holding her hand.

Bill Murphy had answered the phone the same time Laura had gone to clear her head.

'Hi Bill, Sharon here, Is Laura there?' she asked.

Sensing a disappointed tone, he replied, 'No, she has gone on an errand; actually, she dropped the kids off earlier and hasn't come home since/'

He paused now before continuing.

'To tell you the truth, I'm a bit worried about her, she didn't seem herself today. How did ye get on last night? Ye were out, weren't you?' he probed. Sharon winced. Fuck. What could she say?

'Oh right, ah, eh, ye were went out. Just down to your local there in the village. A good night. Laura seemed in good form. I'd say she's fine, look I'd better go, I'll try her again later.' And with that, Sharon hung up the phone.

Shit. She had to get off the phone quickly as she didn't want him quizzing her further. Sharon didn't want to give him the name of anywhere or commit to something. As she didn't know what Laura was or was not going to say. Shit. She needed to talk to her friend.

'DAAD,' shouted his daughter breaking into his thoughts. 'When's Mam home, I'm hungry.' Bill sighed loudly before responding.

'She won't be long now honey, I'll start the dinner,' he replied, walking into the kitchen from the hall. Jessica was sitting on top of the island, her legs resting on one of the stools, a magazine on her lap.

'Yeah right, Dad, I want to live to see tomorrow you know.' She laughed at him. Bill wasn't known for his cooking skills.

He barely ever made anything for the children, his talent extending to helping them pour their cereal in the mornings.

'Enough of that young lady,' he smiled walking over to open the fridge, but his shoulders were stooped and his steps heavy.

A few hours later the house phone rang. Bill jumped from the couch and ran to the hall to answer it.

'Hello,' he spoke quickly.

'Hello there, is that Bill Murphy?' came an unfamiliar voice of a woman.

'It is, yes, what's wrong, has something happened to Laura?' he asked anxiously.

'I'm afraid your wife has just been admitted to the Royal Hospital of Dublin, she's OK though, please don't panic. Your wife is a lucky woman. She was found lying on the beach at Clontarf, absolutely soaked through and unresponsive.'

The woman sounded disapproving.

'Laura? On the beach? What?' His mouth opened and closed several times as he stood staring at the wall.

'A couple out walking on the beach found her and called for help. Your wife is showing signs of pneumonia, Sir and is quite sick,' she explained.

'My god, my god, I'll be there in ten minutes,' and with that he hung up the phone, not giving the nurse a chance to reply.

Gathering the children into the car he sped to the hospital, and true to his word he was there in just ten minutes. Jessica began demanding to see her mother the second they reached the reception area. She was causing quite a commotion now as the nurse would not allow any visitors.

'Jess love, come back, look nurse, I am her husband and I have every right to see her. I need to be with her,' he pleaded, his face visibly pale. The nurse regarded him stiffly.

'Your wife has a caught a small case of pneumonia, she must have been in the rain for several hours before she was found. You can see her, but only for a few minutes. Your wife is weak and needs all the rest she can get,' she scolded.

'Yes, thank you nurse,' Bill replied, looking at the floor.

'Down the corridor, take the second left and the first right. She's in that room,' the nurse ordered.

He practically ran down the corridor to the ward where Laura was, leaving his two disgruntled children in the waiting room. Locating the room, he opened the door, a small smile forming on his face when he saw just one bed.

His smile was short-lived when he laid eyes on his wife. He sucked in a breath and put two hands to his head. There were several tubes coming from her mouth and arms. Her face looked drained, deathly white, and her hair looked like rats' tails. Tears formed in his eyes and began to spill as he approached the bed slowly. His legs shaky now, he fell into the chair beside her bed and took her hand. Bill jumped back in shock at the coldness he felt from her skin. His eyes filled again with tears, and he sighed quietly.

He sat in the chair, swearing softly and mumbling to himself. Jumping in fright, he suddenly heard a gentle voice. 'Come along now, that's enough for tonight, she needs all the rest she can get.' The same nurse spoke more softly to Bill, obviously now taking pity on him.

He nodded his head to show that he understood. However, he did not move.

Bill squeezed his wife's hand and watched her, stroking her face tenderly with the other hand.

'Honestly now, you're going to have to go,' came the voice again, not so gentle this time.

With that, Bill cupped Laura's pale and fragile face in his hands and placed a tender kiss on her face. The lips barely made contact with her skin though as he was terrified of hurting her. He glanced around the room, as if only noticing his surroundings. Two chairs, a table that had an empty vase on it, a locker beside the bed with a jug of water. There was a wardrobe in the corner and a door next to it.

'Love you darling, so much. You are going to be fine. I'll be back tomorrow with Jessica and Ben; they can't wait to see you,' Bill whispered softly to Laura. And with that he turned and left the room.

CHAPTER 5

When Bill arrived home the phone in the hall was ringing. It was getting a lot of use it seemed lately. Normally everyone used their mobile phones to contact each other. Rarely the house phone was used, unless it was Laura's parents or his own. And sometimes he called it too, from work, or when he was out and about.

His son came running into the hall and picked up before he had a chance to answer it himself.

After a few seconds Ben said, 'No sorry Sharon, Mam's in hospital, it rained so bad she got drenched so she's in drying out,' he informed a startled Sharon. Bill sighed loudly and grabbed the receiver from his son.

'Hi, Sharon.' But he got no further.

'Bill, what happened?'

Oh, my god, what was Ben talking about?

'Is Laura in hospital,' came an astounded Sharon.

'Calm down, calm down. Yes, she is in hospital, although not drying out!! She went for a walk on the beach earlier today. It started to rain heavily, and she got caught up in it. Got so wet she had to sit down and rest. She must have passed out because two neighbours found her unconscious and rang an ambulance. The good news is Laura is being well looked after now and on the mend. The doctors told me she'd be fine, but it was vital that she got plenty of rest. They only let me in for ten minutes.'

Sharon was horrified. She should have done more. She should have stayed with her last night despite her protests, or at least drove around to her today.

'I can't believe this,' she cried. Poor Laura. She could only imagine how the poor thing must have been feeling.

'I know yeah, I'm as startled as you are. What on earth was she doing out walking in the rain?' Bill questioned aloud. Sharon felt like screaming down the phone that if he hadn't been screwing Miss Fuck

Head Johnson this wouldn't have happened. Typical men, they were never to blame.

'Yeah, look Bill, I'll probably take the morning off work and go in to see her.' Laura would need her support, now more than ever. She wanted to be there for her friend.

'Ah, there's no point,' Bill said. They won't let you in. I promise I'll phone you tomorrow and let you know how she is. Maybe you can visit Tuesday. I'll ask the nurse.'

Sharon felt like wringing his neck. Laura would prefer her there rather than Bill. But she couldn't say that. What a mess.

'OK,' she said, realising she might have no choice but to wait. All of a sudden he was Mr. Caring Husband! Make you sick. But it wasn't her place to confront him .

'Night Bill.' and with that, she hung up the phone as she couldn't stomach any more from the cheating pig.

When Laura woke the next day to find Bill holding her hand, she felt a rush of love for him. Then, the sickness in her stomach hit her like a ton of bricks when she remembered the reason she was there.

Laura tried to sit up but cried out in pain as her whole body refused to budge as if in protest.

'Darling, you're awake. I was so worried honey, thank god. I love you so much,' he said as he tried to wrap his arms around her.

'Ahh, sorry Bill, but could you back off, I can hardly breathe here, never mind try and hug you,' she snapped, although her voice was low.

Bill sat his forehead creased in a frown.

'OK, sorry pet, I just missed you.'

'Missed me? Huh,' she grunted, after trying to laugh but failing.

'What's wrong?' Bill's brow creased further in confusion...

'Eh, nothing, darling. Everything is fine. What the fuck do you think is wrong? I'm lying here like a dead corpse, not able to move and you're practically trying to have your way with me,' she sighed and sunk further on the bed.

Her husband's eyes were wide now.

'What is it? Please tell me?'

He took her hand and willed her to let him in. His eyes bore into hers. Could she just forget about the whole thing? Pretend nothing happened? After all, they had two children together and he was a good father. Could she break up the family? She sighed deeply and took his hand.

'I'm sorry hun, I shouldn't have spoken to you like that. I'm just exhausted and feel terrible. I know you're only trying to help.'

Bill smiled, visibly relaxing now. He then proceeded to fill her in on how exactly she got there and about the phone call he received.

'OK, look, I'll leave you to get some sleep. I'll bring the kids in later. Oh, and Sharon rang. I told her not to come in today but maybe you'd like to see her tomorrow?' he enquired.

'Fine, yeah,' was all Laura said as her eyes closed in both mental and physical exhaustion.

After doing some thinking, Sharon decided that she had no intention of leaving her visit to Laura until Tuesday. She knew Bill would be visiting in the morning and that he would probably bring in the kids later that day. So, she took a chance and left work at 11am.

Sharon drove over to the hospital and reached it fifteen minutes later. Traffic had been light, thankfully. Please let Bill be gone, she thought. She looked around for his car, which was pretty pointless, seeing as how there were more than two hundred cars in the car park. Sharon got out of the car and walked towards the entrance.

'Hi Sharon.' Turning, she saw Laura's mother, accompanied by her father.

'Hello, Gilly, Hi, Charlie,' she said, 'How is Laura?' enquired Sharon.'

She could see the worry etched on their faces.

'She's OK but is very tired. We didn't stay long. She seems very down. I know the nurses told me she was doing well but I'm very worried about her. '

Gilly sighed. Laura's dad took his wife's arm and reassured her that their daughter was a fighter and that she'd be back on her feet in no time.

'Do you think the nurse will let me in?' asked Sharon.

Although she was going in whether they liked it or not.

'They are only letting family in but say you're her sister and you might get in for a few minutes. I think Laura would be glad to see you. It might do her good,' Charlie said.

'OK, well thanks, see you later, and don't worry, she'll be flying by the end of the week,' assured Sharon as she continued towards the entrance. Thankfully, the nurse who was on duty was very nice. When Sharon said she was Laura's sister, the nurse was more than happy to show her to her room. As Sharon entered, she had to stop herself from crying at the sight of her friend. Laura looked terrible. Sharon took a minute to get herself together and then proceeded to the side of her friend's bed. Laura's eyes were closed. She really had hit rock bottom.

'Hiya, pet,' whispered Sharon.

Laura's eyes opened slowly, and she smiled weakly as she recognised her friend.

'Sharon, I thought you weren't coming in till tomorrow.' Obviously Bill had been speaking to Laura.

'Fat chance, I had to come and see you; sure, you're my best mate, aren't you? Besides, I had to make sure there were no sexy doctors trying to chat you up!' she laughed, trying to lighten the mood. Laura laughed too. '

So, Miss Wandering Betty, how are you really?'

Laura looked at her and sighed.

'I feel like dying... I just want to die. Pity I didn't yesterday.' Sharon was immediately alarmed.

'Ah, I know, I'm just joking,' said Laura feebly, although they both knew this wasn't true.

They chatted for ten minutes until Laura began to close her eyes every now and then. Sharon knew it was time to leave. She had wanted to find out if Laura had confronted Bill, but she wanted to wait till Laura brought it up. She would tell her when she was ready.

'Right Honey, I'll let you be, have a good rest now, won't you?' she said, smiling

'You don't need to tell me twice,' Laura replied sleepily. Sharon kissed her friend and told her she would see her tomorrow. As she left the hospital, she caught sight of Bill and the two kids. She hid behind a pillar until they passed. God, she thought to herself, poor Laura wouldn't be getting any rest today it seemed.

That evening when Sharon got home, she threw herself on the couch and let out an exasperated sigh. She was exhausted herself. Not physically but mentally. There was still no sign of her period starting, and she had avoided doing a pregnancy test. She told herself she didn't need to. However, at the back of her mind she knew that she should take one. At least she'd know one way or the other. Ah, fuck. The thought of this, she said to herself. She took the test out of her bag where it had been since the previous evening. Suddenly she heard a key in the lock and quickly fired the test back into her bag, zipping it up swiftly.

'Hi, love,' said Rob as walked into the room and over to the couch bending his head down to kiss her.

'How's Laura doing, did you tell her I was asking for her?' he said, as he proceeded to the kitchen and dropped his backpack on the table. Close one, thought Sharon to herself.

'Yeah, she's doing OK, very tired, but she's hanging in there,' she replied without enthusiasm. Rob noticed her humour.

'What's up? You've been very quiet since yesterday?'

Oh no, better be careful, she warned herself.

'I'm just tired, need a break.'

And with that, she got up and went to have a shower to try and wash her worries away.

On Friday morning Sharon greeted the nurse she had got to know well as she had seen her for the past four days. Laura was improving and might be getting out tomorrow, all going well. Her friend still hadn't mentioned Bill but by the sounds of things, she had not yet said anything to him. Sharon had an uneasy feeling that Laura might not say anything at all. She was low at the minute and felt she needed someone. Oh fuck, thought Sharon to herself. Please don't let her stay with him. She wasn't looking forward to this visit as she had decided she was going to ask about what she intended to do. Her hands were sweating in anticipation of the conversation to come. She hoped Laura wouldn't block her out. The patient was sitting in a chair beside her bed looking out the window and lost in thought by the look of her.

'Look at you, like Lady Muck, sitting there,' laughed Sharon.

'Ah, I might as well make the most of it. I won't get this treatment back at home from Bill and the kids'.

Sharon stiffened suddenly. Laura had no intentions of leaving Bill. She sighed and sat down on the edge of the bed, facing her friend. They chatted for five minutes about ordinary stuff and then Sharon decided to bite the bullet.

'Laura, look, I know this might be a difficult time to have to deal with what happened, but have you confronted Bill about Rita yet?' she asked as gently as she could.

On hearing that monster's name, Laura's stomach clenched. She froze. Laura didn't want to deal with this. She was currently trying to live with the guilt of considering letting the ocean swallow her up. Never ever would she leave her two beautiful children. She was so ashamed of the thoughts she had. Thinking that they would be fine with Bill. She knew she never ever would have done it, but still… The thought should not have entered her head. Not when she had two amazing children to live for.

And they came first. And always would. Which is why she had come to a decision regarding her husband.

'Yeah, look Sharon, I meant to say to you. Things between Bill and I have been great this week. He has been so attentive, and he has promised to spend way more time with the children and me. I think the thought of losing me made him realise that bitch wasn't worth it. And besides, I'm pretty sure it was a one-night stand.'

Sharon clenched her fists and held her breath. Willing herself not to scream at her and tell her how stupid she was, but she knew it would do no good.

'Laura,' she started gently. 'Laura, are you sure Bill will be just as attentive when things go back to normal? I doubt it. I think you know yourself he won't. Laura, he lied to you, and cheated with that bitch Johnson, of all people. He knows how much that would hurt you, please Laura, please reconsider, you just can't stay with him.' Laura knew she was right, but it irritated her to hear her say it. You'd swear she was perfect. No, fuck Sharon, she had Rob. She'd be able to stay with Bill if she kept telling herself that it was a one-night stand. She thought she could just about handle that.

'Look Sharon,' she said as calmly as she could 'I have made my mind up. As I said, it was probably only a one-night stand and no point in breaking up the family over one silly night.'

Fuck, fuck, fuck, thought Sharon, she didn't want to tell her this, but she had to know.

'Laura, do you remember the night we saw Bill with Johnson?' Laura didn't respond; I mean as if she would ever forget that night.

'Well,' continued Sharon. 'When me and you were outside the woman from the restaurant came out. She asked if you were OK. I took her aside and asked her if she knew Bill and Rita.'

Laura didn't want to hear the rest of this. She knew it wouldn't please her.

'Laura, she told me that Bill and Rita had been seeing each other regularly for over a year. They go to that place at least once a week and sometimes they stay overnight there, and when they don't, they order a taxi into the city.'

'NO, NO, NO!' cried Laura. 'Shut up, you're only saying that because you don't want me getting back with him. You're just jealous because I have a family and you don't!' she screamed at her.

Laura knew before she even said it that it was wrong and that it would hurt Sharon no end, especially if she really did want a family, but she couldn't help herself. She was hurting so much she wanted someone else to hurt too.

Sharon reeled in shock at this outburst. Her heart felt like it had been struck by a bolt. She wouldn't let herself cry. Instead, she got up and ran out of the room and outside as quickly as she could. In the safety of her car, the tears began to fall. She just let them spill, one after the other. Coming harder and faster. She made no attempt to wipe them.

What exactly was she crying for? Was it because Laura was so stupid in staying with Bill? Was it because she thought she was pregnant? Or was it the fact that Laura had known how much Sharon wanted a family? She didn't know. Sharon just sat there crying with hundreds of thoughts going through her head. Suddenly she shot up right as a loud knock startled her. She looked out the window, and through her muffled tears thought she saw Jack Downey, a friend of Sean Dawson, Laura's neighbour, standing there.

She rolled down the window.

'Sharon, it is you. My god, are you OK, what is it, is it Laura?'

Lord, how bloody embarrassing, if ever she wanted the ground to open up and swallow her it was now. Jack was an extremely good-looking man, who herself and Laura used to joke about fancying. They often talked about his sexy demeanor, with his jet-black hair, now with faint grey streaks appearing, bright blue eyes and sallow skin.

They often had drinks together when Sean and his snooty wife, Paula held dinner parties at their mansion. He seemed a bit of a lady's man, always having a different woman by his side. Although in saying that, he was a nice guy. Always made you feel like he was interested in what you were saying and wasn't just making conversation for the sake of it, like so many other people did at dinner parties.

'Hi Jack,' she said now. 'Eh, no, no, Laura's fine, I'm just having some personal problems,' she said, feeling absolutely mortified.

He frowned and looked even more concerned.

'Oh, is there anything I can do?' he asked.

Ye, like what on earth could you bloody do, she thought.

Then a thought struck her. It might give Laura a lift to have some friends rally around her.

'Were you going in to see Laura?' she enquired. He looked a bit uncomfortable.

'Well, no actually, an old friend of mine. I knew she was in, but I didn't want to bother her.'

Sharon smiled encouragingly.

'Look, don't tell Laura you've seen me, but she is a bit down. I think your company might cheer her up.'.

He seemed hesitant.

'Ah, I don't know' he said shrugging his shoulders. Sharon continued.

'Ah, go on. Five minutes will be no harm, I'm sure she'll be glad of the company.'

He sighed in mock defeat and smiled.

'OK, so, if you think it's a good idea.'

She didn't really know whether it was a good idea, but at least it would take Laura's mind off other matters for a while.

'I do, but just make sure you don't tell her you were talking to me, let her think you called in because you wanted to see her.'

Jack smiled again.

'OK, will do, take care of yourself Sharon, I hope things work out OK.'

She winced inwardly, feeling her cheeks burning up

'Eh, ye, Thanks, I appreciate it, but don't mind me. I'm fine,' she said and returned his smile as she wound up her window.

Mmmm…. she thought to herself, wondering if she had done the right thing and if the company of a sexy hunk like Jack Downey would make Laura realise that there was more to life than Bill fecking Murphy!!

CHAPTER 6

Later that day, Sharon arrived home and plonked herself, as usual, on the couch and let out a loud sigh. The confrontation with Laura had taken a lot out of her. However, she knew that this was not the only reason she was exhausted. The constant worrying whether she was pregnant or not didn't help.

'Oh god,' she sighed. 'What on earth am I to do if I am pregnant?' She asked herself. She couldn't lose Rob, she loved him so much.

Why couldn't he like children, why? Sharon wished she could try and maybe talk him round. If she was pregnant, the fact that they were in the situation may make him think differently. At least she hoped. She was flying over to London tomorrow. Rob had planned on coming with her but the company he owned and managed were very short of staff. It was a publishing company with just ten employees in all.

The assistant manager who was supposed to be on duty this weekend, had come down with the flu. At first Sharon was disappointed he couldn't make it. She was glad now however, as she needed some time on her own. She had planned on taking the pregnancy test that evening, but she may as well wait until she was over in London where she could do it in the privacy of her hotel room, without worrying about Rob walking in.

Sharon walked over to the fridge and was about to open a bottle of wine and treat herself to a glass when she decided to have orange juice instead.

'Why are you doing this, stop it. Even if you are pregnant ,you can't keep it. Well. It's between your baby and Rob. SHUT UP,' she screamed at herself.

'Shut up, you're probably not even pregnant,' and with that, she opened the wine and had one glass as if in protest. However, she kept it to only one glass.

The next morning Sharon got up early and had a shower. She wrapped a towel round her slim body and walked back into the bedroom. Rob lay awake. Staring into space. He had been very quiet these past few days. She felt guilty for not being more considerate and asking him what was wrong, but she had been relieved that he hadn't probed her own quietness and so she left things as they were. She should ask him, now though.

'Rob, is there something bothering you? You're very quiet.'

He turned his head to her and smiled.

'No, No, darling, I'm fine, just not looking forward to spending the weekend without you.'

Sharon smiled, although she knew that this was not what was bothering him. She went over and gave him a big hug. She worried about him sometimes. He could be fine for months, and then all of a sudden, he would withdraw for about a week, staring into space in a world of his own. He always reassured her that he was OK and that he was just tired. Sharon never really probed him further. She had hoped he would tell her in his own time.

'Yeah, right,' she joked, 'You'll probably have some young thing in the bed with you the minute I have my back turned!'

Rob smiled mischievously.

'Ah, damn,' he replied. 'I didn't think you'd have noticed.'

She thumped him on the arm playfully and he grabbed her tightly and whispered into her ear.

'You do know you're the only one for me? Forever.' Her body tensed, and her stomach knotted as the thought of losing him made her sick with fear.

'Same goes,' she managed, and kissed the tip of his nose.

He then peeled away her towel and made love to her as passionately as ever and she enjoyed every minute of it.

'You're an owl tiger when you get going,' he laughed.

'Feck off,' she snorted, 'You're not what you'd call a mouse yourself.' She laughed. Sharon looked at her watch and shrieked, 'Shit, I better get my things together; the taxi will be here in ten minutes.'

Rob looked up at her.

'Are you sure you don't want me to give you a lift to the airport?' he asked lying back on the bed, pulling the covers over him.

'No, honestly. It's way out of your way. No, I'll be fine,' she called as she got changed and packed her last few things. At the sound of the taxi's horn she grabbed Rob in yet another hug.

'Relax hun, you'd swear you were leaving for a month, you'll be home tomorrow night,' he assured her.

She hoped so any way.

'Right pet, see you darling, I love you,' he told her.

Sharon called, 'Love you too,' and she ran down the stairs and out the door into the awaiting taxi.

He should tell her. She deserved to know. It wasn't fair that he was keeping something that played such a huge part in his life at one stage, from her. Rob sighed deeply. He knew Sharon longed for kids and his heart broke at the thought of it. Rob loved her so much and would do anything for her. Well, almost anything, he just couldn't go down that road. Not now, not after what happened. He had to tell her. It wasn't fair on her.

But he was too afraid of losing her. She'd hate him. Call him a loser, a waste of space. And he wouldn't blame her. That was all he was. Oh god, he thought. Fifteen years today. Fifteen. And each year it never got easier. Oh Sharon, you deserve so much better than me!

Sharon had a pleasant flight and was relieved to find a driver waiting on her at Heathrow. She signaled to the tall man with the sign with her name on it and he came towards her.

'Hi, I'm Sharon Walsh, work for Beauty Forever,' she informed him.

'Let me take your bag,' the driver said, took her small suitcase from her and directed her out of the airport and into the black Mercedes. Mmmm… she thought, snazzy!

An hour later she was lying on her bed in an upmarket hotel room, a perk of the job. It was a pity Rob could not see this she thought. He'd love it. The room was huge with a large double bed. It had floor-to-ceiling wardrobes with mirrors on one side of the bed and a huge flat screen TV nestled on the wall opposite. There was a large bay style window overlooking the streets below. And the bathroom was bigger than their own back home. The bath looked so inviting. Sharon had promised herself that she would have a long soak before she left. She looked at her watch as she stretched out on the bed. It was 11.15am. The conference started at twelve. Thankfully, it was taking place in the hotel she was staying in. Sharon was dressed, washed and fed so she wondered what to do with herself for the next forty-five minutes. She knew she could do the pregnancy test, but then, if it were positive, she'd have to face the conference afterwards.

No, she thought, I'll wait till it's over. I'll do it tomorrow after the last presentation. Happy at not having to face the test today she decided to go downstairs to the bar and have a mineral water.

She saw several faces that she knew very well and spent her time chatting to them about the launch of the new product. Some of them were from other companies, and here for the same reason as herself. To keep an eye on the competition. Sharon went into the conference with John Casey and Sheila Smith. Both from two rival companies.

However, they were all friends and had many a drink together (and late night) in the past. The presentations went on until 3 o'clock. She found she was starving.

'Hey Shaz, a couple of us are heading to town for dinner, this fabulous Italian restaurant, we should be back in plenty of time for the rest of the presentations at 5 o'clock,' Sheila said.

Thankful that she didn't have to decide on where to eat, she replied, 'Eh, yeah, actually I'm starving, count me in,' and Sharon headed off with the small group. The suspected pregnancy never far from her mind.

By 3 o'clock the next day, Sharon knew it was time to find out whether she was pregnant. She couldn't put it off any longer, for her own sanity, if anything. Was she pregnant? Or was there something wrong with her? She didn't feel pregnant. And for some reason when she awoke this morning, she didn't think she was. Sharon didn't know how she knew. But she did. She wasn't pregnant. However, she thought, I'll do the test just to be sure. She had had a good night last night. They had a smashing meal and went back to continue the conference.

It had finished at about 8pm and then she had stayed in the hotel bar until eleven with the group she had dinner with earlier. Sharon hadn't felt great, so she drank water. Didn't want a hangover either with having to face more presentations today, along with the flight home.

Right. This is it. Time to put a stop to all the worrying. She opened her bag to take one of the two tests out from the pack.

Her hands shook as she opened the box and tried to read the instructions through a blur. Sharon walked slowly to the bathroom and followed the guidelines. She then sat on the edge of the bath and began to sing softly to herself to try and pass the time.

When the time was eventually up, her heart pounded hard in her chest. Her mouth felt dry as she lifted the test from the ledge and looked to see what her future held.

'Oh, good god,' she cried. She ran back to the bedroom to the get the second test as she needed to be a hundred percent sure. Her heart skipped a beat when she couldn't find it. Oh fuck, she cried, oh, no. Please, no. She cringed as she remembered that she had driven herself mad Friday night. Going over and over whether she was pregnant or not. She had got out of bed and had planned on doing it in the toilet while Rob slept. However, she hadn't got very far, she had opened the box and was reading the instructions when Rob had wrapped on the door.

'Shaz, hurry up, I'm dying for a pee.'

She had opened the cabinet and shoved it in there knowing that Rob would not have opened it in the middle of the night. However, she had forgot to remove it. Oh shit, shit, shit, she thought.

Laura awoke on Monday morning to the sound of the rain battering on the window. She turned and found Bill sleeping soundly beside her. He had taken today off work to be with her. Laura had got home from the hospital on Saturday, and Bill along with the kids had been pampering ever since. She was still rattled after her row with Sharon. She felt so guilty. Sharon would probably never speak to her again.

Laura eased herself out of bed and decided to look for a spare dressing gown. She hadn't been out of bed since she got home, apart from her visits to the bathroom. The dressing gown she had in hospital was in the wash as Ben had spilled coke down the front of it. She walked slowly into the spare room where she had some extra bed linen and pajamas. Laura could not locate her second dressing gown. Then she remembered that on Bill's last visit to Brussels he had taken it with him. She went to the other side of the room and looked around, spotting his overnight bag in the corner. Making her way over, she tried to bend down and pick it up but she was too stiff. Making a second attempt, she bent her knees and kept her back straight as she lowered herself to the floor. She couldn't see the bag, as her head was looking directly ahead, trying to keep her body straight. She managed to locate it with her wandering hands and took it up slowly as she rose. She moved towards the bed and lowered herself carefully to sit on it. Laura began to unpack his things. Typical Bill.

Too lazy to do it when he got back last week. She pulled out two shirts, a pair of jeans, and the dressing gown. Ah, ha. Got it. She wrapped the gown around her, as it was quite nippy. Laura put her hands in the pockets to keep warm and felt some paper inside.

She took it out and looked at what seemed to be some sort of letter. Her heart began to pound as she knew now the bag had not actually been in Brussels, nor had he, but wherever he and that tart had been. However, she had been trying to put it out of her mind and pretend it hadn't happened. Slowly smoothing out the paper, she began to read

My dearest Bill,

I'm sorry I didn't wake you, but you looked much too peaceful to disturb. I have a busy day ahead and I know you're going home later to your mouse. Thanks for an amazing weekend; it was a great way to celebrate my birthday. You are just as desirable now as the first night we were together. Like, what's it now? Must be a year at least! Well my darling, enough for now, I must run, Au revoir.

Xxx

R

Despite her injuries and barely being able to walk a few minutes ago, she somehow ran to the bathroom and threw up. Oh, good god. The bastard. She had decided to stay with him for the kids' sake. She had made herself believe it was a one-night stand. Over a year. Sharon had told her that but to see it come from the bitch Johnson's mouth. She had no doubt it was from her. Laura was not only familiar with her writing, but 'Mouse' was the name Rita used to call her - used to torture her with. She began to heave again. Having a sudden moment of clarity, she asked herself, what was she doing? Why on earth was Bill still in her bed? How stupid was she? And to think that bitch laughed at her behind her back. Called her the dreaded nickname – to BILL.

What an *ultimate* betrayal. Bitch. And him. Bastard. All along Laura had told herself that it was bitch Johnson's fault. She seduced him. All men would be the same. But from what she had written in her letter, Bill had been making fun of her too. Well, enough was enough. She wasn't taking any more. And she wasn't going to cause a scene either.

No. She would do this as calmly as she could. Thank god the kids were at school. Bill had got them out this morning and then came back to bed. Laura walked into the bedroom and dressed as quietly as she could. She turned and found Bill awake.

'Hey, come back to bed, you shouldn't be up,' he scolded her.

She sat down on the bed and looked at him for a few seconds. Then she spoke.

'Bill, I had so much respect for you. I loved you with all my heart and soul.

'And I thought that you loved me just as much. But I was wrong. Bill, I know about you and her. I want you to pack your things and get out of this house as quick as you can. I'm going to go over to my parents' house. I'm well enough to drive. I'll be back by 3 o'clock. I want you and your things gone by then.'

Jesus, she thought, how was she being so calm? She supposed that she had been dealing with it for over a week now, so all the fight had gone out of her.

Anyway, screaming wouldn't get her anywhere. Bill's face had drained; he tried to speak but gulped like a goldfish instead.

'But... No, Laura.'

'Yes Bill. I saw you, last weekend in that pub in Wicklow. I was there with the girls. You made a fool out of me. Well, I'm no doormat. I haven't the energy to have a big argument, luckily enough for you, because the neighbours would have had to call an ambulance for you if I did. I could honestly beat you to pulp and not feel bad about it. Because you may as well have done the same to me.'

Bill stammered, 'No, Laura, you don't understand. I met her that day, it was a one-night stand, I swear Laura, it meant nothing, I can't be without you. I love you so much Laura. Please, you can't do this, give me a chance to show how much I love you and want you. You want to break up the family over this? What I've done was wrong, but

I swear, she got me drunk and seduced me, it wasn't entirely my fault,' he pleaded pathetically. Tears were beginning to fall down his face.

'Laura, please, I realised when you got sick…' He stopped, his eyes opening wide. It dawned on him the reason she had gotten sick in the first place.

'Oh god, that's why you were out walking in the rain, 'cos of me. Ah fuck, I'm so sorry.'

He pulled the covers back and tried to embrace her in a hug. She let him for a few seconds and then shrugged him off.

'Yes, that's right Bill, I did. I went walking in the rain. I was so hurt over what you'd done. And yes, you're right again, I shouldn't break up the family over a one-night stand. I should give you another chance… and I was going to. Why do you think I hadn't mentioned it? I was going to give you another chance,' Laura cried.

Bill began to nod his head.

'Ye, please Laura, I'll never neglect you the way I did,' he cried.

'Right again Bill, Jesus, you're getting good at this. Yep, you won't neglect me again, because you won't have the chance. You should really dispose of any dirt when you're finished, otherwise you might attract some mice!' Laura remarked as she threw the letter on top of his chest.

'I'm going now. Gone by 3 o clock. And I mean it. If you're not gone, I'm taking the kids to my folks. It's up to you. Goodbye Bill, we'll talk about the kids once you're settled in your new home, most likely bitch Johnson will take you in. And it won't be a mouse you'll be living with then; it will be a fucking rat!'

Laura didn't know how she found the energy to walk out of the house at the pace she did. Bill had shouted after her, pleading not to go, but she kept walking. She had arrived at her parents' house and had practically fallen in the front door when her mother opened it.

'Jesus, Mary and Joseph, what on earth happened? CHARLIE,' she roared to her husband, 'call a doctor.'

Laura sighed. This was all she needed.

'I'm fine Mum, quit fussing, I just need to rest.'

Her dad came hurrying out to the hall and quickly gathered Laura in his arms, steering her up the stairs and towards her old bedroom. After tucking her in as he did when she was a child, leaving his wife whispering comforting words to Laura, Charlie turned and went off out of the room and down the stairs.

He lifted the phone on the wall in the hall and phoned for a doctor who assured Charlie he would be there in about an hour. Going back to the bedroom, he found his wife sitting on the bed holding Laura's hand. The tears were plummeting down his daughter's face.

'What happened love?' her dad asked, extremely concerned. And though Laura had not planned on getting them involved, being in her old room, and having her mam and dad here comforting her, was such a reminder of her childhood. She felt so secure and safe, and so she told them. Leaving nothing out. She had been going to pretend it was just a rough patch. But didn't have the energy to make up any lies. So, she told them everything. When Laura had finished, her mother was crying, and her dad looked mad as hell.

'The rotten bastard, to think it's his fault you were in hospital and me and your mother felt sorry for him,' he cried. 'How dare he treat you like this, I always thought he was perfect for you, was so happy you married a gentleman. He'll be a sorry man when I get him, I can tell you!'

'Charlie, no, please,' pleaded Laura's mam. Laura looked at her father.

'Dad, give me your word you won't get involved. This is between Bill and me. Please. I just need you and Mam to be here for me. Please don't get involved,' Laura whispered.

'This has shattered you all together, you're all out love,' her mother cried as she held Laura's hand.

'I'm just tired Mam, I'll be fine once I rest.' She look at her dad, probing.

'Dad?'

He said, 'OK pet, I won't get involved. It'll be difficult, but I know you're right. The doctor will be here soon to give you the once over.'

With that, he turned and descended the stairs, as he did not want Laura to see him shed the tears that were falling down his cheek.

Her brother Shane had phoned her several times over the next few days, as her mother had told him what had happened. He wanted to come home and be there for her, but there was no point. He couldn't do anything. Laura knew he had one thing in mind, he wanted to box the head of Bill, which certainly wasn't going to solve anything. No, better that everyone just got one with their lives, it would be easier to handle that way.

CHAPTER 7

The shrill of the phone brought Sharon back to reality. She had been in a trance ever since she realised she left the test at home in the bathroom. She debated whether to answer it but did anyway.

'Hi, this is reception, you were supposed to check out an hour ago, are you planning on staying another night?' asked the girl briskly.

Sharon looked at her watch, shit it was half four, her late check out expired at 3.30pm. What will I do? thought Sharon. The fact that Rob was bound to have found the test and hadn't contacted her must have meant he found it. If he hadn't, she might have stayed on for a while. To work out her options. However, she knew she had to talk to Rob.

'No sorry, I got held up, I'll be down in five minutes,' and Sharon ended the call.

After a non-eventful trip back home, the flight had been very calm, no turbulence which Sharon had been grateful for, her taxi pulled up at their apartment at 8.30pm. There were no lights on and her heart pounded at the fact he was not there. She felt half relived but she needed to know whether he knew or not. She paid the fare and bounded up the steps. Opening the door, the coldness of the place hit her suddenly, making her body shiver. The heating must not have been on all day. Bollox, thought Sharon worriedly.

She switched on the lights and strained her eyes as she wandered around the sitting room area, looking down the hall and around the apartment in general.

'Rob are you here?' she shouted, knowing full well he wasn't. She checked the bedrooms anyway in case. No sign of him. She hurried to the kitchen countertop and her eyes rested on what she feared she would find. A letter. Sharon grabbed the envelope, which had her name in big letters across the front in Rob's familiar scrawly writing; She tore it open;

My Dearest Sharon,

This is one of the hardest things I've ever had to do. I want you to know that I love you more so, very deeply. You have been a part of me and my life for the past ten years and I enjoyed ever second with you. You are an amazing woman. A woman who deserves someone much better than me. I'm so sorry Sharon, but you are a lot better off without me. I know this is a slimy thing to do, especially since you may be pregnant, but you have got to understand that I would be no good as a father.

I only realised when I found the test how selfish I was being. I cannot hold you back my sweet darling. You long for kids, and if we stayed together, you would eventually have resented me for not letting you have children. I would give anything for us to have kids and a family, but Sharon... trust me... The kids don't need someone like me. I know this makes no sense to you.

I don't know whether you are pregnant and if you are, what you intend to do. Either way, I think we should call it a day.

I don't want to hold you back any longer. If you are expecting, and planning on keeping it, I can assure you that I will set up a standing order every week to support you financially. But you must understand, please don't ever ask me to meet the child. It just isn't an option. I know it sounds heartless, but I have my reasons. I've moved out and am staying with a friend until I get sorted.

You can stay in the apartment as long as you like. I know we both own it jointly, but due to the circumstances I am leaving it to you if you make the repayments on the mortgage - you can keep the apartment. If you are not pregnant, we can sell it whenever you are ready, or you can buy me out.

Please don't hate me Sharon, please. I am doing this for you. I really am. I know it sounds like am an absolute selfish waster but that is not true. I'm doing it because I love you and want you to have the life you crave. Because even if you aren't pregnant now, you still have time.

I'm so sorry Shaz... I will always love you…

Rob

The tears started to fall, and she collapsed on the floor waling like a child. No, no, no. She'd get rid of it. Nothing was more important than Rob - no.

Please, she pleaded aloud. *You can't leave me, you just can't.* She cried for another while before deciding to call him. His mobile rang out.

Fuck. Just answer it. She tried again and was surprised to find he answered on the second ring

'Hi Shaz, I'm so sorry,' he said to her the minute he answered. Sharon wanted to keep things light.

'Rob, you big idiot, will you come home. OK, I thought I might be pregnant, but I don't know yet. Probably a false alarm. I've told you a hundred times, I'd rather have you than any child,' she said, trying to sound light-hearted.

'Sharon, you know I can't come home, and I won't be. And I really think if you are pregnant, you should keep the baby. It's what you've always wanted, and you'd be a great mother. I promise I'll support you financially.'

Sharon thought she was hearing things.

'Are you fucking crazy, you go on about how you can't ever be a father and how you hate kids but yet you're telling me to go ahead and have it! Fucking ironic, don't you think!' she screamed at him.

'Calm down, I'm sorry, I just think you'd regret it if you didn't have it. I know you Sharon, I know what you're like.'

'Oh right, do you now, and what do you know? That I'm a sad bitch, so sad that her boyfriend leaves her because he doesn't want kids but encourages her to have it anyway if it turns out she is pregnant!!'

She was still screaming. She couldn't help it. Rob sounded panicked.

'Sharon, please calm down.'

She screamed at him: 'Don't fucking tell me to calm down you pathetic piece of shit, you're some boyfriend, fucking off and leaving me when I might be carrying your child, you're not a man; you're a weed, a fucking weed.'

Rob ended the call saying sadly, 'Goodbye hun, take care of yourself.'

Sharon threw her mobile across the room and didn't care that it fell on the ground and might be damaged. She crawled to her bedroom and it only occurred to her then that all his things were missing. Sharon opened the wardrobe and found only her clothes. She checked the drawers, bathroom, under the bed. There no sign that Rob had ever lived here. She went up to the kitchen; all his belongings were gone. She also noticed that a framed photo that had sat on the mantelpiece of the two of them was missing. It was taken at a friend's wedding fours ago and Rob had loved it. She smiled in bitterness. Why would he want a picture of them when he just dumped her? A reminder every day of their relationship. She just didn't understand him.

Four weeks later, on a Thursday morning, Laura was tidying the house when the doorbell rang. Who would that be at this hour? she thought to herself.

She opened the door and found Jack Downey standing there.

'Hi Laura, how are you doing?' he enquired hesitantly. Laura smiled; this was Jack's second visit since she had been in hospital. He was a very nice man (not to mention extremely handsome) and she had appreciated that he had dropped by the last time. He had only stayed for ten minutes, but it felt nice that someone was concerned about her. Laura had met him the few times she and Bill had gone out with Sean and Paula or been to their dinner parties.

Jack usually joined them, but she hadn't known much about his personal life. Laura was struggling every day to try and keep it together for the kids. She pretty much ran on autopilot. Alarm would go off (not that she needed it, as she was usually wide-awake staring at the ceiling). She would get up and be washed and dressed before heading downstairs to get the breakfast things ready. Laura would let a holler from the hallway up to Ben and Jessica. Ten minutes later,

Ben usually came bombarding down the stairs and in the kitchen with bundles of energy all ready for his day ahead. He was only beginning to come around now after the news of his parents' breakup. The first three weeks had been very tough. But Bill had made a huge effort with him and still spent plenty of time with both the children. In saying that, there was no denying it was still a huge change in everyone's life. Coming back to reality, Laura tried to muster up some enthusiasm to greet her visitor.

'Jack, come on in.'

She held open the door as his large frame proceeded through into the hall. Laura closed the door and gestured for him to go into the kitchen. Jack walked on ahead and down towards the stove, standing in front of it, feeling the heat with his hands. Laura's heart clenched. Bill used to do that exact same gesture all the time.

'Cold out there today,' Jack said. Laura agreed, and they began to discuss the weather while she put on the kettle. She went over and sat at the island on one of the highchairs while it boiled. They chatted easily about nothing important, just things in general, both avoiding the elephant in the room. Laura decided she was glad he called around, as he did manage to lift her spirits, and give her a little bit of confidence back. Laura wasn't entirely sure what his reasons for calling were. She was a hundred per cent sure there were no romantic intentions involved, as he was aware that her marriage had only just broken up. That last time he had dropped by, he had caught Laura off guard. She had been taking in the milk from the doorstep and he arrived as if out of nowhere in front of her. She had just been crying heavily and still had not dressed. She knew what a wreck she must have looked and most certainly would not have answered had the door been closed. Jack had immediately gone to her, taking her arm, and tenderly guiding her back through the hall and into the kitchen.

'Laura,' he had said so quietly she had hardly heard him. 'I am so sorry – I did hear about you and Bill – and with you not being well recently, I wanted to drop in and see how you were coping.'

Obviously, he must have thought she wasn't coping. At *all*. But she was. She just had a bad morning. An invite to a cousin's wedding had arrived for her and Bill, and it had set her off. She had let Jack make her a cup of tea and she spoke to him for about twenty minutes. Not getting into any details, just talking about the general separation and the effects on everyone.

Once she had gathered herself together, she had felt absolutely mortified. Laura had jumped up suddenly from her seat at the table and assured Jack she was fine now, and that she didn't mean to rush him, but she had appointment at 11 o'clock that she needed to get ready for. It took her a while to get him out the door, as he wasn't fully sure she was genuinely OK. He must have thought she might do away with herself, and she supposed, given what happened at the beach, she couldn't really blame him. Maybe he felt sorry for her. Yes, that was probably it, thought Laura. After all, he was a very successful businessman. He had properties all over the world, buying old run-down premises or houses for a fraction of their potential cost, doing them up to a high standard and then selling them off, making massive profits. Well, he had not actually said anything about the profits end of things. But she had remembered Paula boasting about it once. About how their 'best friend' Jack was a self-made millionaire.

'Yes,' Laura thought to herself, 'He definitely just feels sorry for me.'

In which case, Laura didn't really want him calling anymore.

As the days and weeks passed, life wasn't getting any easier for Laura. Every day she woke her heart clenched in realisation that she no longer had a husband, well, a live-in husband. Ben had initially taken it very badly. Sometimes taking it out on Laura by shouting at her and refusing to eat his dinner. But he was now coming back to his old self again. And Jessica, much to Laura's surprise, didn't seem to be too upset. Laura had sat the kids down the day after their father left and explained that mammy and daddy were having some time apart, but they still loved the kids more than ever. She had mustered together all her strength and as calmly as she could answered all their questions and concerns. Most of which she blagged as she had no clue herself what the answers were. Ben had got understandably very upset, asking tons of questions, breaking Laura's heart as the tears flowed down his little angry face. Laura was so glad Jess was there. She had told Ben to calm down and leave Mam alone. She had then issued him with several reassurances that they all would be fine, and of the benefits of having their dad live somewhere else, such as extra trips to McDonalds and the cinema. It seemed to do the trick, it wasn't that it had appeased him, but more that it gave him something to think about.

Jessica had hugged her mother and told her it would be all OK because she would look after her. Laura didn't want to cry in front of her kids, but when her fifteen-year-old daughter told her she would look after her, it proved more than she could handle. She had cried into Jess's shoulder as Ben had stomped off upstairs to phone his dad. Laura didn't know what Bill had said to him, but whatever it was it certainly helped to calm him down.

Her son had been very subdued after that, and Laura had been very worried about him. She had spoken to her husband (leaving out their own differences for now), and so Bill had come around every evening, spending a couple of hours with him. It seemed to have worked, thank god. Ben probably realised that he would still see his dad loads, and it wasn't like he was going away forever. He had spent every weekend with Bill since then, in her husband's small apartment which he was renting. It was about a ten-minute drive away, in the direction of the city centre. Laura was quite taken aback by how quickly Bill had gotten himself a place and she had tackled him about it. She remembered the conversation now.

'But Laura, you told me hundreds of times that it's over and you begged me to move out. You told me it was easier for everyone that I went. I didn't want to. You know I didn't. In fact, why don't I just move back? You weren't thinking properly, Laura. I can go and get my stuff now. I mean, I'll lose the deposit and all that, but I don't care,' he had pleaded.

Laura began to panic. Realising her mistake, she quickly reassured him that, no, he was in fact doing the right thing.

'Look Bill, I'm sorry for having a go at you. It's very difficult for me. But you must have somewhere other than a hotel room where the children can go to and spend time with you, which is more is important than my feelings.'

Feeling the familiar wave of guilt rush over him, Bill began to apologise again, but Laura was in no humour for it. She had sent him on his way quickly after that and was in some respects glad that he had somewhere he could call a base. It was one less thing to worry about.

Her daughter didn't seem as keen to spend as much time there and only went over late on Saturday night, coming home early Sunday morning. Laura got the feeling that she only went over out of a sense of duty, and this worried her. After all, Bill was her father. And a good one at that.

She also knew that Jess worried about her, and that was also why she didn't stay away too long. Laura was doing a lot of writing lately. She normally did all her work from home only going into the office when she really needed to, but this week she had been in every day. Getting out and working hard helped her forget about it. She blocked it from her mind altogether, going to the office and speaking with her boss and a few colleagues. None of them knew that she and Bill had separated, and she wasn't ready to tell them. The office was in the centre of town and was a pain to get to in the car.

It would be easier to get the bus, but she really couldn't face public transport right now, especially at the risk of seeing someone she might have to talk to. Luckily, there were a few parking spaces at the back of the building belonging to the company and as most people got the train or bus to work, Laura usually got a place OK. The office itself was in a rather old building with three floors, the first and second used as offices and the third as a canteen, boardroom and meeting rooms. As Laura usually worked from home, she did not have her own office space, and tended to work from one of the meeting rooms if they were free, opting for the canteen if they were occupied. Her boss had recently referred to her frequent office visits and Laura had worriedly asked if it was OK her coming in.

He had assured that of course it was, but he wanted to get her a more secure place to work from. Laura would rather have stayed on the third floor, as being located on one of the others meant she could not avoid conversation. When it had gotten busy in the past with the canteen and meetings, she would always slip out to a coffee shop for a while. But there would be no avoiding it now. Ah, well, she supposed, she would have to deal with it somehow.

When Laura got home in the evenings, she continued on autopilot until the kids were fed, washed and in bed. It was only then that her real feelings came out. She would sit and cry on the sofa, flicking through the channels being careful that her daughter wasn't going to suddenly pop in to check on her.

Nothing on the TV could keep her attention for long, as something would happen that would remind her of her husband. And she would be off again. Laura was never one to drink at home, but she had found herself these past few weeks consuming close to a bottle each night. She knew this wasn't good but argued that it helped her to sleep for the first half of the night. She promised herself she would give it up for the New Year.

Although in saying that, some nights the wine had no effect at all. She would lie awake going over and over her marriage. The last year. Did she have any clues at all? She didn't. She trusted him fully. Sometimes she wouldn't be able to believe it. She would think it had all been a dream and she would laugh to herself and reach for the phone.

Laura would go as far as dialing his number, but always hung up before it rang, the dream over. And then she would cry and cry. And lie there in a daze until her alarm would take her out of the trance and up, she would get to live another lie, as that's what she was doing. The person who got up, got the kids ready, went to work, came home and cooked dinner; this person, this woman was not her, no.

.

CHAPTER 8

Three months later Laura was getting ready to meet Sharon in town. The past few weeks had flown by, and she was glad of that. She spent most of her time working and looking after the kids. She and Bill still hadn't met up.

He rang her some days to see how she was. Sometimes she spoke to him, other times she didn't. When Laura had finally lifted the phone to ring her friend, three weeks after their row, her hands were sweating with nerves. Sharon had been quite short with her, just answering her questions. In fact, Sharon had been acting strange ever since the argument. They had met several times and each time no matter how many times her friend told Laura she was forgiven, she still felt that Sharon was mad at her.

She would not even have a drink with her. Coffee. Or if Laura was lucky, Sharon would have one glass of wine. Jez, she must have really hurt her.

Laura was hurting too because she felt like she had lost both a husband and a best friend. Maybe that was why she was spending so much time with Jack lately. Well, they weren't dating or anything, but he called around a lot and the kids liked him. Bill hated him. Ben would come home in a bad humour from Bill's sometimes and when Laura asked what was wrong after a half hour of nothings, he would ask her if Jack was going to be moving in.

…Obviously, Bill was putting ideas in his head. She told him of course not, that Jack was only a friend. He had only started to call around again around a month ago. Laura had not heard from him for two months. He had asked her out to the pictures last week, but she said she was busy. She liked him but wasn't ready for a relationship. Her marriage had only just broken up and her feelings were still raw. Christmas had been and gone. She and the children had dinner at Laura's parents' house.

It had been awkward because Ben kicked up, insisting that Bill came with them. Luckily, her husband had the decency to be firm with their son and explain that the kids could have dinner the next day with him and their other grandparents. Lucky them! Ha. Poor Jess. She hated every minute of it. The poison dwarf kept putting Laura down. Which was a disgraceful carry on. Bill's mother should have more cop on than to involve the children in this. She was fuming with her. His mother was obviously hoping Laura would hear her words back. She was extremely distressed that Laura had the cheek to throw her son out. Even though Bill had explained what had happened, she had still taken her son's side. Ah, well. She didn't care. Laura didn't want to waste time thinking about her. She wasn't worth it.

Bill had been very good to her the past few months. He always took the kids if she had to work late as she was being given more and more assignments and he still paid most of the bills and made sure they were provided for. Laura certainly felt that he really was sorry. And she was beginning to feel sorry for him. But she could not take him back. Not after bitch Johnson. She probably could have taken him back if it had been a stranger. But not with her.

'Mam!' screamed Jess.

Shit she thought, I'm standing here daydreaming and I'm meant to be meeting Sharon in fifteen minutes.

Some chance. She looked at herself in her bedroom mirror that was attached to the wardrobe, ran her hand though her hair and grabbing her bag, walked quickly down the stairs.

'Yes pet, what is it?' she asked her daughter who was in the kitchen staring at a pot of soup.

'Will this take much longer; I only have forty-five minutes for my lunch break and I've only twenty minutes left now before I go back to work'.

Laura smiled and went over to the cooker. She stared into the pot to see the soup was boiling wildly trying its hardest to throw itself over the edges.

'Good god, you'll never be no Gordon Ramsey! You're meant to turn the heat down and let it simmer once you bring it to the boil.'

She turned down the heat and placed the lid on top of the pot.

'Now, just let it alone for five minutes and it should be ready, although I'm pretty sure you killed any flavour,' she laughed.

Jessica shrugged her shoulders, taking the spoon her mother had used to stir the soup out of her hand and licking the top of it.

'I don't like cooking' it's not my thing,' she told her mother.

Laura laughed again and turning towards the hall, called back.

'Well, you may start learning missus. You're coming sixteen soon. And you don't even know how to make soup!'

Laura thought this was very funny and continued to laugh loudly.

'Oh, shut up, are you meeting Sharon?' Jess asked.

Laura stopped in the doorway and turned towards her daughter.

'I am yes, I better go. OK darling, I'm only joking, you're a great cook! NOT.'

She ran from the hall and out the front door.

Laura was meeting Sharon in Clontarf in a Mediterranean Cafe on the high street. She smiled to herself. She felt a lot better these past couple of weeks. She was beginning to get her appetite back and she didn't have to pretend to smile anymore, it just came naturally. Not that she was over Bill. She wasn't. But she felt a little better and this pleased her. And it was great that she could genuinely laugh and joke with her daughter, without having to put on an act. As she pulled into the car park, she saw Sharon's car already there, a flashy Audi A4. Sharon loved cars.

Fuck. I hope she's in good form with me today. I wish I could make things better between us, she thought to herself. Laura got out and made her way towards the restaurant, wondering whether Sharon was looking out the window at her. As she arrived, she could see her friend was over by a table at the window, the usual glass of water with lemon in front of her.

Laura's heart sank and she felt herself immediately tense.

'Hiya,' she called, as she made her way towards her.

Sharon stood up to embrace Laura.

'How are you, you're looking fantastic.'

She hugged her for longer than normal, and Laura could feel the weight of the world on her friend's shoulders. What was wrong?

'I'm fine Shaz; more to the point, how are you?'

Sharon's smile faded rapidly. She sighed.

'I'm OK, just working a lot lately. I need more me time.'

Laura wasn't convinced. She shifted uncomfortably in her seat and tried again.

'How's Rob doing?' At the mention of his name Sharon's face drained and she lifted her glass, taking a sip of water.

'Yup, fine, all is fine.'

Laura didn't believe her. Oh my god, she thought, is that what was wrong with her this past while and Laura had been too blind to notice? Too worried about her own problems than to think that Sharon might have some.

'What is it love, please tell me, you're my best friend, I know I treated you very badly and I'm so sorry, but I want to be here for you the way you are for me.'

Laura spoke gently and as encouragingly as she could. Sharon hadn't heard such a tender gentle voice speak to her in such a way in so long that she finally broke down. Laura was absolutely astounded. She would expect this of her other friends, and of herself, but for Sharon to cry like this in a restaurant meant something was seriously wrong.

'Come on, it's OK, let it all out. No one can see you.'

Thank god the restaurant was nearly empty. There were two other couples but both a good distance away. Maybe that was why Sharon sat here. Maybe she had asked to meet up to tell her what was wrong.

'It's OK, I'm fine, honestly, I'm just so tired. I need a break I think, I'm exhausted and it's messing me up.

'Sharon, quit talking shite and tell me what the bloody hell is wrong with you!' laughed Laura, trying to lighten the mood. Sharon hadn't intended telling Laura yet. She knew her friend had too many of her own problems to deal with. Sharon hadn't told anyone. The only people who knew were a couple of Rob's mates. He had had to tell them as they noticed he wasn't living with Sharon anymore; but apart from that no one was the wiser. After the night she had come home to find Rob gone, she had struggled on with her life. Worked, worked and then more work.

She didn't socialise anymore apart from meeting with Laura every now and then. Sharon was very much pregnant. But she didn't even think about the baby. Hadn't even gone to the doctors for an appointment. She was pretending it wasn't happening and that was easy because she spent her whole time thinking about Rob. She'd have to tell Laura sometime; it wasn't fair on her either.

'Rob's left me,' she said suddenly. And she didn't cry when she said it - possibly didn't have any tears left to cry. She stared at Laura's open mouth, seeing she was struggling to respond. She continued.

'Yep, he left me three or four months ago, around the same time you and Bill split.'

Laura's mouth opened again, this time to say something but closed again quickly. She couldn't believe it. She didn't know whether she was more shocked because Rob had left Sharon or because nearly four months had gone by and Sharon hadn't told her.

'Four months,' Laura managed.

'I know, I'm so sorry I didn't tell you, but you had your own life to worry about, and there was me giving you advice about your love life when all along mine was doomed too.

'But Sharon, why? What happened? Another woman?' Sharon nodded her head.

'Yes, typical, they're all the same aren't they, some bitch from the gym.' Sharon didn't know why she was lying but it seemed easier to go down that route than the truth. She couldn't handle the full truth just yet. I mean, she still hadn't coped with it herself yet, so how could she tell Laura?

'The bastard, I just don't understand them, they are all pigs. Oh, Shaz, why didn't you tell me, you know I would have been there,' Laura said taking Sharon's hand in hers.

'I know, but as I said, you had your own problems, and I wasn't ready to talk about it. It was like when the two of us had that argument in the hospital, you knew I was right, but you didn't want to hear it or even think about it. I was the same, I wanted to pretend it didn't happen, and that's what I've been doing. Until now.'

Laura's heart bled for her friend. She always liked Rob. She honestly thought they would be together forever.

The odd occasion when she thought about the kid's thing, she wondered would Sharon ever leave him because she wanted kids, but now it seemed like he hadn't given her a chance to. The prick had been shagging someone else.

'Why don't you move in with me for a while?' Laura suggested. Sharon panicked at the thought. She needed her space to be able to cry, shout and scream whenever she needed to.

'No, honestly, thanks anyway, but I'd rather not, I'm feeling a lot better now as it is.

'Where is Rob now, did he move in with his bit on the side?' probed Laura; she couldn't help herself.

'No, no, he's living with a mate, he said it was just a fling, but he thinks it's time we went our separate ways, he was decent about it.'

Laura was baffled that Sharon was being so calm.

'DECENT? What do you mean DECENT?' Laura couldn't believe her ears; this was Sharon, Sharon take no shit; Sharon cut a man's balls off if he crossed her. Fecking hell.

'What's got into you?'

Sharon looked up at her warily.

'Oh Laura, I just mean that he's been nice to me. Rings me now and then to see how I am and that. He just doesn't love me anymore, so I can't blame him.' Sharon didn't know why but she felt like she had to defend him.

Laura bit her lip. She had been in this position before and so she knew what it was like.

'As long as you're OK, but you do know you can stay with me, no problem, anytime.' Sharon sat back in her chair and smiled tiredly. She wished now that they were having this conversation somewhere else. The waiter was hovering around them, sensing the seriousness of the girls' discussion. Tactically staying away, but at the same time, wanting to take their order.

'I know that, and I'm grateful. Thanks, Laura. Oh, and will you keep this to yourself, I'd rather not discuss it with anyone else?'

Laura smiled knowing all too well how she felt, as this was her a few months ago, and even still. What a pair they were.

'No problem.' Laura felt a little relief that at least she and Sharon were back on old terms again.

'Are we gonna eat or what? I'm famished!' At this announcement from Laura the grateful waiter rushed over.

'Are you girls ready to order?' he asked with a radiant smile, and the two friends broke down, holding their bellies with laughter, and further delaying their order, much to the annoyance of the waiter.

CHAPTER 9

That same Saturday, Bill was back in the arms of Laura and they were about to make love when the doorbell rang loudly, waking him from his fantasy. For fuck sake, he thought, I can't even have her in my dreams. He got up from the sofa and walked down the hall. The sound of the grandfather clock indicated it was five o 'clock. Shit, I have to collect Ben in half an hour, he thought to himself.

He opened the door and in horror tried closing it just as quickly. His efforts were in vain as she pushed her way through the door and into the hall. God, please don't do this to me, he pleaded with the Man above to save him.

'You think you could hide from me darling? Ha, Ha,' Rita laughed. 'You can't live without me dearest, you know it, there's no point in hiding from the truth,' she stated, as she began to take her long coat off to reveal a black sexy bra, stockings, suspender belt, black pants and black knee-high boots.

There was a time when nothing would have stopped Bill going to her and ripping off her clothes. He would just have to look at her and he would get furiously excited, but now the sight of her turned his stomach. He didn't have any interest in this woman, nor any other woman for that matter, but Laura. Even if Angelina Jolie was standing there butt naked, he would not be in the slightest turned on. Because the whole time he kept thinking about Laura, and about her lovely body. He looked Rita in the eyes and sighed sadly.

'Just go. Get dressed and go.' He then walked down the hall toward the small sitting room and left her standing there in total shock.

Never had she felt so humiliated in all her life. The cheek of him.

'Come back here, you were not saying that a few months ago, you could not bear to be away from me. You need me and I need you, there's no point in denying it.'

Oh god. He just didn't have the energy for this, he really didn't. How was he going to get rid of her? Summoning as much energy as he could muster, Bill took the bull by the horns and replied.

'Look, if you don't go, I'll call the guards, make no mistake about it, I want you out of my life for good. What we had is in the past and that is where it will stay. You were just sex and I never cared about you. The sooner you get that through your thick head the sooner we can both move on with our lives.'

Johnson was flabbergasted.

Bill did feel a tiny bit of guilt at the way he had spoken to her and what he had said. He knew it was cruel. But the woman just wouldn't take no for an answer. He felt he had no choice. Rita couldn't believe that Bill was sending her away. She was fully sure that once she turned up on his doorstep, dressed in his favourite little outfit, that he would be putty in her hands. She pulled her coat tightly around her and shouted down the hall at him.

'You'll regret this you waster, you don't know who you're dealing with,' she threatened. Bill had had enough.

He stormed back up the hall and took his phone out of his pocket.

'GET OUT - JUST GET THE FUCK OUT!' He could not take anymore; she was driving him mad. He began to dial a number on the phone, and suddenly Rita realised he was serious about phoning the police.

'OK you chicken shit, I'm leaving. You were pathetic in bed anyway. I've had schoolboys who could do better!' she screamed spitefully, turned on her heels and out the door, slamming it so hard it nearly came off the hinges. Bill just laughed sadly. He didn't care. Nothing she said could hurt him. Because Laura was all he wanted.

After a long lunch with Sharon the two friends kissed and promised to meet up through the week. When Laura arrived home at four o clock her mobile began to ring just as she was entering the kitchen. She searched through her bag, eventually locating it, promising herself to do a tidy out as she had so much accumulated crap in it which made it so hard to find anything in it.

'Hello.' She smiled to herself as she saw the caller ID.

'Mam? Are you back yet? How did lunch go with Sharon?' Jess asked, without taking a breath.

There was no way Laura was going to spill the beans.

'Yes great, she's really well. We had a great catch up. Are you still at work?' she asked her daughter.

'Yes, I am, I'm glad you enjoyed it. Can I ask a huge favour?' Jess hurried on. 'The girls are meeting in town later and going to the cinema; I'm finished here in half an hour, could you drop me in to meet the girls around five? Please?' begged her first born.

So much for a relaxing evening thought Laura. She sighed. 'I suppose I could, but are you not going to your father's tonight?'. Laura didn't want Jessica and Bill's relationship to suffer. She tried to encourage her daughter to spend more time with him.

'Well, I am, but later on. He phoned me already today and I asked him if it was OK if I met the girls first. He said once you were OK, then it was fine with him. I'll be going to his after the pictures; he offered to pick me up. Laura was a bit taken aback.

'Oh.' She was pleased that the two seemed to be communicating and getting on better than she realised.

'Well, OK then sure, I can drop Ben off on the way; it'll save your dad coming over for him.'

Jess seemed happy with this.

'OK great Mam, thanks, I'll be home in half an hour. I don't need anything to eat, Dad, me and Ben are going to get a pizza later.' And with that, her daughter was gone, unaware of how much that comment had hurt her mother.

Laura stood with her phone in her hand and couldn't help feeling a little left out. She was glad to see the kids getting on well with their dad, but she was a tiny bit jealous.

'Mam,' Ben cried as he came into the kitchen. He was about to ask her could he get a new PlayStation game but then he saw the look on her face and asked worriedly, 'Mam, are you OK?'

Laura smiled at her son, he had been quite a handful lately, but she wasn't surprised after the separation and that.

'I'm fine pet, what is it?'

Ben walked over to his mother and put his arms around her shyly.

'I'm sorry for being a bit bold lately, I don't mean it, I love you very much, you're the best Mam in the world.'

Laura was surprised. She might not have been had it been a few months ago before things went bad, but he hadn't really shown her any affection since Bill left.

'Don't be silly, you're not that bad, you're just doing what little boys do, isn't that right?' she laughed and pulled him tighter to her.

'OK, once you're sure you won't throw me out for being bold, will you?' he enquired, eyes wide.

'What on earth gave you that idea?' Laura's heart contracted in pain for her young son. 'Dad said that he was really bold and mean to you, and that's why he had to leave. When I told him earlier on the phone that I was being a bit mean too 'cos I wanted to move in with him he told me that you're the best mother a kid could have and that I should appreciate you more.' Laura's eyes prickled.

She wasn't sure if the tears were because of the nice words Bill said about her or because Ben had been bold hoping she'd throw him out too. Oh, the innocence of it all.

'Darling, do you not want to live with me and your sister?' Her voice quivered. Crossing her fingers discreetly, she prayed silently and breathed a sigh of relief when Ben said, 'I do, but I just wanted Dad to feel better by me getting kicked out too.'

Laura started to laugh, and her heart melted.

'Oh, you big softie, Dad wasn't kicked out. We both decided it was for the best. But we want and love you and your sister very much; you do know that, don't you?'

Ben had tears rolling down his cheek, but she was glad she was having this conversation with him.

'Yes,' he sniffled. She threw her arms around him, relieved that he had opened up to her somewhat and then asked him what it was he originally called her for.

'Oh, I don't know, I can't remember,' he said, deciding that the PlayStation game could keep until another day.

Laura indicated and turned right, heading up the street in the direction of where Bill was now residing.

'Have you got your things darling?' she asked her son. He began to shuffle around in the back seat, checking around him making sure he hadn't left anything behind. He hit off Jess, who pushed him off her with a scowl.

'Ye Mam, I hope he's here though,' he said worryingly. This was news to Laura.

'What, why wouldn't he be? Did you not phone him?' Laura enquired. He shook his shoulders.

'I did, but his phone was switched off.'

Oh, thought Laura, not like him. However, as they pulled up, they could see his car was parked outside the apartment. There was also another car next to it in the visitor's spot, a very snazzy Bentley.

There was what looked like a uniformed man sitting in the front driver's seat and the back windows were blackened so she didn't know whether there was anyone in it. She doubted whoever it was had anything to do with Bill; must have been visiting someone else in the complex.

'Right Ben, off you go. I'll wait here to make sure that your dad's able to take you.'

Ben leaned forward between the seats, kissing his mother happily on the cheek and then jumped out of the car bounding like a little puppy towards the front door. Smiling at him, Laura's face quickly changed. Before Ben could knock, the door swung open, and Laura's heart pounded as she saw who emerged from the house. Good god. No. No Way.

The bastard, he told her it was finished. Jesus, why was she so stupid, she had actually felt sorry for him and the whole time he was still screwing her behind Laura's back. She couldn't believe it. The wind had been taken right out of her sails. He really had managed to convince Laura that he now despised his former mistress. Not so former though, it seemed.

But then thinking about it, she was no longer his other half and if he chose to stay with that cow, well then that was his business. Laura would put on a brave face. Coming back to reality, Laura watched now as Johnson nearly knocked her son over as she stormed past him and towards her awaiting car. Mmm… She did seem angry. But how pathetic that she had a chauffeur waiting on her while she and Bill got up to whatever they got up to. She didn't think anything more could shock her about that woman when, just as Johnson was about to get into the car she glanced over in Laura's direction and recognised her former work colleague.

A smile spread across Johnson's face as she opened her jacket enough to reveal what she had on underneath. Laura had to do all she could to stop herself from spewing. Her hands started sweating and she began to shake. It was difficult trying not to imagine Bill and her in bed together, but she managed it most of the time. Seeing that bitch with that tarty lingerie on put more images of the two in bed and it burned Laura to the core. Just then Jess spoke loudly from the back who until now had been listening to her iPod oblivious to what was happening.

Startling her she shouted, 'Who's that woman? She looks familiar.'
What was Laura supposed to say to this? She couldn't deal with this
right now. She silently cursed Bill for leaving all the hard stuff to her.
She was with the children most of the time and therefore had to endure
endless questions about their separation. She thought she had been
doing much better lately.

She had been dealing with the situation and even beginning to feel
a tiny bit more positive about things. Well, all that was totally gone
down the drain now. In fact, she was most likely back to square one.
Her emotions were all over the place.

'Mam?' questioned Jess impatiently.

'Ehh, I don't know love, must be a friend of your dad's.' and with
that, Laura turned the car around with an aggressive force and the tyres
screeched loudly as she drove off down the road like a cop car in a
high-speed pursuit.

'Mam, Mam, are you OK? Slow down please, you're scaring me,
Maaaam,' pleaded Jess, now leaning forward between the two seats.

However, Laura ignored her daughter's cries. She couldn't slow down, she couldn't, she had to get away, and fast.

'Mam, will you slow the FUCK down!' Jess tried once more, a lot more forcefully though and it seemed to do the job as Laura came back to reality and pulled into the side of the road. Her hands were shaking and her head and ears were ringing.

'Jess, don't ever let me hear you swear like that again.' Laura couldn't believe she was chastising her daughter for swearing after the way she had been driving but it was the first thing that came into her head. Jess looked very concerned for her mother.

'I'm sorry Mam, but it was the only way to get your attention, you could have killed us. Jesus.'

Laura sat back in horror and disgust as she realised that she had once again let bitch Johnson win, and in doing that she had put her own daughter's life in danger.

'I'm so sorry pet, I'm so sorry.'

She couldn't hold it in anymore. She began to cry, putting her head in her hands and leaning over on the steering wheel. Poor Jess didn't know what to do.

'Mam, it's OK, I understand, it was that woman. Well, I'm going to kill Dad when I get him.'

No, that's not what Laura wanted. She didn't want to get her daughter involved. It wasn't fair. She managed to sit up, shake herself off, and turned around to her daughter.

'No, no you're not, we are not together anymore, and your dad is entitled to his own life. Jess, look at me, I mean it. Don't mention this to Dad. If he asks, say we saw nothing. Please.'

Jess didn't say anything for a few seconds.

' OK, Mam, if that's what you want. I won't go to his tonight though, I'll come home.' This was also the last thing Laura wanted. Her daughter needed to spend time with her father. Plus, Laura wanted the house to herself, so she could spend the evening drowning her sorrows alone.

'No, you won't pet, you will go to your dads like you had planned: he is your father, and he is entitled to a girlfriend if he wants. We both have to move on, it was just hard for me to see it with my own eyes. But I'm OK now. And I will be.' Jess didn't say anything. Laura thought best to leave it there.

'So, we better get going or you'll be late for the cinema.'

And that was the end of the conversation.

'Dad!' Ben cried as he ran in to the house. Bill was sitting on the sofa in the sitting room, head in his hands, wondering how he could get rid of Rita for good.

'Fuck,' he shouted as he heard his son's voice and ran towards the front door. A feeling of dread washed through him. Please god, No. But his worst fears were confirmed as he heard the screech from Laura's car as it tore down the road. He looked over to the Bentley as Rita rolled down the window and spoke out

'You'll never win her back now!!' She leaned back laughing as the Bentley reversed out and flew off in the same direction as his wife.

Bill couldn't believe what was happening. Just typical. Bloody typical.

He turned to his son who was hovering behind him, with his bag clutched in his hands, not sure what was going on.

'Ben, why are you here? We arranged that I would pick you up,' he asked crossly. His son's eyes began to water as he wasn't used to his dad being mad.

'I'm sorry, Mam was dropping Jess into town and said she'd save you driving to our house and bring me here.' And then the tears began to poor down his little face. Bill's heart contracted painfully and pulling Ben in an embrace said, 'Oh come here you silly sod, don't mind me, I was having a bad day. Much better though now that you are here.'

He felt bad for speaking to him like that. It wasn't Ben's fault. Bill toyed with the idea of phoning Laura, but he knew there was no point. There was no way she'd believe him. If Jess were in the car, then she would have seen Rita too. Ben was still too young to realise anything had happened. He had been so excited about seeing his dad that he didn't even ask who the woman was. Or maybe he did realise and he was afraid of the answer if he did ask. His daughter would go mad. He would have to try and convince her what really happened. He would explain the situation to her and try and get her on side.

Jess could then convince Laura that he really was finished with Johnson. Yes, that's it, that's what I'll do, and he felt marginally better at this thought. Rita had serious issues and he knew the battle wasn't over with her. She was like a dog with a bone. Although he couldn't help feeling a bit sorry for her. He knew she had a terrible childhood. She never knew her father, and her mother had been an escort. Well, that's what Rita had said, the night he had arrived late to the hotel room they were meeting in and found her sitting down in the shower, the water pouring over her, and a bottle of vodka in her hands. He was utterly shocked. He had never seen her anything but ready to take on the world. Strong, confident and full of determination. He ran to her, and after gently coaxing her out of the shower, and prising the vodka from her hands, he dried her off, wrapped her in a dressing gown he found in the wardrobe and sat her down on the bed beside him. And she began to talk.

It was twenty-five years to the date that she had been raped. Just a teenager. One of her mother's clients decided Rita looked like a better prospect than her worn-out drunk of a mother. Rita had been used to seeing men come and go and understood how her mother could afford to give her everything, and everything she did. The clothes, the gadgets, the weekends away. Everything her mother did was for her daughter. But Rita would rather have been poor and have her mother earn her income in another way. She hated it. Seeing the way they looked at Rita, some with sympathy, others with intrigue.

And not knowing if and when one of them would pounce. And pounce they did. A huge burly man, black hair and a big bushy beard, arms like a TV Superstar Wrestler and who reminded her of Bruno from Popeye; so much so, she could never hear the name Popeye without inwardly flinching. That was the night that changed Rita. She never told her mother what happened. But packed her bags at the age of fifteen and ran away. And swore no man would ever get the better of her again. She never had any respect for marriage as a result – didn't most men seek out sex elsewhere, regardless of their marital vows; wasn't her mother proof of that? She did write frequently and sent her money. But when she received no word back after two months, Rita grew concerned, and returned to find another family living in her house. When the door was eventually answered, she was told that the previous woman was a drunk who took an overdose and died a week after her daughter ran away.

And alas. A hard, cold and bitter Rita was born. After she offloaded her story to him, Rita had fallen asleep. And the next morning when Bill woke, she was gone. Leaving a note 'Early meeting – Sorry – Call you later.' And it was never spoken of again. She had completely closed him off when they had met next time. Didn't want to discuss it and told him to forget about it. It never happened. And so he had. She needed help, badly. Especially now. But that wasn't Bill's responsibility. He had his own problems to deal with. Rita had to sort herself out. And unless she sought professional help, she would never change.

CHAPTER 10

Laura had lifted the phone four times but replaced it just as many, before she could actually bring herself to dial the number. It was a couple of weeks after the dreaded events at Bill's, and Laura was now trying to convince herself to ask Jack to go out with her later. Not a date. Just for some company. To try and make herself feel human again. She hadn't heard from him in a while. He had been around a couple of times and had hinted on one of those occasions about them going out for dinner. But she had quickly dashed that idea.

She wasn't sure what his motives were either. Surely, he knew with her marriage break-up so fresh she wouldn't be looking for anything. But maybe he just felt sorry for her and wanted to cheer her up. She wasn't sure. At the time Laura had wanted no part in it. But now that she knew Bill was still seeing Johnson, she felt that she had to prove she wasn't the only one who could have a life. She wouldn't class it as moving on. As she hadn't; at all. And each day was still a tough task. But she did feel lonely and didn't want to be bothering Sharon with the situation her friend was in.

So, Laura had decided that morning that she would see if Jack would like to go out for dinner some evening, regardless of whether he just felt sorry for her or not. She didn't fancy him, although he was very attractive, she had to admit. There was no way she was ready for anything. He hadn't called in a few weeks, and Laura guessed that he probably wouldn't again. Unless she did something about it. He had made his move, although extremely discreetly, and was quickly rebuffed. Whatever his intentions, Jack would not be used to turn-downs.

She decided she would call him later. He would probably be busy this morning anyway and not be able to talk.

Laura sighed and walked from the hall back into the kitchen. She plonked herself down on the stool, resting her chin on her hand, leaning on the island countertop. She looked out the window and watched the rain lashing against the window pane. How depressing, she sighed. Suddenly she sat up as a thought struck her. A holiday. That's what she needed. It would certainly take her mind off things and the kids could really do with a break after what they had been through.

Where could they go? Thinking about it, she remembered something. Sarah, a colleague in work, owned a villa on the south-east coast of Spain. She had offered it to Laura and the family on numerous occasions, but they never seemed to find the time. She wondered if Sarah still had the place and if so, would she be able to take her up on her offer now? It would be so great to get away for a while. Just a week. It would be plenty. She wondered if Sharon would be interested in going too. God knows, Sharon was having a difficult time of it. Maybe it would be good for her too.

Laura was due into work in a couple of days, so she would ask Sarah then, and see if it's available and when. No point in thinking anymore about it until she found out if it was available. In the meantime, Laura thought to herself, I've got nothing to lose. If Jack says no, so what? She got off the stool and went back into the hall lifting the receiver for the fifth time and dialed his number carefully from the display area on her mobile phone where she had his number saved. The phone began to ring, and Laura's heart began to beat loudly in anticipation.

'Jack's phone,' a woman's giggling voice answered. Laura hung up immediately. Her cheeks began to burn in embarrassment. Shit. He's obviously seeing someone. She felt like such an idiot. Ah, well, that put an end to that she supposed. It was a sign. Her thoughts were interrupted by the shrill of the phone in front of her. It couldn't be Jack as he didn't have the house number, so she picked up straight away thinking it was one of the family or a friend.

'Hello.'

Startled then, she heard, 'Hi, who's this? I had a missed call,' Jack's voice sounded down the phone. Shit, shit, shit. Oh, No. Fuck. Could she just hang up? Bollocks.

Her cheeks were on fire.

'Oh, eh, hi, Jack,' she stammered. 'It's Laura, just seeing how you were.'

What a stupid thing to come out with. Please, ground, open up and swallow me.

'Ah Laura, Great to hear from you.' He sounded genuinely delighted. 'Sorry about that, my friend Holly answered the phone. She's an awful joker.'

Laura wasn't sure what to say now. Fuck. She was no good at this.

'Is everything OK? How are the kids?' he continued. This was getting worse.

'All good, yeah. The kids are great. Much better now. Yeah, everything is fine. I just hadn't seen you in a few weeks and said I'd give you a call. See if you wanted to drop in for a coffee if you're passing.'

Oh, Lord. Did she really just say that? She sounded so, so desperate. Oh, what an idiot. The shame.

Jack seemed surprised.

' Oh, right, ehh, yeah sure. Actually, I'll tell you what. Why don't you meet me for a bit of lunch one of the days this week if you're free?'

Laura felt that she had now pressured him in to taking her out. But she could hardly say no when she initiated the call. Fuck.

'Yeah sure, that sounds good. Are you around Thursday?' Damn it, she may as well just get on with it now.

'We could go down to Harvey's in the Village.' Harvey's was a gastro pub that did wonderful food and was very popular. It was also very casual, so Laura felt comfortable suggesting it.

Jack obviously thought so too.

'Yes, absolutely. Sounds good. Does 12.30 work? Get in before the lunchtime rush?' Agreeing to this and saying their goodbyes, Laura hung up the phone and sauntered again back into the kitchen. She walked down towards the table and sat down on one of the wooden chairs. She put her head in her hands and inwardly cringed. Oh, god. That was so awkward.

The lunch was a success and Laura was so glad she had made the call. Jack was very good company and kept her entertained for nearly two hours over a delicious lunch and dessert. She even had a glass of wine, as did he. They kept things light and Bill's name was never mentioned. Jack had done so much travelling all over the world, that he had tons of interesting and funny stories that had Laura intrigued the whole way through. It had definitely taken her mind off her own situation. After paying the bill, which Laura insisting on splitting, they put on their coats and made their way to the door.

Jack held it open for Laura and they headed out into the cold afternoon, although the sun was shining brightly. As they made their way to their cars which were parked near each other, Jack piped up, 'I really enjoyed myself Laura. Look I know you aren't going to be looking for anything serious so soon after your break-up, but I'd love for us to continue to meet up now and then. I had a great time.' Laura was happy to hear this.

'I'd really like that, Jack. And yes, it is way too soon for me to move on, but I would certainly love for us to meet up occasionally. I had great fun today. I'd forgotten what it was like to laugh so much,' she answered sincerely. They hugged briefly, but it was a comfortable hug, like two old friends and then they went their separate ways, Laura wondering to herself what Bill would have made of the situation if he had seen them.

The following week Laura had another dilemma concerning Jack. She was sitting where she always was when deep in thought, in her beloved kitchen. She was sipping a cup of tea and had the newspaper open in front of her on the table, not that she was taking anything in. There was a work night-out later and the whole company were going; partners/wives/husbands, all invited. Laura had no intention of going, but as she had recently told her work colleagues about her marriage break-up, they kept hounding her to come. Although she had no desire to go, she always enjoyed having a drink with the team and sometimes she got great inspiration for her writing after meeting them all.

They all loved to give their input and feedback to what she was working on, so she felt she sort of had to be there. But she really didn't want to go on her own. She had asked Sharon, but she was away in

Brussels with work. Laura had made the mistake of telling Shelly, one of the girls she was closer to in the office, about the lunch she had with Jack. In which case, now Shelly and a couple of the others kept at her to bring him along.

'Come on Laura. We all know he's not your boyfriend, there's no need to be worrying. What harm is there in bringing him as a friend? It will do you good.

'You said yourself you don't want any pitying glances from the others if you'd be on your own,' stated Mags, the black-haired petite PA to the Managing Director. Mags was a great source of gossip and kept the girls up to date on the recent happenings in the office. Although it was not lost on Laura that she was now most likely the topic of conversation in there. She could just imagine if she brought Jack tonight: 'Marriage break-up one minute, dating someone new within a few months!' Suddenly her thoughts were interrupted as Jessica came into the kitchen.

'Hi Mam,' Jess said as she walked over to the island and grabbed an apple from the fruit bowl. Mmmm... Laura thought. What to do? Should she stay in or just go out and see what happens?

The kids were supposed to be staying at Bill's so she supposed she may as well go.

'Pet, em, I've this work get together thing tonight I told you about earlier. I hadn't planned on going, but I might do now, still haven't decided, but anyway, you're definitely staying at your dad's?' Laura babbled on querying her daughter.

'Yes Mam, are you going to go? Ah, do, Mam. It'll be good for you. I'd feel much better if you went.' Laura decided to bite the bullet and confide in her daughter.

'Yeah, well, I didn't really want to go on my own. I was half thinking of asking Jack Dawson to come with me. Just as a friend like. You know the way we've met up a couple of times and that,' she nervously babbled on some more, trying to gauge her daughter's reaction.

Jess's face changed, and she fell silent. Sensing she had just made a mistake, Laura stood up and walked over to her daughter who was leaning over a stool.

'What is it love? Do you not like Jack? Forget it. I won't go at all I am such an idiot at times. Sorry, hun, I should have thought...' Jess interrupted her mother.

'No, no, I do like him, he seemed really nice the few times I have met him and he seems very fond of you. I suppose it's just about what Dad said last week. About wanting you back so much. You do believe him Mam, he wasn't with that woman, I know he wasn't.' Jessica looked at her with innocent puppy dog eyes, as if pleading on behalf of her father to give him another chance. It broke Laura's heart that her children were being dragged into relations between their parents. That should never have been the case.

The reference to Johnson made Laura's hands sweat.

'Look love, we have been through this, your dad and I are better off as friends. If he wants to date, then that's fine by me. I wish he wouldn't use you to get to me. I've told him how I felt, Jess. I know your dad loves me and I love him too. But would you rather we lived apart and be happy or lived together and fight all the time and be miserable?' Jess shrugged her shoulders and said unconvincingly, 'Suppose so Mam, once you're happy, that's the main thing.' Laura felt angry; she had been so annoyed at Bill last week. Jess had come home that Sunday and 'explained' the situation of how bitch Johnson was stalking her father! Ha, as if Bitch Johnson would run after any man, no matter what status or power he had. Poor Jess, she didn't know that her dad had had an affair with the woman. She just thought she was after him. He had conveniently left that bit out. To think he was using their innocent daughter to try and win her back, it made her feel sick. That was why she had made herself call Jack. Maybe Bill would get the picture and stop torturing the kids, building up Jess's hopes of them getting back together. Ben, thank god, had been spared. If he knew his dad wanted to get back, all hell would break loose. Wild horses wouldn't stop him arranging it.

'So, what are you waiting on, go and phone him. It's better than going on your own. Honestly Mam. I want you to start having a social life again,' Jessica urged her, sounding a bit happier now.

Ah, feck it, thought Laura. What had she to lose? And if her daughter was on board, that was one of her biggest concerns sorted.

'OK then, give me a couple of minutes.'

Jess bounded out of the kitchen and Laura could hear her running up the stairs, undoubtedly to her room. She took her mobile out of her handbag and dialed Jack's number, having no idea what she would say to him. He answered on first ring and Laura was a bit tongue-tied.

' Ehh Jack, Hi. Ehh. How are you?'

Why did she always sound like such an idiot when she called him?

'Hi Laura, good to hear from you. Looking for another lunch date already? I must have made a good impression,' he joked down the phone.

Laura laughed too and this gave her a bit of courage.

'Eh no, not lunch, but eh, see the thing is, I have this work night-out later, everyone's going including partners. It happens at the same time every year. Sort of an employee appreciation night. Anyway – as me and Bill are no longer together, eh, sorry, it's just I didn't want to go on my own and wondered… Oh, sorry, Jack. I am making a mess of this… ' She could her him laughing softly as he said: 'Do I take it you want a plus one? As friends only?' Laura sighed in relief. Thank god he knew what she meant. She felt like an idiot.

'I'm sorry Jack. Yes, that's what I am trying to say. I'm not really used to this.' So, he had agreed to come with her and after chatting about arrangements they decided he would pick her up at 9.

Funnily enough, the call had just ended and she heard her daughter coming back down the stairs.

'So, what did he say? Is he going with you?' Jess probed her. Laura smiled.

'By any chance had you your ear plugged to the floor young lady? Seems a bit suspicious that you land down here the minute I finish talking to him!' Jess laughed and said, 'You know me too well. I did try but I couldn't hear what you were saying. Just a mumble of conversation. So anyway – what did he say?' Laura filled her daughter in on what was said.

'What are you going to wear? Not boring old jeans, I hope!' God. She hadn't considered for a minute what she would wear. But then thinking about it now, yes jeans. Absolutely. Laura regarded her daughter across the kitchen. She was now sitting up on the counter beside the sink. A habit Laura had told her time and time again not to do. There were enough chairs without having to sit on the counter.

'This coming from the queen of jeans, you never take them off you,' Laura teased back deciding not to chastise her for now.

'Yes, but I don't get to go anywhere to dress up, you have to wear something sexy and young, not old and droopy.'.

Ehh. This was getting a bit awkward now. She didn't want her daughter thinking she was going on a date.

'The cheek of you, are you saying I have bad taste in clothes?' She gave a look of mock horror, and Jess came back quickly.

'No, I'm just joking, but you should wear a skirt or something,' her daughter advised her.

'No thank you, for now I'll stick to my boring old jeans, thank you very much. When I need your expert opinion, I will ask for it!' And Laura headed for the stairs and up to her room to rummage through her wardrobe. She had to go through her clothes and make sure she had a decent pair of jeans for tonight at least.

'I'm surprised I got the invite to be honest,' Jack said to her, as the two of them sat in his BMW on the way to where they were meeting the others in a fancy café bar in the main nightlife area of the city. Laura had been there a few times. While it was a nice place, and very trendy, it was always packed, and the music blaring made it difficult to have a conversation. She had been surprised that they had chosen *Moonlight* as the venue for their night out. But Shelly had assured her that the reserved area they were in wasn't as loud, and had plenty of space. Laura hoped she was right. She didn't fancy being boxed in like sardines, struggling to hear what people were saying. Laura squirmed a bit now, not sure exactly how to respond to Jack's comment.

'Eh I just fancied someone with me, I did ask Sharon you know – But she couldn't go. Sorry – You were second choice.' She laughed, hoping she hadn't offended him.

'Well, I feel privileged, all the same, even if I was second best!' He smiled at her and she relaxed. A comfortable silence fell among them for the rest of the journey, and it wasn't long before they had found a parking space and were making their way into the bar.

Laura heard her name being called. 'Over here Laura,' came Sarah's high-pitched voice. Well, at least Shelly had been telling the truth, the music certainly wasn't as loud as normal.

But maybe it was still early. Excellent, thought Laura to herself, she hadn't been sure if Sarah was able to make it tonight, but now that Sarah was here, she would ask her about the villa. She would try and get a quiet moment with her later; she didn't want to be asking in front of Jack.

As they were making their way over to the group, Laura could hear one of the girls speaking. 'Who's that fine specimen of a man that Laura has in tow?' She glanced at Jack who didn't seem to notice the comment although she was sure he had heard it too.

'Hi there, girls and boys, how are we?' asked Laura politely.

'Never mind about that,' said Shelly, 'who's your new friend?' And the group giggled like school children.

Laura would kill her. Shelly had promised her she would be on her best behavior if she brought Jack. Starting with Peter and Matt, who had been with the company from the start, Laura began to introduce Jack to everyone. They were all very welcoming, while some clearly surprised as they had not yet learned that Laura and Bill had separated and now here was Laura with a new man on her arm already. Feck it, she thought to herself. Let them think what they want. Shelly, Mags and Sarah also had been working with the company for a long time, and so Laura was still the newest employee. Her boss and his wife were meant to be coming, but they didn't seem to be here yet.

'Sit down here, plenty of room, Peter, go up there and get Laura and, sorry, what's your name?' enquired Sarah as she flitted her eyelids at him.

'Jack,' he relayed, and seemed a bit too pleased with himself thought Laura. Poor Peter ran to the orders of his workmate as it was quite obvious, he fancied Sarah. She had slept with him once apparently and then dumped him. He was distraught; thought that they were going to make a go of things, but Sarah wasn't interested.

She wanted a man with money, and although Peter's job paid well, it was not well enough for all the things she wanted to be bought and places she wanted to be brought. Just then Laura's boss Terry arrived, smiling as usual with his beautiful wife on his arm. The girls didn't like Terry's wife. They said she was stuck up her own ass. However, she had always treated Laura with respect and Laura couldn't help but like the woman despite the protests of her friends.

She moved over as if to signal to her boss's wife to sit down and she did hesitantly, afraid that she might be misjudging Laura's actions. Peter came over with the drinks and went back to the bar for more when he saw his boss. Rose, Terry's wife, was sitting quietly now and Laura felt sorry for her. They started chatting and despite the dirty glances she got from the girls, after a few minutes they all joined in.

Jack was chatting with the lads and seemed to be getting on well. Laura was glad she had brought him.

The night flew in and Laura could not remember the last time she had such a good night. They laughed constantly, and she nearly forgot about the past five months. She had also managed to nab Sarah for a chat when they were in the bathroom. Sarah was delighted at the prospect of helping her friend and said no problem; of course she could use the villa. But she would have to check availability as they usually rented it out if family or friends weren't using it.

It was March now, and Sarah reckoned there would be a week free at the end of April, if that wasn't too early, but she would have to check.

But the end of April would be prefect for Laura as she didn't want to wait too long to get away and the kids would be on their Easter holidays, so she wouldn't have to take them out of school. She would wait until Sarah confirmed the dates and then she would call Sharon and see if she would join them. The thought of it was getting her excited. As they were making a move to go home, Jack took out his keys to signal that he would drive. However, Laura wasn't as keen, as he had been drinking.

'Jack, I think we should take a taxi, you've had a few drinks.' She looked at him questionably.

'Ah. I only had two and a half, didn't finish my last one, I'm fine, don't worry.' Laura didn't know how many he had had as she hadn't been watching and most of the drinks had been on Terry. But Jack did seem OK though, so she decided to go home with him in the car.

Thankfully, they arrived at Laura's safely and she was in a fix as to whether to invite him in or not. Oh, what the heck, a cup of coffee would not do any harm.

'Would you like to come in?' she asked cautiously, afraid he would turn her down and shatter the little bit of confidence she had gathered.

'That would be lovely,' he said.

Shit. Laura's heart started to beat very fast. What would she do now? Bollocks. Jack was an extremely good-looking man, and very sexy, it was only now that she was beginning to realise how much she was attracted to him. Or was that the drink talking? They made their way into the kitchen, sat on the high stools and began exchanging stories from the past about funny things that had happened to them.

The whole time, Laura was getting braver. And angrier. She kept thinking about Bill and what he had done to her. And decided to throw caution to the wind and take the plunge. Bill was doing it, why couldn't she. It wasn't as if she didn't know Jack. She had sort of been seeing him these past few months. He put his hand over hers as if reading her thoughts and cupped her face with his other hand. Laura's heart began to do somersaults.

'You're beautiful,' he said, as he kissed her gently on the lips.

At first, she didn't respond, but when he put his hand on her thigh, she honestly thought a bolt of lightning had struck her. Laura grabbed Jack by neck and pulled him close to her. She began to kiss him, slowly at first until the two of them were wrapped around each other. Jack being the big strong man he was, lifted Laura, and whispered to her.

'Directions madam.' She giggled like a schoolgirl and pointed in the direction of the stairs.

Climbing the stairs proved difficult and the two of them had fallen several times on the way up, hurting themselves slightly but not enough to stop them. He laid her on the bed and started to kiss her neck. Slowly he undressed her and continued downwards with his kisses. On a normal, or sober occasion, Laura would have been mortified, but it felt too good to stop him. Boy, was she glad she had tidied up down there. Suddenly she began to panic.

'Jack, it's been a long time since I was with anyone else,' she couldn't help blurting out. But he soothed her and said gently, 'Don't be worrying Laura, just enjoy yourself.' And so, Laura took his advice, relaxing and fully immersing herself in the experience. Afterwards, Jack flopped down on the bed beside her and took her in his arms.

'That was amazing, you're so beautiful.' Laura smiled sleepily and the two cuddled up together and fell into a deep satisfied sleep.

CHAPTER 11

Sharon opened her eyes and squinted as the sun shone brightly through her bedroom window. It was a Friday morning and she had taken the day off so was grateful for the lie-in. She was five months pregnant at this stage and stroked her tummy as she had come to do now every morning she woke. She had come to terms that she was having a baby, and when she realised that Rob would not be coming back, felt such a surge of guilt. Guilt that she had ignored the life growing inside her for the first few months.

Sharon was now doing her best to make up for it though. She didn't drink any alcohol, not even one glass of wine after a heavy day at work. She was eating healthily and had decided that she and her baby would be enough for each other. She felt such a protective force for her unborn child, and each time she thought back to the time when she was willing to give up her baby for Rob, she felt like vomiting. How could she have been so stupid? Nothing, not even Rob, was more important than this baby. This baby was now her life.

'Then why haven't you told anyone about it?' she kept asking herself. Although naked it was obvious, Sharon had managed to conceal her belly with flowy tops and baggy jumpers. Even Laura who she had met several times in the past month had not realised. But Sharon knew she would not be able to hide it for much longer. Rob had phoned several times recently.

She told him that she wasn't pregnant, so he began to ask what she wanted to do with the apartment. Sharon did not want to discuss it and fobbed him off every time. Rob had got the picture, as he hadn't mentioned it in the last few calls. Sometimes Sharon wondered why he cared for her so much. He always sounded so considerate and concerned on the phone, yet he never made an attempt to arrange a get together or anything.

He certainly had Sharon confused. Yet she didn't spend as much time thinking about him as she had done at the start. Her baby was her main focus and therefore her thoughts were full of things like, boy or girl? What colour will she do the nursery? Will she stay in the apartment or find a house in the countryside? So many questions and so few answers. Sharon knew she would have to tell Laura about the baby soon.

She was bursting to tell someone and talk about her little precious gift, but she knew she would have a hundred and one questions to answer as soon as she spilled the beans. She couldn't face the third degree. Not yet. She would tell Laura; she'd tell her soon. Maybe she would call out tomorrow afternoon for lunch and let her know. Yes, feeling happier at the prospects of confiding in her friend about the baby, Sharon picked up her mobile from beside the bed and called Laura's number. They could go shopping for baby clothes and discuss names.

'Hello… ha, ha, stop it you big oaf, hello,' came Laura's squealing girlish voice. Sharon was amused.

'Hi Laura, how are you? Good by the sounds of it?' She smiled softly into the phone.

'Oh, Hi Shaz. Sorry I haven't called all week. How are you?'

Laura was happy to hear from her.

'I'm fine yeah, I was hoping maybe to call out to you tomorrow, have some lunch and a bit of a catch-up?'.

Sharon hadn't really spent any time with her other friends since she found out she was pregnant. Carol, Gabby, and Becky all led busy lives, so she had managed to dodge any potential meetups by claiming it didn't suit.

'Yeah, sure, no problem, come to mine around one if that suits and I'll cook us some lunch, chicken stir fry, your favourite,' Laura giggled loudly.

'Laura, do you mind me asking, but eh, what exactly are you doing?'.

It was beginning to get on Sharon's nerves now.

'Oh, I'm sorry Shaz, Jack is here beside me, he won't stop tickling me, hang on, stop it now, or I'll have to get cross.' Sharon heard Jack's husky voice in the background.

'Oh, now you're talking.'

Laura said: 'Sorry Sharon, he's a big kid.' Sharon had enough.

'Right! I can see you're busy. OK, look, I'll be round about one tomorrow. See you then.'

She hung up the phone and her heart reeled in hurt and rejection. She was jealous. How could she be so selfish? Her friend had been having such a tough time this past year, and now she had found someone who could make her happy. And she was jealous. Stop being a bitch, she said to herself. Laura had phoned Sharon last week and filled her in on her new very *early stages* relationship. To say she was shocked was an understatement. She thought it would take Laura years before she would consider dating someone else. But then when Laura had told her what had prompted her into action, she understood. Bill. Still up to his antics. Sharon wondered if Jack had told her that it was, she who had sent him to see her in the first place. Obviously, he hadn't, and Sharon was not going to say anything.

Laura seemed quite taken with him; she had only been dating him for three weeks now.

Yet to hear her talk about him you'd swear they were a married couple. Laura had said Bill wasn't impressed about the new relationship. He had called over several times pleading with Laura to give up Jack and get back with him, that he couldn't bear to see her with someone else. Sharon couldn't believe it, but she actually felt a little bit sorry for Bill. Originally, she had backed her friend one hundred percent. But when Laura had told how he claimed Johnson was chasing him and he didn't want to be with her, she began to doubt the situation. Although Laura did not believe him, Sharon felt he was telling the truth, as if he did want Johnson, he would be living with her. Ah, well, I suppose he got what was coming to him, sighed Shaz, as she lay back on the bed and drifted into a deep sleep.

Sharon called round to Laura's at one on the button the next day, anxious to share her news with her friend. She just hoped that the irresistible Jack wasn't there. Stop, Sharon scolded herself. That's not fair. As she got out of the car, another car pulled up behind her, and Ben hurtled from the house at full speed with a sports bag hanging from his back.

'Hi Shaz, Mam's inside. See you later.' And with that, he jumped into the car. The woman behind the wheel who Sharon did not recognise smiled and waved at Sharon, which she returned. Once the car pulled off again, Sharon made her way to the front door which was slightly ajar.

'Hello, anybody home?' joked Sharon… ' Laura called out: 'Come on ahead, I'm in the kitchen hun.' As she made her way into the kitchen, Sharon felt herself praying they would be on their own. Thankfully, it was just Laura who was sitting at the island in the middle of the room, a holiday brochure in hand. On seeing Sharon, Laura jumped up and hurried to hug her friend.

'Sit down Shaz. Lunch is ready, I'm just keeping it warm on the cooker.

'Glass of wine?' asked Laura although she knew that Sharon would decline. She had been wondering lately as to why Sharon never took a drink anymore. As she reflected on the last few times they met, and looking at her now, Laura slowly realised with horror and disgust with herself, that her friend was very much pregnant. How had she not realised before? She knew how. She was too wrapped up in Jack to think of anyone else.

She felt like such a bitch for not being there for Sharon. If she was honest with herself, she wasn't sure how she felt about Jack. He was a good distraction though, and when she was with him, it took her away from reality for a while. She thought that was probably why she was seeing so much of him lately. She certainly didn't love him. Maybe she would in time. But she wasn't sure. Anyway, one thing was for definite; she was going to start giving Sharon a lot more attention. But she wasn't sure how to approach the situation.

Should she mention it? Or let Sharon? She would see if Sharon mentioned it today and if not, she would say it to her. Laura poured them both orange juice from a jug in the fridge, set down the two lunches and added a plate of garlic bread from the oven.

'Now dig in! I have some lovely desert for afterwards – low calorie of course!' lied Laura.

'Ah this is lovely; your stir fry is defo the best in Dublin!' laughed Sharon.

Sharon regularly told people that to order a stir fry in a Dublin restaurant was a waste of time once you had eaten Laura's, as nothing could compare! They ate their lunch chatting amicably and when they finished Laura put the kettle on and took out the cheesecake from the fridge. After making the tea and sitting back down, while tucking into her first mouthful of cheesecake, Sharon said out of nowhere, 'Laura, I'm pregnant.' Sharon had been working her way for the past forty minutes trying to find the best way to tell Laura.

She had planned to go through the motions and telling her a bit more before dropping the bombshell but in the end, she couldn't help it. She just wanted to get it out there. To make sure she wasn't going mad and imagining it. Telling Laura made it real. She really was pregnant and expecting a baby. She was quite excited now about it. Although she felt anxious and nervous as she waited on Laura's response.

Although Laura had realised earlier that Sharon was pregnant, she had no idea if Sharon was happy about it or not. So, she was not sure how she should respond.

She decided to be honest and show her true feelings; Sharon was her best friend after all.

'Oh, my Lord, No Way! Oh, Sharon. That's great news! Isn't it? Or is it? How do you feel?' she exclaimed coming around the table and taking Sharon in her arms, careful now to avoid her tummy area. She gently pushed Sharon back a bit and looked down at her.

'My word, how did I not notice? I am so sorry Sharon. I have allowed myself to get so caught up in Jack that I couldn't see what was going on with you.

'How are you, sweetheart?' she cried. Sharon had tears rolling down her cheeks, but she was laughing.

'Yes, I am happy, very happy. Although at the start it was a different story. But I have dealt with it now, and I am really excited about it. I'm due at the end of August.'

Laura was so relieved that her friend was happy. It was now early April, and although originally Laura had been going to ask Sharon to go to Spain with them, she hadn't in the end; she had been working her way up to asking Jack if he would come instead. Although when she thought about it, he didn't make much of an effort anymore with the kids. But anyway, that was out the window now. She would make Sharon come. She needed it.

'Sharon, I know this is short notice, but my friend at work Sarah is giving me the loan of her villa in the south of Spain for a week. Myself and the two kids are going in just over two weeks' time. Please come with us. You could do with the break, and we have so much catching up to do. I feel so guilty for not being there for you. It's so true, the saying, that you never know what is going on in people's lives.

'Please say you'll come. The villa is free, and we just have to pay for flights, which are great value at the minute. Or I could buy them for you if you can't afford them. It's supposed to… ' but Laura didn't get any further as Sharon interrupted her ,laughing.

'Good lord Laura, will you calm down a bit and let me get a word in! To be honest the sound of a holiday right now would be great. I'll have to check with my doctor to see if it's OK to fly, but I think that would be until much nearer the end of the pregnancy.'

Laura was so delighted she jumped in the air and then gave her friend another hug.

'Ah that's wonderful. And I am going to spoil you. Now, sit back down there. I am going to make a fresh pot of tea and I want all the details of what's been happening the past few months. No more cover-ups! I want it all. Including about Rob!'

So, Sharon didn't fight her on this and did just exactly that. From her trip to London, the pregnancy test, the letter from Rob, everything.

If Laura had been feeling guilty earlier about not being there for Sharon, she felt a thousand times worse now. That's it; she would cut back a bit from seeing Jack and spend more time with her friend. Besides, if Jack really liked her, he would understand. In fact, he was due to come round later, but Laura had now changed her mind.

'Sharon, there's a new film out this weekend with Nick Gleeson in it and I am dying to see it. Jack doesn't really like the cinema, and it would be too old for the kids. Would you come with me this evening? And maybe we could go for dinner after it?'

Sharon would love to spend an evening other than sitting in her apartment staring at four walls, but she did not want to intrude either.

'Are you sure, is Jack not coming over?' she asked. Laura thought quickly.

'No, not tonight, he has some business dinner that he said would be too boring for me,' Laura was not lying. He did mention he had a dinner but had planned on cancelling it.

'Great, OK, well I better head off then so I can have a shower and get my things together. I have a few bits to do.

'What time is the film?' asked Sharon. Laura flicked on her mobile and quickly checked the cinema listings.

'The one I want to see is at 6.30. Which means we will be out by 8.15. Plenty of time for dinner. Does that suit? Do you want me to collect you?' asked Laura.

'No, No, in fact, I think I should collect you, seeing as how I cannot have a drink anyway.'

Laura replied, 'Nothing stopping you having a glass of wine or two! I insist. I'll pick you up at 6.10.'

Sharon smiled.

'Thanks Laura. You have no idea how much better you have made me feel. It's as though a huge weight has been lifted off my shoulders.'

'No problem Sweetheart, and remember, I will always be there for you, and the baby. I'll do all the babysitting you need and I'll even hold your hand when you're pushing your dear one out!!! If you want!!' laughed Laura… '

Sharon laughed.

'Ah, stop reminding me of what's coming! I'll see you later, thanks again for lunch,' and with that, she went out the door to her car. Laura picked up her phone and called Jack straight away to cancel.

She told him Sharon had asked her to go out and she didn't want to say no as she hadn't spent much time with her lately. He seemed fine with it, said no problem at all; That he would call her tomorrow. With that all settled, Laura decided to lie down on her bed for an hour. She was exhausted with all the activity.

CHAPTER 12

'That was one of the best films I've seen in a while,' said Sharon as they made their way out of the cinema that evening. It had been an action thriller, which would not normally be her choice, but she really enjoyed it. She was totally absorbed and didn't let her mind drift once throughout the film.

'Yeah, it was good, wasn't it? I was afraid it might be a bit shit; you know when films get a brilliant write-up, and then when you go to see them, you're wondering if it's the same film you read about. They can be such a let-down at times. But I have to admit, I wouldn't throw Nick Gleeson out of bed for eating crisps!' laughed Laura. 'He was hot stuff all right. And had a wonderful charisma about him'.

They walked along the street and turned a corner into a small square. They decided to go to a new steak and seafood place that had opened a couple of months before called 'Harrys Place.' They had not booked a table, so were not sure if they would be able to eat there.

Laura pushed opened the door and Sharon followed in behind her. The

restaurant was buzzing. It seemed it had two floors.

'Hi, can I help you?' asked a young girl not much older than Jessica.

Laura took charge.

'Hi, Sorry, we don't have a table booked but we were wondering if

you could fit us in? Just the two of us please?' The young waitress

looked down in her book for a minute or two, and then excused herself

for a brief second. She was walking around the restaurant looking at

the tables.

She turned and made her way back toward them, a big smile on her

face.

'You're in luck, there is a couple at the back there who are just

finishing up, if you wait a couple of minutes, I'll just get the table

cleared.' Laura and Sharon were delighted. The food must be good to

be pulling in such a crowd. But then it was Saturday night.

After being seated comfortably, and after both women had glanced

around to see if they recognised anyone (they didn't), they gave their orders. Grilled salmon for Laura and a 10oz steak for Sharon. Well, she was eating for two, as she had pointed out laughing! Laura and Sharon were totally relaxed and filled their time talking about both the upcoming holiday and the baby's arrival. Laura could not wait to get away for a week with Sharon and the kids.

They could have nice dinners like this every night. With guaranteed lovely weather. After an enjoyable evening, Sharon asked, 'What time is it? I'm pretty wrecked to be honest, ready for my bed.'

Laura looked at her watch.

'It's nearly 10 o'clock. Sorry for keeping you so late. I forget how much tiredness can hit you when you're pregnant,' Laura replied, glancing around her to see most people were still sitting drinking bottles of wine.

'I just want to run to the bathroom,' said Sharon, 'I see a sign that says they're upstairs. Only I am bursting. I would wait till I get home, but not looking forward to managing these steps!' she sighed.

Laura flicked through her phone looking at news updates and friends' posts on social media as she waited for Sharon to return. She had a small drop left in her wine glass which she now finished as she saw Sharon coming back towards the table. Laura frowned at Sharon's expression. She seemed quite serious suddenly.

'Shaz, you OK hun? Is it the baby?' She hoped not, not now, when Sharon seemed to be finally moving on and looking forward to the future.

'No, nothing like that, me and the baby are fine... Well, it's just that... I'm not sure whether...' Sharon stumbled.

'Oh, spit it out Shaz, what is it?' cried Laura.

'Look, it's probably nothing, but I just saw Jack up there in the corner having dinner with some woman. It's most likely innocent, but I just thought you should know,' Sharon said quietly. Although she knew it was anything but innocent. She saw him holding hands with this woman and the way they were looking at each other It certainly wasn't a business dinner as Laura had mentioned earlier. But she hadn't the heart to tell her friend; she had too much heartache in the last while without Sharon adding to it.

'Oh,' said Laura, not sure what to think. 'I'm sure it's just a friend, or the business colleague he spoke of earlier. He has several female acquaintances from work. He's often spoken of them. Did he see you?' she asked.

'No, I don't think so. He had his back to me. I didn't recognise the woman. Yes, you're right. Most likely nothing,' Sharon lied.

Laura decided she would casually ask him tomorrow what he had done tonight. If he told her the truth, she had nothing to worry about. If he lied, well, she would deal with that then…

'Hello,' Laura sighed into the phone. It was 11am Sunday morning and she still hadn't bothered to get out of bed. She had been scrolling through her phone when it rang. She had seen it was Jack and knew it must have been him ringing the house phone five minutes earlier. She just hadn't the energy to get out of bed and answer it.

'Hi honey, how are you? How was the cinema?' Jack asked seemingly full of energy.

'Was good yes, really enjoyed it. Sharon was on great form. So, I was delighted we went. Got home around 10.30pm so it wasn't too bad. How about you? What did you get up to?' Laura asked, her heart beginning to beat a little faster.

'Oh, my business dinner was cancelled, but a friend of mine, Carol, who I used to work with as it happens, phoned me on the off-chance I would be around. She was up in Dublin for the day. She lives in Cork now. So, we went to Harry's Restaurant in the Square, do you know it? Fabulous food. We had a nice night; I was home around the same time as you, though.'

Laura felt massive relief as this revelation, although for some reason she didn't let him know that she had been there too.

They talked for a bit, and though he wanted to come around, Laura put him off until some evening during the week. She didn't have the energy to put on a show, and she was looking forward to spending some time with Ben and Jess. Maybe they would watch a movie and get a take-away. She'd have to be careful with the takeaways though, they had one each week at their dad's, so she wouldn't make a habit of it. Laura herself had a bit of the munchies from having too much wine last night, so a take-away was just what she needed to sort her out!

The week before they were due to go away; Laura sat at her desk trying to work out if she would fit another column in before Friday or would she just make do with this one.

While she loved her job, she was getting a bit tired of it. As a rule, she had no interest in the 'Celeb World', so it was difficult to keep up the passion. But what else would she do? Yes, she had great office skills; maybe she could look for some office manager roles. Or admin. Laura didn't want a big high-powered job like she had in the past. She wanted something with less pressure but which she enjoyed. The money would come in handy now, although she still had good savings from her earlier career. She had also been left some money from her granny who died five years ago.

So financially, she was comfortable. Not comfortable enough not to work at all. Plus, she hated to think of it now, but if her and Bill got a divorce, it was going to cost money. Laura didn't allow herself to think of those things for long, so she put it to the back of her mind. Her mobile shrilled and she saw Sharon's name flash up on the screen.

'Hi, Shaz, are you nearly set for Sun, Sea and Sandy Beaches?' asked Laura with a smile.

'Oh Yes Laura, I can't wait, really. I'm taking Friday off to give myself a chance to get everything sorted. What time is the flight on Saturday? You're picking me up on the way to the airport, yeah?' asked Sharon excitedly.

Laura and Sharon had seen a lot of each other in the short time since their night out. Laura called over to the apartment after work some weekdays and Sharon visited once or maybe twice on a weekend. While Laura was still seeing Jack, she wasn't seeing as much of him. He seemed a bit disappointed when Laura told him that Sharon was going with them to Spain. He probably thought Laura would ask him, and in fairness, that was Laura's fault. She probably hinted it a couple of times. Well, she was trying to make it up to him and was doing a nice dinner for him tonight. Ben had football training and Jessica was going to a friend after school.

'Yes, I'll pick you up. The flight is at 11.45 so I'll collect you around 8.30am. The kids are so excited. Even Jessica was much more enthusiastic than I thought she would be. Ben did sulk for a bit, when I told him Bill wasn't coming, but he soon got over it when he heard the villa was situated on the beach and had its own jet skis. He wanted to go there and then when I told him there was also a private swimming pool! Ha. You should have heard him: 'You mean a pool, all for me? No one else will be in it!!' At which I had to tell him that you, Jess, and myself might be partial to the odd swim or dip! But he said he didn't mind that!! ha. The little pet! Anyway, other than that, how are you? Any word from Rob?' Laura enquired. Sharon was smiling thinking of the excitement Ben must be feeling of going on holidays for the week.

She has all that ahead of her with this little one, she thought as she patted her stomach.

'Yeah, I'm fine. No word from Rob lately, which is strange. He had been phoning me regularly, maybe twice a week, since he left. And I haven't heard from him in two weeks. I hope he is OK,' Sharon said, concerned. Laura thought the whole thing was strange. When Sharon first told her what happened, she kept telling Sharon to go and find Rob, and find out what happened to him in the past or find out what's the cause of his behavior.

Because there was obviously something. But Sharon wouldn't budge. She said it was up to him to come to her. He had left. Rob knew how much Sharon wanted him. She wasn't going to humiliate herself any further. If he wanted to explain, he knew where she was.

'Sharon, don't you think it's time you told him you are pregnant? He has had plenty of time now to get his head around whatever was going on in that mind of his. Maybe you should let him know. Then see what happens,' Laura said. Sharon thought Laura was right. She had been thinking the same thing the past few weeks. She wanted to let him know that he had a child on the way.

She wouldn't demand anything of him or be rude or call him names. She planned on just telling him she was pregnant and due in August, and then hang up the phone. But he hadn't called in two weeks and when she tried him the other day, his phone went to voicemail.

'Yes, I had decided that I was going to tell him. But then I didn't hear from him. And when I tried to reach him, he had his phone switched off. I'll give it till we are back from Spain. And then I will try again if I don't hear from him before that. We need to sort things out for once and for all. I feel strong enough now to deal with it.'

CHAPTER 13

Rob stared at the computer unaware that his work colleague was watching him. Suddenly two hands covered his eyes and a voice came.

'Guess who?'. Rob took the hands away and annoyingly turned around to see Fiona Collins standing behind him

'Don't do that to me'!

Fiona said, 'Oh, sooorrrryyyy, but you were in another world; I was just trying to get your attention.'

Rob tried to mask his anger. It wasn't fair to take his humour out on his colleagues (well, his staff really, but he preferred to think of them as colleagues). The last thing on earth that he wanted to do was have a bit of banter with Fiona Collins.

'Well, you have it now, what do you want?' Rob barked. He didn't mean to sound so harsh.

'Tetchy, you haven't been yourself the past few months and I was hoping you might come out for dinner with me tonight. Cheer you up a bit,' she replied.

Rob counted to ten in his mind and breathed slowly. Calm down. Don't snap her head off.

'No thanks Fiona, I have things to do. Thanks, though. I know I haven't been much fun lately. But I'm heading away for a couple of weeks to clear my head. Hopefully, when I'm back I'll be my normal jolly self,' Rob joked, trying to make up for his earlier rudeness. It seemed he was forgiven as Fiona said, 'Sounds like a good idea, and maybe we can hook up when you're back.' And with that she winked at him, turned, and walked out of the office. No chance, thought Rob to himself. He had demons he needed to put to rest, and if he was successful, he had every intention of claiming back the woman he loved.

'MAAAAM, look at the size of the swimming pool! It's SOOOOO Cool!' exclaimed Ben loudly as the taxi pulled in to the driveway.

'Ben, keep your voice down love, and take it easy,' smiled Laura. It was 3.15pm and the sun was shining brightly in the sky. Their flight had been pleasant enough, thankfully as, like Sharon, Laura was not the best flier. Any sign of turbulence and she would start a round of Hail Mary's! They had a nice time at the airport before leaving Dublin. They had a lovely breakfast and then browsed the shops. She treated both Ben and Jess to new swimwear, and even bought some for herself. Why not? This was a new Laura. She had pre-booked a taxi at the airport so they didn't have to wait when they arrived. And the journey took just thirty minutes to the villa.

The villa itself was located on the edge of a seaside resort. The taxi took them off the motorway and sped down a winding road for a couple of miles. The view of the town was beautiful with the ocean glittering in the background. Laura could really feel the excitement setting in. They began to see shops, hotels and other buildings and knew this was the start of the resort area. The taxi then made a right, in the direction of the sea, and drove downhill about two hundred meters where he pulled up on the right-hand side of the road to which they could see a gorgeous whitewash villa.

'Here we are,' the driver said in faulting English. The villa had whitewashed walls surrounding the property, with a garden that looked to go the whole way round the house.

The pool was to the left of the house, overlooking the sea, with sunbeds spread around it and several small tables with parasols.

'My lord,' said Sharon, 'Who did you say lent you this place? It is stunning. I cannot wait to explore inside! They are obviously not short a bob or two to own something like this!'

Sharon had been a bit worried about coming away for a week, given the situation, but when she saw the villa, it was hard not to feel the excitement bubbling up inside her. Like Ben, she too could not wait to try the pool. Laura had told her that she had to tell the kids that Sharon was pregnant, as they would notice it in Spain. But she hadn't told them anything about Rob; as far as they were concerned Rob and

Sharon were still together. But then the story was really for Jessica's sake; Ben wouldn't really take it in.

'It is so beautiful,' Laura replied, 'I never realised. Sarah just said she had a three-bedroom villa in a nice location in Spain. She never actually said anything much about it. I am quite surprised that she never mentioned how fabulous it was. I know she bought it years ago, and at a very good price. The area had not yet been discovered by tourists. It was only when the area became a resort that the property prices began to rise. So, with renting it out most of the time, she is probably able to cover the mortgage,' explained Laura.

The taxi driver had asked if they wanted him to drive up to the front door (it was only about fifty meters from the gate), but Laura said no, not to worry, as she knew she had to rummage through her handbag to try and find the code to the gate and she didn't want to keep him waiting. As she eventually located the four-digit code and punched it in, they heard a click and the gates creaked open. Laura wondered if there was a smaller pedestrian gate somewhere as she didn't want to have to keep opening and closing the gates as they came and went. As she glanced around the garden from the tarmac path that led to the house, she spotted a little gap in the wall over the far side of the swimming pool.

There was a gate there also, but it seemed one that could open and close by hand. Ah, that would be much easier, thought Laura to herself.

'It's so hot,' exclaimed Jess taking off her sweater. She had a sports vest on underneath. 'I can't wait to jump in the pool, hurry up Mam, I want to change into my swimwear,' she begged, as Laura fumbled with the keys in the front door. When, finally, she found the right ones, she opened the door and Ben and Jessica flew past her nearly knocking her over. Sharon laughed.

'God love them, they are just excited. I think we all would like a swim though, it would be very refreshing, especially after the flight and everything'.

The house had a small hallway, with stairs directly in front to the right. There was a door immediately to their left, which looked like the kitchen, and both Laura and Sharon proceeded into it. Ben and Jess had raced upstairs to claim their bedrooms. Well, Jess would be sharing with Laura as it was only fair to give Sharon her own room. The kitchen was very spacious, with white marble worktops and a workstation with stools propped up against it. There was also a table and chairs for six people. The room spread out to the right into a sitting room area, where there was a fireplace, two couches, a large cream rug, and a flat screen TV. There were patio doors that led out to the back of the house, and to a patio area. Sharon walked over and fiddled with the glass doors. She managed to open the locks and pulled back the sliding door. She stepped outside and the view took her breath away. It was so peaceful.

She could see the sparking ocean, and the beautiful beach in front of the house was practically deserted. Most people went to the main beach, which Sharon could see way over to the left. It was very busy with people sunbathing, swimming and doing water activities. She judged it was probably a ten-minute walk to the dead centre of the resort. Perfect, not too close, not too far.

'Breathtaking, isn't it?' Laura said as she came out behind her. She handed Sharon a glass of cold fizzy lemon.

'I found a note that said there were the basic provisions in the fridge, just so we didn't arrive to nothing. And to thoroughly enjoy the villa as much as we can.' Sarah also left the names of the best restaurants in town and some ideas for sightseeing if they fancied it.

It seemed she had thought of everything – doctors' numbers, hospitals, takeaways, taxi firms, etc. Laura felt so grateful to her friend. She would have to buy her something nice to say thank you. She would also treat her to lunch or dinner when she got back.

'She also left instructions on how to get the jet ski to and from the water should we decide to use it!! I somehow cannot see you taking advantage of it, but I am not sure I will have much choice with Ben and Jess,' laughed Laura. Sharon smiled sadly. Rob loved jet skis. How many times had they rented jet skis on holidays? Sometimes one each, sometimes they would share one.

'Ah, yes, I see it over there. I wonder how we are supposed to get it down the beach. I know you can just walk through the gate there and you're practically on the beach, but I can't see the jet ski fitting through that!' said Sharon.

'Sarah has said that there is local man named Michael Smith who we need to call when we want to use it. He will arrive and hook up the trailer and drive it down to the beach. She also said he will help us get started off and that,' Laura replied.

'Michael Smith? He's obviously not Spanish so!!' joked Sharon. Laura had thought the same.

Must be an Irishman who had retired over here and lived in the area. Anyway, she couldn't see them on the jet skis today or even tomorrow, so she put the jet ski out of her head for now. At that moment Ben flew past them in a hurry to get to the pool. Laura's heart hammered as she wanted to check out the pool area before he got in it.,

'Ben, wait, don't get into the pool yet, I want to… ' but it was too late. In he dived, not a care in the world, and thankfully, she could see his head emerge half way up the pool. He turned and smiled at his mother.

'Mam, it's so great. The water is lovely.

'Ben, you should not have jumped in there until I told you. You didn't even know how deep it was. You could have hurt yourself. How deep is the water? Can you stand up in it?' enquired Laura worryingly. Although she knew she was being a protective mother, she couldn't help it.

'I can stand in this part,' Ben exclaimed triumphantly, and then he swam back up the pool and said, 'But I can't stand here. I can if I hold my nose and go under water. I think you could stand in it, though,' Ben replied.

Laura knew Ben was an excellent swimmer. He had won tons of competitions in the last few years through school tournaments and had progressed to the 'All Irelands' several times, never clinching first place, but he did get second one year.

'Stop worrying,' smiled Sharon. 'He's fine.' They both turned to see Jess coming out in her new bikini. She had a beautiful figure and Laura became aware that it wouldn't be long until Jess started having boyfriends. She shuddered at the thought, wanting to protect her daughter from any potential hurt that would surely come her way at some stage. She would most likely have several relationships before she settled down. Laura always encouraged Jess to travel. To go and see the world.

She wanted her to get a degree from college first though. Once she had a degree, the world was her oyster. Laura didn't mind what she studied. She wanted Jess to be happy. But she also knew an education was so important. It would mean that Jess could spend several years travelling and living abroad before she got a proper job. The degree would be her safety net. Jess never really passed comments about college; she would just shrug her shoulders and say she would see when the time came. Well, next year would be her final school exams, so there was not a lot of time really. Anyway, Laura would worry about that then. For now, they were in Spain, and she intended to enjoy it.

'Jess, love, that bikini looks great on you. Ben says the water is lovely. Myself and Shaz are going to get changed and have a dip,' said Laura to her daughter.

'Oh, Mam, you should see upstairs. The rooms are gorgeous. And the bathroom has a jacuzzi. Two of the rooms have a small balcony, look.'

She turned and pointed towards the small balconies on the back of the house.

'Mam, you and me have the biggest room but only because it has two beds, I would have let you have it otherwise, Sharon. But your room is lovely too. And we both have balconies. Except Ben, his room is at the front, and it's quite nice too, but it doesn't have a balcony, which he doesn't care about anyway. He didn't even look at the room, just threw his bag down, got changed and ran back outside!' laughed Jess.

'Ah, Jessica, I can't wait to see the rooms. I am sure mine will be just fine,' said Sharon.

'All I need is a bed in mine, I don't mind the size of the rooms, and you're very good to think of me though. Come on Laura. Will we take a look?' Sharon asked. Laura, who was now dying to get back inside and investigate further needed no more encouragement. 'Yes, absolutely, let's go!'

After an enjoyable afternoon spent by the pool, they had all strolled into town, wandering around the shops and browsing the little stalls. It was a very pleasant area, with plenty of bars and restaurants, but it wasn't too noisy. No groups of loud drinking louts, which was reassuring. Well, they hadn't seen any yet, so fingers crossed this just wasn't an area that attracted those groups. They found one of the restaurants that Sarah had recommended. It was on the promenade, with plenty of seating out the front, looking out at the ocean. They were all starving, having only eating snacks here and there since breakfast. It was now 8pm and Ben's stomach was rumbling loudly! They all had three courses, which were wolfed down quickly by everyone, especially the mouthwatering deserts. Laura and Sharon had Banoffee Pie and Jess and Ben had Malteser Cheesecake.

Laura was thankful to Sarah for recommending this place. It was not expensive, had great food and the service was spot on. After fixing up the bill, they decided to walk back to the villa via the beach instead of the road. The sand was still warm as they all took their shoes off and paddled in the water. Ben had seen the jet ski earlier and had asked her about it a hundred times. He was driving her mad.

But Jess was quite keen too. It seemed Laura had no choice but to put a call in to this Michael guy tomorrow at some stage. Maybe arrange it for tomorrow evening, or the following morning. She might actually go for a spin on one herself! She had never gone on one in the past. Always let Bill ramble around on them, with the kids wrapped tightly to his back. At the thought of Bill, Laura felt her heart contract. It was their first holiday without Bill. Laura was surprised that she hadn't thought of him much.

OK, so it was the first day, but still. She wasn't moping about or wishing he was here. She hadn't really thought about Jack either. He had texted earlier to see if they got there OK .She had replied and said she would ring him later. Men, they could take a back seat for now. She intended to enjoy this week as much as she could. A dog barked up ahead, and ran after a stick, which its owner threw into the sea. Laura smiled, thinking of Barney. He was staying with her parents this week. She wasn't worried about him. Her dad loved having Barney. No doubt he would take the dog everywhere with him. Barney loved sitting in the front of the van, head proudly looking out the window. Her parents were glad she was going away. They said it would do her good. Well, she hoped so too.

CHAPTER 14

The next morning Laura made scrambled eggs, bacon and toast for breakfast. She had made a visit to the local grocery store earlier that morning; it was only a minute's walk away. She poured glasses of orange juice and then shouted up the stairs. She was surprised Ben wasn't up yet and, in the pool, but then given the long day they had yesterday, he was probably tired.

'Breakfast ready for anyone who wants it. It's just gone ten o'clock.' Laura walked back into the kitchen and sat at the workstation reading a local newspaper for the expats who had emigrated to Spain.

It had been in the letterbox this morning. As she flicked through, she looked at a photo taken at an event in an Irish Bar called *Paddy's Place*. She laughed at some of the antics of the people in the pictures. The pub looked like good fun. Maybe they would take a ramble down there tonight for a drink. They had pool tables too, so Ben would be happy. Laura jumped as she heard her phone ringing, it was Jack. She put it on silence and let it ring. She had phoned Jack last night when they got home. A woman had answered like before, giggling and saying,

'Jack's phone.'

It had been 11pm. Why would a woman be answering his phone at that time on a Saturday night? Laura didn't know what to think. She thought her original interest in Jack was probably more to do with getting back at Bill in her own way and proving to herself she could move on. But reflecting on it, it was much too quick. She didn't love Jack. She enjoyed his company. But she certainly wasn't going to go down the road of worrying about other women.

She could do without that. Laura decided she would take the week away to think about it, but it might be an idea to part ways with Jack when she got home. Her phone shrilled again and this time it was Bill. She answered it.

'Hi, Bill. How's things?' she asked in a warm voice. She wasn't going to be accused of being a bitter ex.

'Hi, Laura, how are all of you? Did ye get there OK? What's the place like?'. Laura laughed.

'Slow down. Now I know where Ben gets it from.' Laura filled Bill in as much as she could and then said she had to go and dish out the breakfast.

'I miss you all, I really wish I was there,' he said quietly. Laura sighed. She didn't need this. Not now. Thankfully, Ben came into the kitchen and saved her from replying.

'Hang on Bill. Ben, here, your fathers on the phone.' Ben's eyes lit up as he grabbed the phone and started to tell his dad excitedly about everything they had done so far.

After the morning swim and a walk around the town, they stopped for lunch in an Italian café. Ben had started asking again about the jet ski, so she promised once they got back to the villa, she would phone the man Sarah had left details for. Sharon seemed thoroughly relaxed.

'You OK, Shaz?' asked Laura gently.

'Absolutely Laura, I love it here. It's so peaceful. I feel so much happier out here. Wouldn't it be great to own an apartment here? If only we could work from home! I would seriously consider moving out.'

Laura was surprised. She knew it was a lovely place, and they were all enjoying it, but Sharon was really taken with it. Laura was glad to see her so happy. In fact, Laura didn't know how much Sharon was taken with the place. They were only on their second day, and already Sharon was wondering if there would be any marketing jobs there. She thought there would have to be, being such a touristy area. The only thing is, it was probably very seasonal. Anyway, it was just a thought. She couldn't possibly move here. How could she? Especially with a baby on the way!

Michael Smith arrived at 8am the next morning. Laura had phoned him the evening before. He sounded a bit quiet but was pleasant enough. He advised her he couldn't help them the evening before; he was tied up, but that he could be there this morning. He told her that he would have to get there early as he had to work that day, so he would launch the jet ski for her, get them all set up, and then he would come by this evening after work. Michael told Laura that if they intended to use the jet ski over the few days, that there was an area on the beach they could put a lock on it overnight, or when they were not using it. It would save them having to bring it back and forth each time. Laura was delighted with this as she knew Ben would be ecstatic.

Laura had been in the kitchen attending to the breakfast when she saw a man out the back in a white van. At first, she thought he was trying to burgle the place but then she realised it must be Michael. He was so used to the place he obviously just got on with it. Still, she felt it was a bit rude, not to announce himself. Laura opened the patio door and walked out towards him. He wasn't exactly a handsome man, but he had strong features. He was tall, with broad shoulders and looked quite fit. Laura guessed he was in his late forties. He wore a serious frown as he went about getting the jet ski onto the trailer hitched to his van.

'Eh, hello there, I'm Laura. Can I take it you're Michael?' Laura enquired, a hint of sarcasm in her voice. Michael looked a bit startled as he looked up from what he was doing. He stood up straight and looked at her briefly.

'Hi, Yes. I'm Mike. Sorry about not knocking, I was afraid you were all still in bed. Didn't want to disturb you until I had this all hooked up and ready to go. Do you have the lifejackets?'

OK, she thought to herself, no small talk. Just down to business.

'Eh, no, sorry. Not sure if Sarah has any.'

He went back to fiddling with the boat and jet ski,

'She does yeah, in that small hut there, I'll get them now,' he said. 'I have a key. Who exactly will be using this, Laura?' he asked.

Again, Laura was taken back by his abruptness. It wasn't that he was rude. He was just so blunt.

'Eh, myself, my 16-year-old daughter and my 12-year-old son.' Jess had turned 16 only the week before. They had a small family party, which Bill came to, and then she went with her friends for a meal in town followed by the cinema. At least that's what she told Laura. And she had no choice but to believe her. She didn't think that Jess would be up to no good; she didn't seem the type. But then you never really knew. Laura had wanted to give her a big party in the house, invite all her friends, but she insisted she didn't want one. So, Laura and Bill had given her money and bought her a new iPhone, which she seemed delighted with.

Michael interrupted her thoughts suddenly; shaking his head.

'Your son will not be allowed use the jet ski on his own. He is too young. You must be 16. And even then, they can be quite tricky,' he informed her. Laura's heart sank. Ben was so looking forward to going on the jet ski. She couldn't disappoint him.

'OK, sure he can come with me, and his sister also, can bring him for a spin, I am sure we will manage,' Laura replied sweetly.

'I mean it, Laura; do not allow your son to drive it on his own. He could be killed, or cause a serious accident. Jet skis can be as powerful as a car,' he warned Laura.

OK, she thought, when Michael had gone, there goes that idea of letting Ben have a go. Laura would just have to brave it and take Ben out herself.

She wasn't sure how good Jess was on jet skis. Michael walked over to the hut, unlocked it, and came out with four or five life jacks which he threw in the van.

'Right, I'll meet you all down on the beach in twenty minutes. Just there,' he said, pointing to a certain area of the beach. And with that he got in the van and drove out the front gate. He obviously had a key for that too as she hadn't opened it for him. Well, thought Laura, what a very unpleasant man. He seemed to have a right chip on his shoulder.

When Laura went back inside, the other three were tucking into breakfast, Sharon doing the honors of dishing out the food. Laura filled them all in on the situation briefly and watched Ben's face crumble in disappointment.

'Don't worry Ben; I'll take you out for some cool spins.'

'I love them. And I can go quite fast,' Jess told her brother. Ben's face brightened somewhat with this news. While Laura was glad that Jess cheered her brother up, she wasn't sure she wanted Jess to be zooming around in a jet ski with Ben on the back. She realised she should have never mentioned the subject. She should have just pretended it was broken, as Ben would have seen it either way. Ah, well. Too late now.

The difference in how Michael spoke to Laura and how he spoke to the kids was unbelievable. He was like a different man. He was explaining gently to Jess, making sure Ben was listening, how to drive the contraption and all about the safety requirements. His voice was gentle, and patient and he even cracked several smiles when Ben would ask something a bit silly. Like, 'Will the sharks eat us if we fall off'? Laura was supposed to be getting the lessons as well, but he just seemed to ignore her. Sharon noticed it too. She was sitting on a towel, relaxing with a book. But she was observing the goings on around the subject.

This Michael guy seemed to have a bit of a problem with Laura. Sharon hadn't really spoken to him as there was no need, so they didn't know if it was people in particular, he didn't like, or just Laura! Sharon looked out at the peaceful ocean. She still had heard nothing from Rob. The longer the pregnancy went on, the more she wanted to tell Rob. Surely when she confirmed she was having his baby he would come around? She had no interest in any other men. She could never see herself taking up with another guy. She loved Rob so much; it still hurt her to the core. But having this baby meant she still had part of him. As she stroked her growing belly, she smiled, watching Laura and the kids. Laura was such a good mother. She had come through so much in the past six months. And here she was on holiday with her children without Bill. Or Jack.

Thinking of Jack, Sharon's face clouded over. She had a feeling now that he was bad news. She felt incredibly guilty as it was all her fault, they were together. She persuaded Jack to go see Laura when she was in hospital, which set off the chain of events. Sharon never told Laura what she had really seen in the restaurant that night, but she had a feeling that Laura wasn't as committed to Jack as Sharon first thought she was. Laura had hardly mentioned him since coming away, and when Sharon did mention him, Laura didn't seem keen to talk about him. She would leave it for a few days, but then she would ask Laura about it gently. And if Laura was having second thoughts about

Jack, Sharon wanted to make sure she steered her in the right direction this time!

Laura let Jess go first on her own, as she had no desire to show off her own jet skiing skills with Michael watching. She would definitely make a show of herself. Jess was a natural. Gliding through the water, no problem to her. Poor Ben was bouncing up and down on the beach, shouting at Jess to come back and take him.

'Are you comfortable to take the jet ski out on your own?' Michael asked Laura suddenly.

His words seemed a bit kinder than his early remarks. Laura was absolutely terrified to take the jet ski out on her own. She had never driven one and all this talk of them being so dangerous and could kill people, was making her even more nervous. But she didn't want Michael to know that.

'Yes, I'll be fine. No problem. You can go on now if you like. Thanks for all your help,' Laura replied.

'No sorry, no can do. If you intend to take out the jet ski, I want to see you drive it first. If anything happened to you, I would be responsible. I need to be sure you know how to handle one.'

Laura was infuriated. Who did he think he was? The cheek of him.

'I am not a child and I don't need your permission to drive one, thank you very much. And I'm 39 years old; I think I can be responsible for myself,' Laura fumed.

Michael smiled and put his hands up.

'Sorry, sorry. My fault. I didn't mean it to come out like that. It's just I have dealt with a lot of tourists and jet skis over the years, and have encountered so many accidents, a lot due to people not knowing how to handle the thing. I didn't mean any offence. If you are sure, you can handle one, no problem. I will leave you to it. Just make sure Ben doesn't go out alone. He is so excited; he might easily try it when you're not looking.'

Laura was surprised; first at how nice he was being now, and secondly, at the length of his conversation. He was really confusing her. Laura really wanted him to show her the ropes. She would feel so much better. She supposed she should stop being stubborn, as her and Ben's safety would be at stake. She needed to learn properly, and not by herself. Michael sensed that she would like him to help her, so he said, 'Look, poor Ben is going to wet himself unless he gets out there. Jess is coming back now. I'm going to take Ben out for a spin myself if that's OK with you. When we come back, I'll take you out. Explain about the different controls. And then you can try it. Is that, OK?'

He felt guilty. He knew he had been very short with her earlier, but he was after having a huge argument with his ex-wife over their daughters. Honesty, the woman drove him insane at times. All she cared about was herself, and how she could benefit the most. Never mind what was best for their daughters.

'Ehh, yeah, that would be great. Thank you,' Laura said, and then she walked over and sat down beside Sharon. Sharon looked at her, lifted her sunglasses and gave her a big wink followed by a smile.

'HE obviously had a change of heart, not bad looking either, especially when he smiles!' laughed Sharon' to which she received a playful dig in the arm from Laura.

CHAPTER 15

Laura flopped on the bed, exhausted. They were just back from spending the day on the beach, including using the jet ski for most of it. Sharon had gone into town earlier to look around and the kids were in the pool. Laura enjoyed today, even if it started off a bit shaky. Michael had been great in the end. He had taken Ben spinning around the sea, in and out of the waves; Ben screaming in delight. When it was Laura's turn, Michael went a lot slower. Once she had watched him and knew what to do, she switched places with him. She was very aware of him being so close to her.

There were two handles on the back of the jet ski, so she didn't have to put her arms around him to hold on ,which she was grateful for. It took Laura a few minutes to get the hang of it, but once she did, there was no stopping her. She pulled the throttle back and flew over the waves. Michael was shouting at her in her delight,

'You dark horse, I think you've done this before.' She drove around for ten minutes and then came back to the shore. She had been delighted with herself as it meant she could take Ben out now herself and not have to leave it all to Jess. She thanked Michael again and he said his goodbyes and left them to it.

She slept for an hour and then went downstairs to find Ben and Jess watching TV and eating crisps. Laura did not have the energy to go out again, and she was sure Sharon probably wouldn't either.

'Is Sharon back?' she asked them.

'Yeah, about ten minutes after you went up. She went for a lie down as well. Still up there.' Jess replied without taking her eyes of the TV screen.

'How would you guys feel like getting a pizza in? I don't think I want to walk back into town, I know it's not far, but I'd rather stay in.'

'YEAH, PIZZA. Can I have a large one to myself?' asked Ben. Laura smiled.

'Jess? OK with you?' Laura asked.

'Yeah, no problem, I'm easy.' Laura decided she would make herself a cup of tea and read her book for half an hour. She didn't want to disturb Sharon yet. A quiet night would do them no harm as they were going to a Marine Adventure Park tomorrow. Sharon was going to stay at the villa and do her own thing. Laura was lucky with Jess. She knew a lot of teenage girls could be a real handful. But Jess was great. And took an interest in everything.

It made life so much easier. Sharon had asked Jessica if she wanted to stay with her instead of going to the park, that Sharon might go to the local shopping mall if she wanted to join her.

But while Jessica didn't want to admit it, she still had a very childlike streak when it came to having fun. Laura knew she was looking forward to the park as much as Ben, but she wouldn't admit it. Jessica had thanked Sharon, but said she better go with her mam, to help with Ben! It was nice of Sharon to ask, though.

The Marine Park was just like any other park they visited when on holidays before. However, they enjoyed it. It had all the usual animals and they attended a Dolphin Show which was very entertaining. The park had a water land section with slides and swimming pools and they had great fun in the afternoon, especially as it was so hot. They arrived back to the villa around 4pm. Sharon was sitting reading her book beside the pool.

'Good day?' she enquired.

To which, Ben proceeded to give her a full run down of the day's events!

'What about you, did you go shopping?' asked Laura. She hadn't really got a chance to have any private conversations with Sharon yet. She must find the time over the next day or two. Check she was OK. Although Sharon looked more than OK. She was glowing. And seemed very relaxed.

'Yes, I went to the shopping mall. Was huge. Bought a few things. Maternity clothes and that,' replied Sharon, although she didn't tell them about her visit to the recruitment place.

'Sounds good, do you want to chill here for an hour or two and then maybe head down to that Irish Bar *Paddy's Place*?' Laura asked.

'They do food too. We could have something to eat, a couple of drinks and head back?'

Ben and Jess were happy to do that, and Sharon agreed.

Paddy's Bar was like the usual Irish bars located in Spanish tourist resorts. But there was a cozy feel to it. They chose to sit inside, as they were tired being in the sun all day, and had planned on going back to the beach tomorrow, so some shade was much needed. They chose a table and ordered their food, Laura getting herself a glass of wine, Sharon having a mineral water. Jessica asked if she could have a glass of wine as apparently all the parents let her friends have the odd one. Laura sighed and thought she may as well do it in front of me than behind my back.

She promised Jess she could have a glass after the dinner. At least then Jessica would have a full stomach, so the wine wouldn't be as hard on her. They enjoyed their meal and the pub was beginning to get busy. Laura went to the bar to get herself and Jess a glass of wine when she bumped into Michael, who was also waiting to order a drink.

'Ahh, I see you found the best pub in the town,' he smiled.

God, Laura thought, he seems like a different man to the one I met yesterday morning.

'Let me get our drinks. I think I owe you a bit of an apology. I shouldn't have been so abrupt with you yesterday morning. I was having a bad day and took it out on you.'

Laura couldn't help but agree with Sharon. There was something nice about him, especially when he smiled.

'Oh, you don't need to buy us drinks. Sure, I should be buying for you, helping us out like that yesterday,' Laura said.

'No, let me, what are you having?'

Laura gave in and told him the order. He asked her to sit back down and he said he would bring them over. Sharon once again gave her a cheeky wink and knowing smile. Laura glared back at her, before giving in to a smile too.

Jess was all excited at the prospect of her first glass of wine. Well, her first glass of wine in front of her mother! Laura hoped she hadn't had too many in the past behind her back. When Michael came back over, Laura insisted he joined them. Ben and Jess were playing pool which left the three of them, but Sharon suddenly stood up, claimed she was wrecked tired, and would see them at home. Laura knew what she was doing and could have killed her. She could feel her cheeks burning. They bid her goodnight and resumed conversation. Michael had been telling them that he had lived in Spain for eighteen years. He had married a Spanish woman who lived twenty minutes inland. They had two girls, the oldest 18. Michael had separated from his wife ten years ago but stayed in Spain to be close to his daughters.

However, he was now thinking of going back to Ireland. He wanted to open a pub/restaurant as he had run so many of them over the years. He had also saved up quite a lot so had the money to do it. But he wouldn't go unless his eldest daughter got into Trinity College in Dublin which was one of the most prestigious universities in Europe.

His daughter Natalie wanted to do Journalism and had applied to Dublin at her father's request. But Natalie would also like to go to Ireland as she had visited so many times over the years to her father's family in Wicklow. However, her mother Paloma, did not want her daughter going anywhere near Ireland. She didn't care that it was such a good university and would do wonders for her daughter's career. It was so difficult to get in to. Paloma didn't want Michael to be happy, so she kept causing arguments by demanding that Natalie go to a university in Spain. She did not however have much choice, as Michael would be funding his daughter's education.

He was involved in property and had made a nice few bob over the years. But Paloma still phoned him regularly just for an argument about it. Isabella was just 14. So, they had a few years yet to make plans for her. If he moved back to Ireland, she could come stay with him for the holidays, at Easter in the summer and Christmas. He also intended to come over to her some weekends.

Laura told him bits and pieces about her own life. She didn't get into the details. Just that she was recently separated but getting on with things. She talked about work, but how she was getting a bit bored of what she did and was thinking of going back to the office end of things.

They had a good chat and Laura was really enjoying his company, but Ben was getting restless and wanted to go home. He had tired of playing pool and losing to Jess who proved to be a surprising good player.

'Michael, can you unlock the jet ski for us tomorrow morning? We're going to the beach,' Ben asked as they were getting ready to leave.

'Sure, Ben. No problem. Although I have to go to Malaga in the morning, but I should be back around midday. I'll drop down to you on the beach and get you set up then. Is that's OK?'.

Ben shouted, 'Cool,' and with that, ran off heading for the villa.

They spent the rest of the week between the beach, the pool, the town, and a little time sightseeing. Laura could not believe how quick the week was going. Ben and Jess were having a fantastic time. She had spoken to Jack a couple of times but not for long. She didn't mention the woman who answered his phone. It didn't matter anymore. She decided she was not going to pursue the relationship once back home. She had moved on much too quickly. Laura wasn't ready for a relationship. But it had taken her till now to realise it. At least it was early days. He might be disappointed at first, but she was sure he wouldn't sit around moping too long.

Herself and Sharon had a good catch-up last night. They were flying back tomorrow so Laura pinned her down when the kids went up to bed, grabbing the chance to have a quiet chat. Sharon was anxious to talk too. They had sat up for hours chatting and getting things of their chest. It was therapeutic for both of them. When Sharon had probed about how she felt about Jack, Laura told her the truth. That she wasn't sure anymore, and was considering finishing things.

When she had said this, Sharon then confessed that she thought there was much more to the woman in the restaurant that time she saw them, but she hadn't wanted to upset her friend. Laura was glad she told her, as it cemented her decision to end things with him. She also told Sharon about looking for a new job. Sharon encouraged her and told Laura she would help her write up her CV if she wanted, and to create a LinkedIn profile for her. Sharon explained that LinkedIn was a website specifically dedicated to businesspeople. You could do loads of things from a work perspective like arrange potential business meetings, get business news updates, and check out what jobs were available in the marketplace. Recruiters tended to use the site a lot to look for potential candidates for clients. So, Laura was delighted. She only now felt a new chapter in her life starting; Jack was in the old life, associated with Bill.

This holiday had been such a good idea. Sharon had spoken to Laura at length about Rob, her feelings for him and her hope that they would reconcile. But at the same time, Sharon admitted that she was going to look into jobs abroad in Spain, as she had enjoyed it so much. It wasn't that she hadn't been to Spain a hundred times; she had. But this time something felt right about it. She didn't know if it was the location, or the villa or what it was. But she felt like a new person out here. She hadn't much family left back home. Her mother had passed away ten years earlier and her father now had a new partner, who Sharon was not that keen on. She only saw them once or so a month. Could be longer. Her only brother lived and worked in New York. They were close as brothers and sisters go; they spoke on Skype a lot. But the separation made it difficult for her to confide in him.

Thinking of the apartment back in Dublin depressed her. She didn't want to raise the baby there. Fine, she would wait till the baby was born. But Sharon was really beginning to consider relocating. She would look into it more once back home. Laura encouraged her also. If this is what she wanted, she should go for it. Laura asked about Rob, what if he wanted her back, and Sharon said that if he truly wanted her back, he would go with her wherever she was going, considering she'd have his child by then. But then she might not go anywhere. There was so much to find out. And how much would it all cost? Sharon had invested in some oil shares seven years previously. She knew they were doing well as a larger corporation had taken the company over a year ago. She could cash those in if she needed; it would give her a nice few pounds to get started. She knew she would have to do a lot of research on this one. It would be such a life-changing decision. At least it would keep her busy for the summer back home and until the baby came.

CHAPTER 16

Laura scrolled through the jobs listing website. It was the end of May and they had been back a month now. She and Sharon had managed to finally get her CV in shape last weekend, and she was only getting around to looking up jobs. She was sitting at the garden table, as it was a beautiful Saturday morning. Laura had to squint to read the words on her laptop as the sun was shining in her eyes. Any of the jobs that she thought would suit her were all nine to five thirty, five days a week. While Laura didn't mind hard work, she didn't fancy working full time from morning till night.

She would like something a bit more than part-time though. Truth was, she didn't know what she wanted. Nothing grabbed her enough now to apply to anything, so she shut the screen and sat back in her chair with a sigh. So much for a new chapter in her life. She was more confused now than ever. Laura had told Jack that she wanted to call things a day after she returned from Spain. She didn't want to string him along. Jack had obviously sensed her coolness towards him in the last few weeks as he had said he felt she was having a change of heart. He was disappointed, said they could have been great together.

But he understood and respected her decision. He did say that maybe in six months or a year, if she felt up to it, they could take things up again. However, Laura quickly quashed that thought.

'Jack, you're a lovely man, and I am sure you have women queuing up for you. Don't be waiting on me to move on. To be honest, I don't think we would have worked out anyway. We can always be friends but that will be all it will ever be,' she said.

Again, he was disappointed, Laura felt he probably had suggested it just to save face a bit and not because he wanted to rekindle their romance at a later stage. Anyway, it was done now, and they parted on good terms. But the problem now was Bill. He had been coming over, spending more time in the house. As summer was on the way, he was mowing the lawns, cutting the hedges, fixing up the trees, etc. And afterwards she would make him something to eat.

They would all sit down and eat dinner and chat away laughing and joking. It was so like old times. Laura had caught Bill watching her on several occasions over the dinner table as the kids laughed and teased each other. She knew he was willing her to give him a second chance. Her feelings had reignited for him again in the last month, with seeing so much of him.

Bill was being more attentive than he ever was. Laura was not stupid though. She knew a lot of this was in order to win her affections. She did know though that Bill would most likely keep it up for a long while if she chose to take him back. But if she took him back, could she ever trust him again? All those trips abroad? She could ask him to give up the business trips – but no, she would not do that.

It was his job. If she couldn't trust him to go away without shagging some woman first chance he got, then she couldn't take him back. There would be no point. But then maybe she should take him back for the kids' sake? Until Ben was old enough, until he was finished school. Ben was nearly 13. Could she take Bill back for another four or five years? No. That's not the right thing to do either. If Laura was going to take Bill back, it needed to be for the right reasons.

It had to be because she believed they could put the affair in the past. And move on. And make their marriage work. During the daytime when Laura was busy, either writing her column, doing the housework, or spending time with the kids, she wouldn't contemplate taking Bill back. It was only when she was alone at night in bed and felt such utter loneliness that she began to let her mind wander. How long was he gone now? Seven months. It felt so much longer.

She had agreed to let him take her and the kids to a show in the city centre later that evening. And then to Eddie Rockets afterwards. Laura knew she was giving mixed signals to both her kids and to Bill.

It wasn't fair to get their hopes up if she did not intend on giving Bill a second chance. She sighed loudly as she watched a robin hop around the garden, with no worries on its shoulders, only where it would source its next meal. To be a bird, thought Laura, flying free with no worries. Well, you're not a bird, she thought, and you better make a decision soon and stop keeping everyone in turmoil! And with that she got up and went back into the house to prepare for the day ahead of her.

Sharon was feeling so nervous, her stomach was sick. She couldn't eat, or even drink a cup of coffee. And it had nothing to do with the pregnancy. Rob was calling over in an hour. An hour!!! My god – She hadn't seen him in so long. He had only phoned twice since she was home, and she had not been able to work up the courage to tell him about the baby. And now he would see her, with her protruding belly. He had asked last week if he could call around for a coffee and a chat. Sharon wasn't sure what to think. She had agreed, as he needed to find out sooner or later. She had put on the most flattering maternity clothes she could find. Never one for a lot of makeup, she put on a small bit of foundation and mascara, and a touch of lip-gloss. She looked over the apartment and saw brochures on *Moving Abroad*. Sharon picked them up and hid them in the cupboard. She had no intentions of revealing her plans to Rob until she found out what his intentions were. Sharon had done a lot of research in the last month;

both on the web and making phone calls. There were a few jobs in the south of Spain that would have suited her perfectly, some even coming with a relocation fee and accommodation, but they all needed to be filled in the next month. With the baby due in three months, Sharon wouldn't really be able to fill a role for another seven or eight months. She wanted to spend some time with her baby before going back to work.

If Sharon was being realistic, she would most likely have to take a gamble. She would have to move to Spain without a job. Get herself set up out there with a house and a nanny. And then look for job out there. She had enough money to keep her going for at least a year, so it was an option. The only problem was if she didn't get a job, she would have to come home. And then what? Go back to her father's? No chance – she didn't think she would even be welcome there as Wendy, his new partner, had little time for her. Wendy would not like to be put out by having Sharon and a little toddler shacked up with her. So that's what she had to decide. Would she go? And if so, when? She was due to finish work in two months' time. That would leave a month before the baby's due. But she would not be allowed to fly at that time. So, if Sharon was going to go, she would have to wait until the baby was at least a month old. Mmmm… that would be around end of September. October.

She would think about. Sharon had no idea what Rob wanted. She did know it was something about the apartment.

Sharon was calculating her half of the apartment as collateral in Spain, so they needed to discuss the sale of it, whether Rob wanted her back or not!

There was a knock on the door and she heard Rob's voice

'Sharon – It's me.'

At least he didn't have the cheek to let himself in, she thought. She was so nervous; the palms of her hands were dripping with sweat. This is stupid, she told herself. You have nothing to be afraid off. He left. Not you. You have a future with your baby to look forward to, with or without him. And with that, she felt a bit more confident and waddled over to the door to let him in. Once she unlatched the door, she quickly turned around and walked back into the apartment. She stopped at the couch and turned around to face him.

He looked dreadful. Sharon couldn't believe it. He hadn't shaved in weeks, maybe months! He looked so scruffy. This was not the Rob she knew. What was going on?

'Rob, what the hell? What's wrong with you?' she exclaimed.

'Eh, Sharon, I think we can put me on hold for a bit, while you tell me WHAT THE HELL is going on. You're pregnant. You told me you weren't!' Rob shouted.

Sharon got a bit of a shock and sat back on the couch. Rob was immediately remorseful and ran to her side.

'I'm so sorry. Sorry, Sharon. I shouldn't have shouted at you. I just can't believe you didn't tell me.'

Sharon felt a bit better now that he had calmed down. She told him how she tried to tell him so many times, but she just couldn't work up the courage to do it, as she knew how much he hated kids. Rob took her hands in his and said,

'Sharon, I don't hate kids. Don't ever think that. I love kids. I just don't want to have any of my own. I would be no good for them,' he said as tears ran down his face.

Rob didn't know what to do now. He had gone away to Switzerland for a few weeks, where he skied and mountain trekked and done as much as he could to clear his head. He had decided that he was going to try and win Sharon back. He felt that maybe in time, they could have a kid. But not yet. He knew he looked like shit but until he knew if Sharon would take him back, he couldn't bring himself to clean himself up. The passion had gone out of life once again. But could he stand by her now? I mean, the baby would be here in a few months, he thought to himself. He couldn't get his head around it.

Rob stood up, he wanted to run away, but knew that he could not. He had to tell Sharon. He would tell her. And then he would leave.

'Rob, for god's sake, what is it? I think I deserve to know why you don't seem to want our child. The truth? At least give me that much,' Sharon said.

But she wasn't crying or upset. She was much stronger now that she wasn't just looking after herself but had to protect her baby as well. Sharon knew by the way Rob was behaving, that whatever happened today, he would not be back with her any time soon. Whatever he had going on, he was far from over it. Rob sat on the couch opposite her. He put his head in his hands.

CHAPTER 17

'I never told you this. And my friends and family were all sworn to secrecy. I couldn't speak about. The pain was too raw. And I haven't spoken of it in fifteen years until a couple of weeks ago. I started seeing a councillor to try and help me. It has helped, a bit. But I still need more sessions, a lot more.'

Sharon sat as still as a statue on the couch. She could feel her heart pounding and her stomach was sick… what the hell is going in… she felt terrified.

'Go on,' she urged him gently. Rob paused before continuing.

' OK. But hear me out first if you can. Before the questions come.' He paused again.

Then he went on shakily.

'I had a fiancée who I met twenty years ago. I was 19 years old when we first got together. She was from England and worked over here in Dublin. She regularly went home for the weekend to her family. As we got more serious, she took me home with her. To Manchester. She had a large family and I got on great with all of them. She had two brothers who were very protective of her as she was much younger than them. Her father was also very close to her and was wary of me at first.'

Rob stopped to take a breath. Sharon thought she was in a film. She didn't think this was real. It didn't feel like it was happening to her.

He had a fiancée! From England!

'What was her name'? she asked. Rob looked up, and then back down again, as if the effort of looking at her was too much.

'Lizze,' he said. 'Lizze Babington. She was an accountant with one of the big English banks. They had a branch over here which she was sent over to manage the financial department. Originally, she had intended going back, but when she got pregnant, we decided we would stay in Dublin. And I did the decent thing and proposed. We were young. I was 23 and she was just 22. But we were happy.'

'PREGNANT?' Sharon said, shocked.

'What, you have a child in England?' Rob looked up once again, realising asking her to refrain from questions till the end was impossible. He was crying heavily.

'No, no, no. I did have a child. I did…' and he started weeping so heavily that Sharon moved over beside him and took him in her arms. What the hell happened? She wasn't sure she wanted to hear the rest of the story. She knew the worst was to come. After a while, he spoke more softly.

Sharon gave him the box of tissues from the table.

'Her father always told me to make sure I took good care of her. To never let anything happen to her. He said that she was the baby of the house. And the fact that she was living in Ireland they couldn't watch out for her.'

Rob paused for a couple of minutes, and then continued.

'It was on a weekend to Scotland it happened. If it had been in Ireland, I would not have been able to continue living here. Mark was twenty months old. He was the most gorgeous little boy you have ever seen. Full of smiles and laughter, always wanting to play and run around. He was the apple of our eye.' He paused again.

Sharon felt as though she was having an out-of-body experience. To think he had a child at one stage! A real living toddler. And never told her. As if sensing her frustration, Rob went on.

'One day, we went for a drive up the Highlands and stopped in several places for some pictures. It was a windy enough day although the sun was shining. I'll never forget it, as long as I live on this earth,' he whispered. Sharon didn't think she could be any more shocked. Rob had a son called Mark. Who was nearly two! Or had one. She really didn't want to hear the rest of the story, but she knew she had too.

'We stopped in a spot called Devils Canyon. It was such a steep drop and people had fallen off years ago and died. But it hadn't happened in a long time as they had made it safe. There was a small fence to stop you falling over. I got Lizze and Mark to stand at the fence to take some pictures. It was getting even windier and Lizze said she'd had enough. The weather was too bad for Mark. That we should be getting back. But I told her no, just a couple more.

There was a small break in the fence, which Lizze was standing under my instructions. She was perfectly safe as she was holding the side of the fence with one hand, and had her other hand on Mark's shoulder. I was taking the pictures and when a flock of birds in their hundreds started flying through the canyon behind her, I told her to just wait a second till I got the birds in the background. I hadn't finished speaking when a gust of wind blew Lizze a bit off balance and her hand came off Mark's shoulder.

'On hearing me say there was a flock of birds, Mark turned around and took a few steps forward, reaching out towards them. The wind howled again, pushing all three of us forward. Mark had no chance. He went straight away. Fell over the ridge. Lizze screamed and went to grab him, but he was gone, and the wind knocked her over the edge. She managed to hang on for a couple of seconds and I grabbed her hand. I begged her to hold on. But she couldn't. Or wouldn't. I saw the look she gave me.

'The look of disappointment and sadness. She blamed me for what had happened. And she was right. She was calm when she finally fell. She didn't scream. I think she wanted to follow our little man. Rather be dead than alive without him… And that's it. That's why I can't have any more children. For two reasons – One – I couldn't even look after the one I had. His blood is on my hands. What type of a father puts his two-year-old on the edge of a cliff on a windy day?' he cried, and then continued. 'And secondly – I don't think I would be able to look at another child, and not feel such immense pain and sadness for the loss of Mark and Lizze. I know that's selfish.

'And not fair on you. But surely you understand.' He leaned back against the couch; all energy gone from him. He looked white as a ghost.

Sharon also sat back. She was stroking her stomach. She could not imagine the pain anyone could feel losing a child. And she understood why Lizze went.

Oh, she let go alright. Of that she felt sure, as Sharon thought she would most likely do the same if ever faced with such a heart-wrenching situation. Although she felt sorry for Rob, she was annoyed with him also. How could he put them in such danger? She knew they had been young, but still. Such a waste of life. Sharon's head was all over the place. She still loved Rob, loved him so much. And this explained a lot about his behavior at times in the past. However, she needed time to digest this. And the fact he had a secret life before her...

She knew she should probably be comforting him.

'Rob that is one of the most horrific and saddening stories I have ever heard. To think what you must have gone through. I do understand now why you are acting like this. However, I think you should have got help years ago. After it happened. And not waited until now. And you shouldn't blame yourself. Yes, what you did was stupid, but you had no idea that you were putting either of them in real danger. It was a freak accident.'

Sharon was trying to say the right things. Although she had no idea what the right things were to say. Her head felt like it was going to explode.

'That's what the doc says,' Rob replied. Sharon leaned forward and took his hand in hers, she met his eyes and gently said, 'But Rob, this thing with not being able to have another child because it will remind you too much of the past, is something you need to get over. Because if you don't, you will live a long life of unhappiness.

'You need to move forward for your own sake. If you can't sort yourself out, you will never be able to be a father to our child. You will miss out on so much, and so many happy memories. But I can't heal you. You need to do this for yourself. If you can't, then the baby and I will move on. And we will live our own life. But we would much rather you were with us.'

Rob looked at Sharon.

'I don't deserve you. I love you so much. I never thought I would fall in love again, and then you came along. And I started to realise that maybe I could be happy again. As long as I blocked out the past. But I should have dealt with it. And not hidden it away. It's only coming back to haunt me now. I want nothing more than to be part of you and the baby's life. I just don't know if I can,' he said sadly.

Sharon knew this herself. They spent another half hour talking and she kept reassuring Rob that it was an accident. It wasn't his fault. She then approached the topic of the apartment.

'Rob, I know you need time to sort things out. Please do that. Go away and do what you've got to do. If you can get through this, we will be waiting for you. But if you know in your heart that you can't, then be honest with me and let me know. As I will want to move on.' She stopped, waiting to see if he would respond. He didn't, so she continued. 'I am not putting you under pressure; I don't expect a decision before the birth. I understand this will take longer. I suggest you check in somewhere that can help with these things. But next year is a new year. And I won't be waiting anymore. So, you have six months to get your head together. In the meantime, I want to sell this apartment, whether we stay together or not.

'I don't want it to go immediately but hoping to get rid of it in a few months' time.' Sharon took a deep breath, tired after the long speech. Rob sat there for a minute, deep in thought.

'Sharon, do what you want with the apartment, I want you to have it. No matter what happens. I owe it to you. If you sell this though, where are you going to live?' he asked her.

Sharon didn't want to start discussing Spain with him right now. It was a conversation for another day. And to be honest, if things between them didn't work out, she didn't want him knowing anything about it.

'I am looking to move closer to the sea. And I also want a house, rather than an apartment. There are some nice two and three-bedroom houses with a view of the sea not far from Laura. And they wouldn't break the bank. I could rent somewhere until I decide where to buy. And if the worst happens, I can stay with Laura. She has a spare room that has its own en-suite, so I'll be OK for somewhere to stay. Rob, I want you to take half of the sale. It wouldn't be fair for me to keep the lot. We both put a lot in to it.'

But Rob wouldn't hear of it.

'No, you have enough to be worrying about Sharon. We have a lot of the mortgage on this place paid off, and you should get a good price for it. I want you to take the lot. I'm feeling bad enough as it is, so I am probably being selfish by making you take it, as it's only to make me feel a bit better. But anyway. You take it. Let me know if you need any help with anything. Estate agents or solicitors. I am going to try my utmost to sort myself out, as I would love to be there for you both. I just can't promise anything. In the meantime, keep me updated, won't you? Even a text to let me know if you have any buyers or anything. I will keep in touch though. To check on you and the baby.'

Sharon thought about this for a minute.

'No, Rob. I don't want to hear anything from you until you have made your decision. You need to take the time out with no distractions. I might need you to sign a few forms to do with the apartment which I will text you about if that's the case. But other than that, please don't phone me. Or call around. Even if you haven't decided before the baby is born. Just leave us be. I would rather me and the baby get used to being on our own in case it will be permanent. I do expect a decision by the end of the year though. I mean it. Next year is a new year for me, regardless of what you decide,' she told him firmly.

Rob did not seem too happy about this. He was a bit taken aback by Sharon's blunt approach; he was used to always coming first with her. But this was not the case anymore. Not that he blamed her. But he knew he had no choice. He rose slowly from the couch and Sharon rose with him. He touched her face and stroked it gently. He looked down at her belly.

Sharon thought he was going to stroke that too, but he turned quite abruptly and walked towards the door.

'Thank you, Sharon, you are a very understanding woman. Most women would want nothing to do with me; tell me to sling my hook. Or else they would insist I stand by them. You are giving me a choice, and for that I love you even more,' he said to her from the doorway.

'Rob, it has to be your choice. If I forced you to come back through emotional blackmail, it would never work out long-term. You need to come back to us, because that's what you want to do. Not because it's what you are being made to do. That's the only way you will ever be truly happy. Follow your heart, and do what makes you as a person happy.' Sharon felt like someone else was talking and not her. How was she doing this? Saying these things?

'Don't try to live your life to please other people, otherwise you will always be unhappy and will live a life of regrets. So that is what I am asking you to do. Then at least if you don't come back, I will know it truly is for the best,' Sharon managed to finish. She didn't know how she was being so strong. She felt like throwing herself on the floor and begging him to stay.

But she knew that was pointless. Even if he did stay, it would never work out. He had to come back of his own accord. And if he didn't, she would be crushed. But she would not dwell on it. She would move on. For the baby's sake.

Sharon knew enough women who held grudges and used their children to hurt the fathers. She thought this was so wrong.

A child should never ever be used as bait by a mother or a father. She thought about Laura and how brave she was. Even after Bill had cheated with her worst enemy, Laura still wouldn't hear a bad word about him in front of her kids. She recognised the importance of Jess and Ben retaining a stable relationship with him. She could have easily stopped them seeing him, by feeding them with vile stories, but she was a step above that. She didn't use them to get at Bill. So many women did use their children, and not only did they end up hurting their ex-husbands or ex partners, but they always end up hurting the kids just as much. It was such a selfish thing to do.

'Right, I'll be off now. You take care of yourself. If you need anything at all, just let me know.'

He smiled sadly. He kept his eyes on her face. And then he turned and walked out of the apartment.

CHAPTER 18

Bill ended up back in Laura's bed by pure drunken stupidity. It was a couple of weeks after they had gone to the show in Dublin, which had been a great evening. Bill had asked her several times to go out for dinner with him, just the two of them, ever since. Thursday morning the doorbell had rang, and she opened it to two dozen red roses and a card:

Dinner Friday Night – 7.30pm – La Massimo xx Bill.

He had worn her down and so she decided to go. It was only a meal after all. Both Jess and Ben were originally supposed to stay with her parents, but they now were staying with their own friends instead.

La Massimo was an amazing Italian restaurant that had just opened a year ago. It was based out in Howth, on the pier. They had never been there as a couple before. Laura felt more comfortable with this. She would rather not have old memories haunting her. She certainly hoped he had never taken Johnson there. And here was the start of it. If he had taken Johnson there. Laura knew she needed to put Johnson in the back of her mind if she was going to move on. But it was way more difficult than she realised. She had been in the office yesterday and Bill had texted her to say he would collect her at 7pm. She had been going to drive, to ensure she didn't drink much. But she let it be. Maybe a few glasses of wine would relax her.

When Bill picked her up, he had more flowers. He both smelled and looked great. Laura began to feel her heart quicken. Could this marriage really be salvaged?? They ended up having a really nice evening. Laura managed to forget about Johnson and they both had several bottles of wine between them before heading next door to the pub for more drink. They got a taxi home around 2am and they were both very drunk. Once in the taxi they were already kissing. She was sure the taxi driver must have thought they were a very new couple, and not actually been married for the last seventeen years! When they got back to the house, they didn't have another drink; they just fell up the stairs, tore each other's clothes off, and made passionate love a couple of times. Laura thought it was a couple of times. She wasn't entirely sure.

When she had woken, she had one of the worst hangovers she had had since uni. Laura usually always made sure to drink plenty of water when she got home from a night out. This always helped alleviate the hangover. But alas, last night was a different story. Bill turned towards her, pulled her in to him in a cuddle

'How are you this morning, Sweetheart?' he asked groggily. 'I don't know about you, but my head is bursting,' he groaned. Laura wasn't sure how she felt about Bill being back in her bed. The pain in her head wouldn't let her think straight.

'Suffering,' was all she could manage. Next thing, Bill jumped out of bed.

'Wait there love, I'll get you some tablets and water, back in a tick'.

Laura lay back in the bed. There were some merits to having him there she supposed. But what happens now? Did she tell him to leave? Especially before the kids came home. She looked at the clock, my god, she thought. It was 11.30am. She never slept that late. Thank god the kids hadn't arrived back yet. But she had spoken too soon.

'Mam,' came Ben's shouting voice as she heard the front door burst open. Oh, no, she thought. She heard Bill greet their son and Ben's excitement at his father being there. Laura couldn't hear what was being said, but she dreaded to think. She heard Ben's footsteps running up the stairs and he burst into her room.

'Mam, Dad said you both had a great night. And he stayed here because he had too much to drink. But where did he sleep? He says the spare room, but I don't believe him, look his phone is on his side of the bed, he slept in here, didn't he Mam? Are ye back together now?'

Ben was asking questions at two hundred miles an hour. Laura's head was busting and she couldn't deal with this now. Bill walked into the room and smiled over at Laura.

'Ben, son, come on. Your mother needs a bit more sleep. And my phone is over there as I helped your mother to bed last night. That's all. I did sleep in the spare room. Come on now.

'Let's go downstairs and you can tell me what you got up to at Alan's house.' He put his arm around Bens shoulders and steered him towards the door.

Laura gratefully swallowed the two tablets Bill had just given her and felt very relieved that he had taken control of the situation.

She drifted off back to sleep and woke again at 1.30pm. Shit, she thought. She better get up. Laura had no idea if Jess was back or if Bill was still downstairs.

'Hi Mam.' Jess was sitting at the kitchen table reading OK Magazine. 'Rough night on the tiles!' Jess joked. Laura smiled and ruffled her daughter's hair. She went to the fridge and poured herself a glass of orange juice.

'Where is Ben?' she asked, not wanting to make reference to Bill.

'Dad's taken him to his football match. It's at 2 o'clock. So, they won't be back till around 4.15. So, is what Ben says true? Did Dad stay over with you last night?' Jess teased. Laura groaned inwardly.

She didn't know what to say.

'Eh, Ye. He did. We both had too much to drink. So, your dad left his car and we got a taxi home. He stayed in the spare room,' Laura replied without looking at Jess.

'Yeah, right Mam, Ben said he checked the spare room and the bed had not been slept in!' Jess laughed.

Good lord, thought Laura. The cheeky little git. You had to be up early to catch these kids out now.

'How did your dad take Ben to the football? His car is in Howth,' she asked Jess now, avoiding the bedroom conversation.

'He phoned his friend Sean and asked him to help him out. Sean picked Dad and Ben up around half hour ago,' Jess explained.

Good thinking, Laura thought. She sat down at the table across from Jess.

'Do you want to go into town with me and do a bit of shopping?' Laura asked. It was the last thing that she wanted to do. Her head was still throbbing and she the thought of shops made her want to puke, but it would be nice to spend a bit of time alone with her daughter.

Jess laughed again.

'Like you're in any state for shopping! Ha, thanks Mam. But I'll have to pass. I switched my shifts at work, I actually start in 15 minutes, so I got to go now,' Jess said as she rose from the table and grabbed her things.

She walked over to her mother and kissed her head.

'Bye Mam, and it's really great news about you and Dad,' and she ran out the door heading in the direction of the local shop. Oh no, thought Laura. Is that what they think? Please, no. She wasn't ready to take Bill back. Yes, she spent the night with him.

But that was just a first step. It was such a pity Ben had caught them. She was only confusing them by having Bill stay. It wasn't fair to them, especially Ben. Jess was older, and understood the way the world worked. But Laura was sure she still hoped her parents would get back together. Oh, no. What a mess. Laura picked up her mobile phone and rang the only person she knew she could talk to.

'You SLEPT with him!' exclaimed Sharon, half in shock, half laughing. 'And you got caught by your 12-year-old son! Ha. Sorry Laura. I know I shouldn't be laughing. It is funny though. Having to explain yourself to your kids.' Laura sighed and accepted the cup of tea Sharon handed her.

They were sitting in Sharon's apartment; barely an hour after Jess had left for work. Laura had been grateful that Sharon was in and had invited her over. It wasn't a conversation for the phone. Laura took a biscuit from the table. She had the munchies from all the drink the night before.

'Oh Sharon, what am I supposed to do?' she groaned.

Sharon felt the same type of conversation come on as she had had with Rob.

'Laura, you need to do what makes you happy. What do you want? If you still love Bill and would like to give it another chance, then go for it. God knows how hard he has worked to try and get you back.

'But only take him back if you really want to make another go of it. Don't do it to keep the kids happy, or him, for that matter. It won't work out in the long run,' Sharon said.

Laura looked closely at Sharon. At 38, she was such a beautiful woman. She looked so much younger. Laura was a year older at 39 but felt she looked mid 40's! Sharon was so strong and so brave. Laura did not think she could cope if she was in her situation.

'When did you get so wise Shaz?' she asked her friend. Sharon smiled and then let out a sigh.

'Unfortunately, through experience. I told Rob what I am telling you. He has to work out what he wants for himself. Not for me, not for the baby. But what he wants. And that's what you have got to do too'.

Laura thought about this.

She knew what had happened with Sharon and Rob as she had filled her in last week. Laura was so shocked. She was split in her feelings about Rob at the minute. She felt tremendous sadness for what the poor man had gone through. It was a horrific accident, and was certainly not his fault. She understood his guilt and how he must feel. Laura thanked god quickly that both her kids were okay. But on the other hand, she was annoyed with Rob.

Yes, so he went through a tragedy many years ago, and yes, he had always made clear that he didn't want kids, but come on. You can't go on hoarding something like that all your life. And then taking it out on your loved ones. Laura sincerely hoped he came to his senses and realised the life of happiness he had ahead of him with Sharon. She hoped he wasn't going to throw it all away. He would only end up miserable for the rest of his life.

It would be tough on Sharon, especially at the start. But Sharon would move on. She had beautiful looks and a bubbly personality. She was also extremely smart and driven. Sharon would be snapped up quickly, baby in tow or not. She knew her friend would survive. But Rob may not. Laura really hoped he did. She sighed.

'I would like to take things slowly with Bill. Maybe go out to dinner with him once a week for a while. And after a couple of months, then see how things go. I don't want to rush into anything, as I am not sure how I feel. I am also still quite resentful of the Johnson affair, and I don't know if I am strong enough to put that behind me and move on with him. It has a habit of raising its head, particularly when me and Bill are getting on well. And once I think of it, I close up and hardly speak to him again for a while. It's so hard to know.' Sharon thought about this.

'I actually think that's a great idea. Go out with him once a week and as time progresses, see how you feel. You will only know after being out with him a good few times whether you can put the affair behind you. If you can't Laura, then there is no point. It wouldn't be fair on either of you.'

Yes, Laura thought, that's what she would do, take it slowly and see what happens.

Chapter 19

When Laura got back from Sharon's, Bill and Ben were in the kitchen making dinner.

'Mam, Dad is going to stay for dinner. He is helping me make chicken and mushroom pasta for you. We know it's your favourite. I even have the garlic bread ready to put in the oven,' Ben told her proudly. Laura didn't know what to think. It was nice to see her son and Bill working together in the kitchen. But she wanted to take things slowly.

'That's lovely Ben, thank you,' said Laura not wanting to dash Ben's excitement.

'We won't serve up until Jess is home from work. And I think your favourite Jurassic Park movie is on later'.

'Mam; can Dad stay and watch it too? Please? Please?' he begged her. Bill could see his wife's discomfort.

'Look Ben, I'll stay for dinner, but then I'll have to head home, I have things to do,' Bill said.

'Are you not going to collect your things, Dad, and then come back here? You and Mam are back together, aren't you?' Ben cried.

Oh lord, Laura thought. This was so complicated. How was she going to take it slow with Bill when the kids were involved? It was just going to be too difficult. She didn't want to give up on her marriage just yet. But she couldn't drag the kids into the middle of it. Laura made a decision.

She didn't think Sharon would agree with her, as Laura was not making the decision for herself, but for her family.

'Yes, your father is going to collect his things and then come back here and watch the film with us,' Laura said, with a slight smile. Ben jumped in the air and shouted with joy.

'YEEEESSSSS. I knew you would get back together. Wait till I tell Jess. She owes me a tenner! We had a bet!'

Bill was looking over at Laura with absolute delight. Laura went over and tended to the dinner. She then turned to Bill and said, 'I'll walk you to do the door, Ben, sit down and read your comic, I have the dinner in hand,' which Ben was only happy to do now that his parents were back together.

'Laura, you will not regret this, I am….' Bill started when they were on their own.

'Look Bill. If I had it my way this is not the way I would do it. I would rather take things slowly, and not have you move back in straight away. I don't know yet if we can save our marriage, I truly do not know if I can put your affair behind me enough that we can move on and be happy. But I do not want to give up without trying. You will have to be patient with me Bill, and as I said, this does not mean we are one hundred percent back together. I just don't want to keep confusing the kids with you coming over every weekend. I'd rather just give it a go, and if it works out great. But if it doesn't, you have to respect my decision and we'll both move on.

'Oh, absolutely Laura. It will work out though. It will be different this time; I'll make sure it works. I love you so much. Thank you Laura. Thanks…' Bill replied like a flushed schoolboy. Laura interrupted him.

'OK, enough Bill. And drop the red-carpet treatment. If this marriage is going to work, start as you mean to go on. You can't keep this happy-to keep-anything-for-me attitude up all the time. I just want you to be yourself,' Laura told him.

Bill looked a bit hurt but nodded his head. He grabbed his keys and went to kiss her. Laura turned her head away

'Don't push your luck!' She laughed and gave him a gentle shove out the door.

Bill had been back a month now and Laura was happy enough with how things were going. Obviously, it was still very early days. Although they were sharing the same bed, they had not made love since the night they had dinner. Laura asked him for time, and he respected that. She was sitting in her parents' house having a cup of tea. When she told her mother and father that she was going to give Bill a second chance, they were not too pleased. They didn't say too much, but Laura could tell. She explained that it was just a trial though as she didn't want to throw her marriage away without giving it a chance. It was understandable that her parents were not keen about Bill coming back. They knew how much he had hurt their daughter. It would be different, they said, if it had been a one- night stand, but the fact he had a year-long affair, they just couldn't accept it.

Her parents were quite old fashioned though, so Laura was surprised they weren't happy that she was giving the marriage another go.

'As long as you know our door is always open. Even if you just want to come over on your own and stay a night or two. Anytime. And we won't probe. Just come and go as you please,' her father said at the time.

She had taken them up on the offer, and stayed one-night last week, and last night with them. She just felt she needed a bit of time away from Bill. He seemed to understand and was happy to spend the time alone with Ben and Jess.

'Are you happy, love?' her mother asked her now. Laura had to think about this. She thought she was happy. Wasn't she? She wasn't sure to be honest. The biggest elephant in the room between her and Bill was the fact she still had not slept with him again. Maybe she would have a few drinks and it would help. Laura couldn't do it sober at the minute, as every time they made an attempt, all images and thoughts of that bitch Johnson would come into her head. Laura would real backwards and say she was sorry, but she just wasn't ready. Would she ever be ready? She just didn't know.

She needed more time.

'I'm happy enough Mam, thanks. It'll work out in the end,' she reassured her mother. Laura still had not applied for any jobs. She would take some time out later and apply for a couple. She knew she didn't want to keep writing the column and she was getting eager to move on. She was also losing interest in her work and that wasn't good. It was evident in her column. So, Laura had to spend more time than ever trying to insert some passion into them.

Laura's mobile suddenly rang and she didn't recognise the number. It was a Saturday morning, who would be calling her?

'Hello,' Laura said into the phone.

'Laura, Hi,' came a familiar voice although she could not place it.

'It's Michael, Michael Smith, we met in Spain? The jet ski man?'

Good god, Laura was extremely surprised. What on earth was he phoning for? Did she leave something behind? But surely, he would have phoned sooner. He had her number from it being on his contact number about the jet skis when they were on holiday.

'Oh, Michael Yes, how could I forget? What a surprise to hear from you!' Laura laughed nervously.

'Yeah, I know. I hope you don't mind? It's just my daughter was accepted at Trinity College so she will be moving over here with me. I remember you said that you were looking for a new job, and that you were hoping to get back to office/admin. Did you get something?'

Laura didn't know what to make of this. He was obviously in Ireland at the minute.

'Eh, no, I haven't got around to really applying for anything yet. I was just thinking about it before you phoned actually. I really need to get myself in gear!' She laughed.

'Oh, that's great, well great for me hopefully. Look, sorry, I know I sound all over the place, it's just I have a job that might interest you. Would you be free for a coffee later this afternoon? Or Monday if today doesn't suit?' he asked her. Laura was immediately intrigued.

'Yeah, I can do today, no problem. Are you in Dublin?' she asked him.

'Not at the minute, I have a house in Bray, but I am heading up that way shortly. You live out near Clontarf, don't you? How about I meet you at the Marine Harbor Hotel there on the main street?' Laura knew that Bray was in a different county but only about an hour from Dublin City.

'Yes, perfect. `it's now 11, so would 2 suit you?'

That would give her time to go home and have a shower. Check up on the kids and then head in to meet him.

'Cool, sounds good. See you then, Laura,' and with that, the phone clicked off. Laura sat at the table thinking of the little time she had spent with him in Spain. After the initial bad start, they had gotten on quite well. She had bumped into him another couple of times in *Paddy's Place* and he always sat with her and the others for the night. He had also spent a bit more time with them on the jet skis, particularly on the last day as Ben kept hounding him for just one more spin. Laura had grown quite fond of him. Could she work for him? Well, she didn't even know what type of job he had in mind yet. She wouldn't count her chickens; she would just have to wait and see.

Laura pulled in to the car park of the hotel at 1.50pm. She was eager to find out what Michael had to say to her. Bill was a bit taken aback about the whole thing. She had to explain how she knew him, and the kids told him how he had helped with the jet ski. Bill also knew that Laura had been looking for a new job lately; well, hoping to come across something suitable.

Bill had been so delighted to be back at home at first. And so grateful to Laura for giving him a second chance. However, although Laura was perfectly polite towards him and they seemed to be getting on well, she just didn't seem her old self to Bill. She had definitely changed. The old Laura used to seek his opinion on everything. Nowadays, she just got on with things, and only really asked his opinion if a subject happened to arise when they were talking. But then he supposed she had been on her own for the past seven months and got used to it. He wasn't sure if she was happy though. She had been going through the motions all right, but he was worried that she might change her mind. When he found her putting on some nice clothes in the bedroom after the shower, and she told him about Michael and the job he might have, Bill was pleased for her. He wanted Laura to be happy. Maybe if she could get a new job, she would get a little bit more like her old self. Oh, he didn't mean depending on him or seeking his approval. But some of the old passion and flare for him she once had. Bill really hoped that wasn't gone forever.

CHAPTER 20

Laura got out of the car and made her way into the foyer. She walked across to the bar entrance and looked around the room. There was Michael, sitting over beside the window, a cup of tea or maybe coffee in front of him, engrossed in the newspaper. Laura wasn't sure why, but her heart quickened. She just realised she was actually very nervous. As she made her way over toward him, he looked up and his serious frown broke in to a wide smile. He was more handsome when he smiled.

He stood up and came to greet her like an old friend. Michael's tan stood out much more now, in comparison to everyone else in the bar.

'Laura, great to see you. Thanks so much for meeting me. And sorry for the early morning call,' he said. She sat down beside him and a waiter came over to see what she wanted. Laura ordered a pot of tea and a scone. Michael ordered another for himself.

'So,' she began. 'You moved back to Ireland?'

'Yep, sure have. As I said earlier, I am in Bray for now. I do love it there. But my new venture is in Howth. So, I will look for something closer to rent while I get the place up and running. Then I'll decide whether to sell or keep the house in Bray.' Michael said.

He went on to explain that he had started building a pub/restaurant close to the Marina in Howth, and that it would take a year to complete before opening. He had got planning permission for the premises at the end of last year but had not done anything until he knew what university his daughter would be going to.

He told her it would also have ten bedrooms, not hotel size, but would be more than adequate for tourists. He would offer B&B and dinner packages. That was all going to plan. Howth was just fifteen minutes from Clontarf, further along the coast.

Michael explained that his daughter would live in the house in Bray and commute up and down to Dublin by train. It wasn't that far a journey. Natalie wasn't due to arrive for another six weeks. Her course started in late September, but she would come a few weeks early to familiarise herself with Dublin and the journey.

'My word, Michael. It's full steam ahead for you. But with no disrespect, where do I fit in all of this? I have never worked in a pub or restaurant, and to be honest, I don't think I would want to,' Laura told him honestly. No point in pretending. If he was looking for a bar manager or waitress it was not her.

'No, No, I know that. Well, it's just since we started building a couple of weeks ago my phone hasn't stopped. My email and voicemail box are always full. There are so many enquires and paperwork that need to be done. What with building materials, stock for the bar, suppliers for the venue, health & safety checks, tourist agents wanting to offer joint packages and the list goes on. I can't cope with it as I am on site a lot working with the builders, I knew I would have to set up an office, but I didn't think I would need to for at least another few months. But I need one now. Would you be interested in helping me out? It's just I don't know anyone personally in Ireland who would be interested and I am always wary of strangers, which I think you realised yourself when I first met you! Sarah, the girl you work with, trusted you with her villa, so I know I could count on you,' he said.

Laura was startled. Manage an office for him. For this pub/restaurant/B & B. And if it was on Howth Harbour, you could bet it was going to be a busy place. She didn't want to have to work somewhere putting in stupid hours every day. As much as she loved a fast-paced environment, she still wanted to clock off at a decent time each day.

'Michael, I am flattered that you asked me. I really am. And as exciting as it sounds, I don't really want to work five or six days a week, from morning till night. I want to work, definitely. But not full time,' Laura explained. 'Also, I wouldn't know where to start. Maybe you need someone young to support you, not an ol' one like me! she laughed.

But Michael wasn't put off.

'Laura, the office will eventually need five maybe even six office staff. To get started I would want you, who would be the boss, and one other full-time person. You could come in each day say 9am to 2pm? Would that be OK for you? Five days a week. I would give you a work phone though and may need to call you sometimes after 2pm if it's urgent, but other than that I wouldn't bother you. And you can recruit the new person yourself. Someone would have to work Saturday, so as times goes on, you could recruit people as you need them, obviously running it by me first. But I wouldn't expect you to work long hours. Just to get the office set up, equipment needed like photocopier, fax, scanner, etc. The first person you hire should probably be a receptionist/PA. She can deal with all the calls and emails. Which would free up your time to deal with more important things like the tourist agencies, the suppliers, the invoicing etc.? Am I getting your interest yet?' he asked.

Laura had to admit to herself, she was becoming very excited now. She loved being in the middle of a big project; having to juggle several things at a time. And she would only have to work till 2pm each day. She would be home by 2.30pm easy and then would have the rest of the day to herself. It sounded too good to be true.

'I am definitely interested now Michael, I must admit. But it's all a bit of a whirlwind.'

'I know,' Michael said, 'and I am sorry for rabbiting on, but I am just so passionate about the place. To be honest, I had the foundations for the place down the time you were in Spain. I didn't want to say anything about the venture as I didn't know what I would do if Natalie hadn't come to Dublin. I would have been disappointed, but I probably would have come anyway, but I kept it to myself until I had made the move. I don't like to jinx things,' he told her.

Michael went on to tell her the salary he had in mind which Laura was more than happy with. It was a lot more than she was currently getting from the newspaper. She would have to hand in her notice. She was on a month-to-month contract, so it wouldn't be a problem.

'Can I tell you that I will think strongly about it? It sounds great to me Michael, and I am so grateful that you thought of me. However, I just want some time to think about it. Maybe run it over with my husband and that,' she said. Michael looked a bit surprised.

'Yes, no problem. Take your time. Your husband?' he questioned her. 'I thought you had separated.' Laura felt her cheeks go red, and she felt embarrassed.

She was not sure why.

'Yeah, we were. We got back recently. It's just a trial though. It may not work out, but we said we would have another go for the kids' sake,' Laura quickly answered.

She wondered why she was explaining herself to him.

'Ah, I understand. Don't I know the feeling? Been there, done that, bought the t-shirt! Isn't that the saying?' he smiled. Laura looked surprised.

'You've done the same as me? Given your marriage another go for the kids' sake? Did it work?' Laura didn't know why she was asking him such personal questions, but she couldn't help it. Michael looked at Laura sadly and smiled.

'Every relationship is different. So don't compare. But yes, we did give it another go for the kids' sake, and another and another. It never worked out. Too much resentment on both sides. We finally realised we were only making the kids unhappy, and we were both miserable. The best thing for us was to separate. But as I said, that doesn't mean it won't work for you,' he said gently.

Laura remembered Sharon's words 'Don't do it to keep someone happy, only do it if it makes you happy. Otherwise, it won't work out long-term'.

Laura thanked Michael for the meeting, changing the subject quickly, and stood up to go.

'I must get going, I have to pick Ben up from football practice,' she lied. Bill was with him and would bring him home. But she just felt she had to get away. She had had a personal moment with Michael and it felt strange. She wanted to clear her head. Michael shook her hand and told her take her time, just give him a call when she knew if she wanted the job or not. Laura turned and walked out of the hotel and straight to the car. She drove out of the car park and headed for home but intended on stopping at Clontarf Beach so she could go for a walk. As she pulled up in the gravel area for cars, she realised she had not been here since she had ended up in hospital eight months earlier. It felt like eight years earlier. It was crazy. Nothing exciting had really happened in her life in the past ten years apart from the bullying in her job that time. But it seemed that she had ten years of events happen to her in just eight months. Laura's head was all over the place. She decided to go for a long walk. Thankfully it was a beautiful warm day so hopefully she shouldn't end up in A&E again.

Sharon was finding it difficult to move about now. She was over eight months pregnant, and had nearly six weeks to go till her due date. She still had two weeks left at work. But she was in much better shape in the last couple of months.

She had decided that she was most certainly going abroad once the baby was born. Sharon had opted, though, to go to Gibraltar instead of Spain. Gibraltar was next to the south tip of Spain and was a British Overseas Territory. The weather was also beautiful there and they had lovely beaches.

The property wasn't bad on price either. The idea for this change of heart first came through a message she had received on LinkedIn.

It was from a recruiter in Gibraltar asking if she would be interested in a marketing director role, based in Gibraltar. The salary was forty percent more than what she was currently on, and they offered a relocation fee along with three months free accommodation to allow you to get settled in. Sharon had immediately called the recruitment agent. Thankfully, she was woman who had three kids herself. Sharon felt that she really understood. Obviously, she didn't tell the agent much about her personal circumstance.

But what she did say was that she was expecting a baby next month, but then planned to move to her aunts in the south of Spain. Sharon told her once the baby was three or four months old, she would be looking for a job then. The agent explained to her that she couldn't hold this role, but that Gibraltar was always looking for marketing people, and these, ninety percent of the time, came with a similar package to this one. She advised Sharon that she might be better moving to Gibraltar instead of Spain, as there wasn't as much marketing work there, plus you needed Spanish in most cases. Sharon felt much better after speaking with the agent who promised to call her in a few months to see how things were. She then had started to research Gibraltar, and the more she read about the place and the culture, the more excited she got.

It would be like living in Ireland or the UK but in the sun. She trawled through stories of people who made the move, about family life there, about nannies and babysitting facilities. It seemed like such a better option than Spain. God works in mysterious ways, she thought. Spain wouldn't have worked out. The agent was right, she didn't even speak Spanish, although she had been learning through an app she had downloaded on her phone. But she wasn't near good enough to even hold a conversation yet. Sharon still intended on learning Spanish though, especially as she would be so close to Spain itself.

The more she thought about it, the more Sharon realised that she wasn't really missing Rob anymore. She began to wonder if she even wanted him back in her life. She had gotten so used to being on her own, her and the baby, inside her. She spent so much time talking to the little bundle, wondering if it was a boy or girl. Sharon didn't mind what it was. She would love it either way. But what if Rob decided he wanted to come back into the fold? Sharon wasn't too sure anymore. She would go on planning her and the baby's future and worry about Rob when the time came.

CHAPTER 21

Laura had decided that she had nothing to lose. She may as well take the job. Otherwise, she felt she would regret it. She hadn't bothered to discuss it with Bill. She just told him about the opportunity and that she thought she should take it. Bill agreed with her. He could see how happy she was since returning from her meeting with Michael. Laura handed in her notice that Monday. They were all sad to hear she was leaving, as they were good friends. Sarah teased her about Michael.

'I send you to Spain for a week and you come back with my Handy Man in tow!' she laughed. Laura laughed too. But Sarah reassured her that Michael was an honest and decent man. She knew he was divorced and had two kids but did not know much about his personal life. He didn't really talk about it with many.

Her boss Terry wished her well, and told her to make sure she contacted them for the launch of the venue. He promised her some free coverage and free advertising

'Only for a certain time period though; we'll have to start charging you at some stage,' he joked! Laura got working on ideas for remaining columns. She wanted to make sure that they didn't lack in quality just because she was leaving. But she was very motivated now, as she was so excited about her new role.

Her boss was on the lookout for a new columnist. He had a couple of interviews lined up for next week. He asked Laura to sit in on them with him. Of course, she agreed, no problem.

Laura was due to have lunch with Sharon on Friday. Thinking about Sharon made her realise her friend didn't have long to go till the baby was here. Laura had vowed to be there as much as possible when the baby was born. Well, she could help out at weekends and in the afternoons after work. She didn't want Sharon being totally alone, she had such little family.

She was also a very private person, and only a handful of her friends knew exactly what was going on in her life. Laura wondered about Rob. Sharon never mentioned him anymore; had she gotten over him? Or was it too painful for her to talk about? Sharon certainly didn't seem upset, or down in the dumps. If anything, she was the opposite. Laura hadn't seen her friend so happy in a long time.

The pregnancy obviously suited her. And she was so strong, coping on her own the way she was. Laura would give her the hamper she had for her when she saw her this Friday. She had bought a huge basket months ago, and had been adding baby things the whole time that would come in helpful for Sharon. Nappies, creams, baby grows, vests, outfits, powders, chocolates, baby toys, wine - she had an assortment of everything and anything in it. Although she wouldn't be able to lift it herself, never mind Sharon who was a month away from giving birth! She would get Bill to bring it by for her.

Bill... Mmmm ... What would she do there? With getting offered the new job and handing in her notice, Laura began to realise she didn't want Bill's opinion on anything; she just didn't care what he thought anymore. It was as though she had lost all respect for him. As a husband, that is. Not as a father. She was trying to make the marriage work, but she had been lying to herself the past month. She wasn't happy. She didn't want to be with Bill anymore. But she did not feel ready yet to face more drama.

Laura decided she would wait until she got settled into her new job, and then see how things were. Maybe by then, she would feel differently. He was really making an effort, with both her and the kids.

He cooked dinner three nights a week, took his turn to walk Barney; something he never used to do, helped with the school runs and was constantly asking Laura if she needed him to do anything for her. To be honest, she was feeling a bit smothered. He was trying too hard. She wasn't used to him ever being like this. So, it was hard to get a handle on. She wasn't sure she liked it.

Laura preferred the way things used to be to an extent. She was glad she was a stronger person now, and that Bill took more time with the kids and treated Laura with more respect. But doing all these extra chores, walking the dog, bending over backwards, it was just too much. It wasn't normal. Maybe his behavior would calm down. Well, she made her bed so she better lie in it for a while. She can't just throw him out when he was only just back. He would argue that they hadn't given it enough time. And he was probably right. Time, maybe that would solve everything. But deep down, Laura knew they had no future as husband and wife.

'Gibraltar,' Laura said, surprised. 'Why the sudden change of heart? I thought Spain was the plan?' she asked her friend. They were in Sharon's apartment and Sharon was turning down whatever she had on the hob cooking. There was a knock on the door.

'Hello, Sharon, Laura, can you open up please, this thing is heavy!' came Bill's weary voice from behind the door. Sharon looked up in surprise, but Laura just smiled at her and said, 'Hang on, I'm coming,' and went to the door to open it. She had to grab the side of the basket as it was slipping from his fingers as he came through the door.

'Over there on the table,' Laura instructed as the two struggled with the weight of the hamper.

'Good lord Laura, what on earth…?' Sharon laughed and went over to inspect the contents. The hamper was done up in sparkly cellophane wrapping with two huge bows around it, pink and blue.

'I thought this would come in handy for you,' Laura said. 'It has all the practical stuff you will need, along with a couple of essentials,' she laughed as she pointed to the wine and Baileys in the basket. Sharon was delighted.

Although she already had loads of stuff bought, it was such a thoughtful gesture and she knew she would use it all. Especially the alcohol! Once she had stopped breast feeding, of course! Sharon went over and hugged Laura.

'You're so good to me Laura. I really appreciate it,' she said, and she felt tears begin to prickle in her eyes at her friend's kindness. Then she realized, she better acknowledge Bill who was standing there awkwardly.

'And Bill, thank you so much for doing the honors! You must have something to drink, tea, coffee, beer?' she asked him.

Bill was dying for a cup of tea after carrying the hamper for a full five-minute walk; he couldn't get parked out front.

'Tea would be great, eh, that's if you don't mind, Laura? Sorry I don't want to intrude,' he said, eyeing Laura nervously. Laura did mind and would rather he leave and went back to work, but she realised she was being unfair. He had done her a favour taking the time off and bringing the hamper over.

'Of course, I don't mind Bill. Here, I'll stick the kettle on. Sharon you sit down.' And Laura busied herself making the tea. Sharon and Bill chatted among themselves, catching up on how each other were keeping. Bill knew that Rob and Sharon had separated, but Laura just said they hadn't been getting on. She didn't go into details. And tactfully Bill never mentioned it.

'Right, I better be off. Enjoy the hamper, and if I don't see you before the little bundle arrives, best of luck with it all. I'm looking forward to seeing the baby. Let's hope it has its mother's good looks,' he joked. He gave Sharon a kiss on the cheek and left to go back to work.

Sharon stood up and turned the heat on under the pot on the cooker.

'I made some beef stew. Sorry, I know it's only lunch time but I'm craving hearty food at the minute.' She laughed. Laura was actually hungry as she had skipped breakfast, so stew was perfect. She would have a salad for dinner later and the kids and Bill could have the lasagna she cooked yesterday.

'So,' Sharon said as she dished out the food. 'What was that all about?' Laura genuinely didn't know what she was talking about.

She frowned.

'What was what about?' Sharon put the plates on the table followed by a big jug of water.

'Come on Laura, you and Bill? He looked so nervous around you. It was obvious he was wary of saying the wrong thing. He kept looking over at you to get your approval on different parts of the conversation, but you just ignored him! Did you have a row?' probed Sharon. Laura sighed loudly and put her spoon down. She may as well tell Sharon how she was feeling.

'Let's eat first. I don't want this delicious food going cold,' and with that, they both tucked in.

Afterwards, Laura confided in Sharon about how she had been feeling. Everything from when he first came back right through to now, even being frustrated at him accepting a cup of tea. Which Laura knew was wrong. She was being very petty. But she couldn't help it.

Sharon knew then the writing was on the wall. Laura took him back too soon and for the wrong reasons. But she wasn't going to say I Told You So. She admired Laura for giving Bill a second chance, a lot of women wouldn't. Then there are women who would take him back in a heartbeat. But at least Laura had tried. Sharon knew it wasn't going to work out with Bill for Laura. But she didn't want to say that. Laura had worked it out for herself.

'Laura, you've gone through so much and so many emotions in such little time, you probably need to take a little break. If you think it's not going to work with Bill, maybe to make yourself feel better, you two should head away for two nights. Spend a bit of time together alone, without the kids. At least then you really will know whether your marriage is doomed or worth saving. And you should do it soon; one, because there is no time like the present, and two, because I don't want you going away too close to this baby's scheduled arrival!' Sharon laughed.

'I'll go and stay in your house to keep an eye on Ben and Jess, why don't you head off somewhere tomorrow?' Sharon encouraged her. Laura thought about the prospect off spending two nights alone with Bill and it filled her with dread. NO, she couldn't. Not yet.

'No Sharon, thanks though. And it is a good idea. But I have too much on the go, with trying to finish columns for the next couple of weeks and getting ready for the new job. I just don't have the time. But I will go. A few weeks after the baby is born, I'll organise it.'

They both knew she was making excuses, but neither said anymore on the matter.

Laura changed the subject

'Oh, by the way, Carol wants to meet up again before the baby's born. I know the last time the five of us had lunch was a bit awkward, as you and me were both fending off questions! But I think they realised we didn't want to talk about the men in our life, so I am sure this time would be nicer. You up for it? I was going to arrange something for next week? Just the five of us again?' Laura asked. Sharon smiled remembering the last time they met. Carol, Becky and Gabby kept asking her and Laura about Bill and Rob.

The girls hadn't seen much of one another since that fateful night in Wicklow. They weren't the type of friends that needed to be in contact all the time. But usually when they did meet up, they just picked up where they left off and had a great time. Obviously, they wanted to know what had happened with Bill, it was only natural for them to ask. Laura had answered as best she could but didn't feel comfortable. Then when they found out Rob and Sharon had gone their separate ways, the questions were fired at her.

The girls didn't mean any harm. But both topics were still quite raw and Sharon and Laura would rather have a good time than talk about their problems when they all met.

'Yes, suits me. I am after all, a lady of leisure now,' giggled Sharon. She had finished work two days ago.

'Sharon, tell me about Gibraltar, I was so caught up in myself I forgot to ask you,' Laura said guiltily.

'Don't be silly Laura. I'm happy to be here for you. When you think about it. It's quite crazy that we both are going through one of the most difficult times in our lives at the same time? I mean, the chain of events even started within weeks of each other. It's crazy,' Sharon pointed out. Laura smiled to herself. Yes, it was crazy.

But she was glad in way, as the two of them realised in some way what the other was going through.

'It sure is. But we'll get through it. And you have an amazing baby to look forward to,' she smiled. Sharon then went on to tell her about her plans for Gibraltar and how they had come about.

Laura agreed, once she heard all the details that it sounded like a better option, given the work opportunities. They talked a bit about Laura's new job and Sharon teased her a bit about Michael, and how he had conveniently remembered Laura was looking for a new job. Sharon believed that Michael had a soft spot for Laura.

'Give me a break Sharon, I think the men in our lives are enough to be dealing with at the moment!' she said jokingly.

CHAPTER 22

Laura shivered with the cold in the Portacabin and put her hands to her ears to block the loud screeching noises coming from the building works. When she had arrived, there was no one around that she felt she could ask anything. Anyone on site was busy operating machinery or digging foundations. She phoned Michael and he had told her to wait there and he would be with her in ten minutes; that he was just in a meeting. He told her to make herself a cup of tea from the kettle in the canteen.

Canteen, ha. One kettle, one toaster and half a pint of milk placed on a table in a portioned-off room counted as the canteen. Although it was August, the place was like an ice box. The sun was shining outside, but the cabin was located in the shade of some high trees, so it wasn't getting through at all. She had made herself three cups of tea by the time Michael had arrived over an hour later. He apologised profusely; he had got held up. He then took Laura on a tour of the building site and introduced her to the site manager and anyone else he thought she might need to know.

Laura enjoyed that part. He then told her that her first job was to make the portacabin more of an office. Make a list of what was needed and he would take her to the shops and help her pick the stuff up. This sounded fine to Laura. She had the list made by 12 o'clock, but there was no sign of Michael. She didn't want to keep ringing him. Eventually he called her at 12.30pm and told her he would take her for lunch. That he would pick her up in ten minutes. But Laura was beginning to learn and told him that she would love to have lunch with him but that she would meet him somewhere. She was within walking distance to plenty of restaurants.

She told him she would take a walk and when she decided where to go, she would text him and let him know. He could meet her there. She knew he was going to be late, and she was starving, as having been too nervous to eat any breakfast or dinner the night before. Laura had picked a nice café that had plenty of room and a lovely menu outside. She supposed it being a Monday it was quiet; people usually brought their own lunch.

No doubt it would be much busier later in the week. She texted Michael the name of the place 'Benny's' and ordered a coffee while she waited. She was sick of drinking tea. She would give him ten minutes, she decided. And then she would order. An hour later Laura paid the bill and made her way back to the portacabin. Michael had not showed. He had sent several texts, apologizing that the meeting had run over. But he would be there. She got tired waiting, ate her lunch and left. She bought the paper on the way back to give her something to do. At 2 o'clock Michael phoned her and told her to go home. He was really sorry but he had got called to another meeting with a supplier he had been trying to get a hold of for ages. There was no point her waiting on him. He would see her at 9am in the morning. Laura was quiet with him on the phone, said that was fine, she would see him tomorrow. She was feeling so disappointed about the whole thing. Maybe she made a mistake. But then it was just her first day.

She had to give it a little time. The office wasn't even workable yet. It would be fine once they had the equipment in. But the next day wasn't much better. She realised Michael was certainly overrun. He had no word when it came to timing, not through his own fault, but he had so much going on. Laura had told him that she needed him to sit down with her for one day or even half a day. A few hours. With no interruptions. And go through everything that he wanted her to do. She just wanted the general concept of what he wanted. If he gave her the names of people to contact for the different jobs, she would manage the whole lot. She wasn't asking him to give daily tasks, but more to explain what projects he was needing to be done. That way she could just get on with her job and would only need Michael to sign off on stuff. Michael had agreed that was a great idea.

He said once they came back from getting all the equipment, they would sit down and he would turn his phone off for a couple of hours. Laura enjoyed the morning; she felt she was making headway. They had bought two large-screen laptops, a colour printer, a couple of desk phones, a fax machine, three heaters, three flat-pack office desks with three office chairs, stationery, and a fridge. It was certainly enough to get started. Laura was looking forward to going through her responsibilities with Michael. However, they had only sat down and someone came knocking on the door.

'Sorry to bother you Michael but I couldn't get you on the phone. Alan Jones from the council is here,' Michael's foreman told him. He apologised to Laura, but she said it was fine; to go on ahead. She would make a start on the things they bought. An hour later she had done as much as she could. She had unpacked the heaters, printer and fax and had assembled the chairs, which was easy enough.

She had made phone calls yesterday to arrange for Wifi and a landline to be put in. But they couldn't come in until next Monday morning. She didn't try to assemble the office desks as they looked a lot harder to assemble than the chairs. They weren't big desks, two of them would fit in the front part, and one could go down the back, in the room past the canteen. She also dragged the fridge to the canteen and plugged it in.

There wasn't much else she could do; only another tidy over which she had already done several times. She looked at her watch. It was 11.30am. No sign of Michael. She decided to go back to the same café as the day before and have a sandwich or scone. She took her time and once again bought the paper on the way back. Still no sign of Michael. Laura was beginning to get very irritated when he popped his head round the door.

'Ah great. I see you're sorting the place out. It's definitely taking shape. Fancy some lunch?' he asked her. Laura bit her lip. Breathe, Breathe, she told herself.

'I already had lunch. But thanks. Look Michael, I know how busy you are, but this is never going to work out unless you give me some of your time without running off.' she told him. Michael sighed.

'I know. Look. I can only apologise. To be honest, it's not normally this bad. For some reason everything seems to be happening at once. Look,' he said, handing her a book with about twenty sheets of paper in it.

'Could you start going through these for me. Just get a notepad and log each one into it. Date, Time, Supplier, Cost, Vat, Contact, etc. You will have to put it on to the computer from there. But it might be easier to get started by logging them in a notepad. I should be back in an hour. If I am not here by 2pm, go home. And I absolutely promise you I will meet you here at 9am, on the button. I won't make any other arrangements or even answer my phone. Deal?' he asked her.'

Laura was happy just to be given some type of work to do.

'Yes, OK. If I don't see you later, we'll catch up first thing. I'd very much like to have my project plan formulated by the end of the week so I can make a fresh start on what has to be done on Monday.' She smiled at him. She couldn't stay mad for long.

He was being very nice to her and he did give her the job even if it had been a disaster so far.

'Sound's great. See you later,' and with that, he was gone. Not only did Laura write down the details of each invoice, but she photocopied each one and stored them in a folder. She just realised she hadn't bought a filing cabinet. Well, she could just add it to the list. Laura then powered up one of the new laptops and spent half an hour getting registered and downloading the various software's she would need.

She then opened up Microsoft excel and began to create a new ledger. She had the invoices inputted within another half an hour. It was now 2.15pm. No sign of Michael. She knew he wouldn't be back today. Laura switched off the computer and the heater in the corner. She grabbed her things and headed for home. She decided to stop for a nice walk on the beach. There was a slight breeze but it was a mild day. She wouldn't have needed to use the heater if she had a proper office; the portacabin was so cold and dreary. She didn't know if she could get used to it. The office in the main building wouldn't be ready for five to six months. She shivered at the thought.

The next morning Laura dressed down. No point in wearing nice slacks and shirts when she didn't even have an office to go to. She put on her jeans and a polo neck jumper. It took her longer than usual to get to work as the traffic was very heavy. She pulled in at 9.10am and her heart sank when she could not see Michael's jeep anywhere. He drove a Mitsubishi Pajero, black. She got out of the car and went to make herself a cup of tea. It was very cold this morning, so she turned on two heaters. No sun shone today, and it looked as though it was going to rain. Laura heart sank even further as she wondered what to do until he arrived. She had no internet so she couldn't even browse that.

There was no 4G reception on her phone either, so she couldn't use that for the internet either.

She had covered yesterday's paper from back to front. She played a game on her phone for an hour and then got bored. Laura had an uneasy feeling that this was all a big mistake. It had been too easy for her. No interview, just an informal job offer. Too good to be true. What would she do now? She needed her own money coming in. Last thing Laura wanted was to be dependent on Bill. Suddenly Laura's phone began to ring.

About time she thought, but she didn't recognise the number that was calling.

'Hello,' Laura said. 'Hi, is this Laura Murphy?' a warm cheery female voice asked her. Laura confirmed it was her.

'Congratulations, I was told to tell you, that you are now the proud godmother of a bonny little lass named Sophia. I'm one of the maternity nurses here at the hospital. Sharon asked me to ring you and let you know. She is just having a sleep.' Laura was rendered speechless but recovered quick enough to respond.

'She had the baby, the baby, she had it? It's a week early, oh my god, oh my god, how is Sharon? When did she get there? How is the baby?' Laura knew she was firing a ton of questions at the nurse but she couldn't help it.

The nurse laughed.

'Calm down, everything is fine. Both ladies are doing great. Sharon was lucky, she had a quick labour. Came in last night and had the baby at 4 o' clock this morning.'

Hours ago, thought Laura. She couldn't wait to see her, Sharon, and the new baby, Sophia.

'Can I come visit now?' she asked the nurse.

'Well, normally, friends are only allowed in at visiting time, but you're her closest friend, so please do. She needs someone to share the magical moment with.'

Laura immediately phoned Michael. Before she could say a word, he said, 'I know I know, I'm sorry.' Laura was so sick of hearing that, she felt like telling him to shove his job up his you know what.

'No, it's not that.' Laura interrupted. 'Sharon has just had her baby. I need to go to the hospital to be with her,' Laura explained.

'No problem, go ahead. Take a day or two if you need it. Just give me a call when you're coming back in. Actually, it will give me a chance to clear all the stuff going on at the minute and so it will be quieter when you get back.'

Laura didn't really care anymore. She was over it. She honestly didn't know if she would come back, but she wasn't going to tell him that.

Chapter 23

Sharon had been just going to bed when she felt her waters break. She couldn't believe it. The baby wasn't due for another week and Sharon thought she would go over by at least a few days. She had been so relaxed the whole way through the pregnancy. She hadn't been worried about the birth one bit. Now however, she was terrified. She started bawling as she sat on the floor, back against the wall. She felt all the hurt, disappointment and anger from the last nine months come to her all of a sudden. She howled like a mad woman. Not in physical pain. But in emotional pain - who had she been fooling? There was no way in hell she could cope without Rob.

He was her soul mate. She loved him so, so much. She wished more than anything that he was there with her right now. Sharon knew she should alert the hospital that her waters were broken. But she was so upset; she couldn't even hold a conversation. She had been such a fool. She should have fought for Rob. Not given him a choice. She wanted him. Here with her. Her and their baby. That's where he belonged.

She had never experienced such emotional pain like it. She had been kidding herself for so long. What an idiot. All high and mighty.

'Only come back if that's what you want to do for yourself.' Ha. Bullshit. He had responsibilities. He should be here.

Sharon knew she needed to calm down. She suddenly began to feel what she assumed were contractions. She bent over and started the breathing exercises she had practiced at the pregnancy yoga classes. After the pain subsided, she managed to get herself up and over to the phone. She called the maternity unit and told them her waters had broken and her contractions had started. The nurse asked her how far apart the pains were. Sharon wasn't entirely sure, but reckoned around two to three minutes. The nurse told her to get a taxi immediately. They were also aware that Sharon lived on her own.

That was why they wanted her the minute her waters broke as she had no one watching her. It took ten minutes for the taxi to arrive in which time Sharon had had several more contractions. She managed to grab her hospital bag and anything else she needed and plonked herself in the taxi. The driver looked terrified, and put the boot down, tearing off down the road, praying desperately that she didn't give birth in his taxi. He pulled in right up to the door and jumped out. He ran around, opening the door and guiding her out of the car.

Thankfully, there was a hospital porter waiting for her with a wheel chair. She thanked the driver, who looked immensely relieved he had got her there in one piece. The porter then whizzed her up to the maternity section where a nurse she recognised took over.

'Ah, Sharon, love, how are you my dear? Not long now sweetheart,' she smiled.

She was brought into a private room and the midwife came in to check on her progress. She told Sharon she was progressing quite quickly, she was 5cm dilated. All of a sudden Sharon experienced a severe contraction. She screamed, although keeping her voice as low as possible as she didn't want to be one of those annoyingly noisy women who give birth.

The pain was so intense.

'I can't do this, I just can't do this,' Sharon panicked. The midwife and nurses were around her.

'It's OK, take it easy. Don't fight it. The more you try and relax the easier it will be. You can do it. You're strong,' they coaxed her.

I can't do it, thought Sharon. I can't. Not without Rob. Oh, why was she so stupid? She couldn't do this on her own. Another contraction overtook her and she thought she would pass out. 'Epidural, epidural,' she managed, breathless.

'I'm sorry,' one of the nurses said, 'you are too far gone to get the epidural.' Sharon felt like hitting her. She wasn't going to make it through.

'Keep going, keep going.'

Sharon felt like telling them all to shut the hell up. She wasn't running a bloody marathon. But she knew she was being unfair. They were being so nice to here. As another contraction began to take hold Sharon bent over, head down towards the bed.

She felt a hand slip into hers, and she grabbed it so hard, she hoped she didn't hurt the nurse that was holding it. But then she felt a strange sensation. She felt as though she knew the hand. She had held it before. How on earth could you recognise a hand? As the contraction passed, Sharon looked up with effort and standing there, holding her hand, with tears dripping down his face, was Rob.

Laura had gotten directions to Sharon's room. She had been apparently moved to a private room because of her company health insurance policy, which meant Laura could visit at any time. She opened the door slowly and was astonished to see a man with his back to her staring out the window, a little bundle being cuddled in his shoulder. She looked to the bed and saw Sharon was asleep, but there seemed to be a smile on her face. Maybe it was her brother Mike, it couldn't be Rob, could it? She had only been talking to Sharon yesterday morning and she made no mention of him, so it couldn't be him.

But it certainly looked like him from the back.

'Rob?' Laura questioned quietly. He turned around and it was obvious he had been crying. But his face lit up when he saw Laura.

But it quickly became serious again as shame washed over him.

'Laura, meet your god-daughter, Sophia.' Rob handed the baby to her. The baby's eyes looked back up at her, searching Laura's face, taking everything in.

'She is just so beautiful, absolutely beautiful,' cried Laura.

She gently touched the baby's fingers and placed a kiss on the tip of her nose. She then looked up at Rob in confusion.

'I know, I know. I have a lot of explaining to do. But not here. Not now. The very short version is I have been a complete idiot. I am so ashamed of myself. I love Sharon so much. And this baby is everything to me. I can't believe I haven't been there for Sharon the whole time she was carrying this little treasure. But I intend to make up for it. For the rest of their lives.'

If someone had asked Laura yesterday, what would she do if she were ever to find herself in a situation like this, she was sure she would have told them she would have gone crazy at Rob; the way he had treated her friend. But somehow now, in the actual situation, any fight left her. It wasn't her business and she had no right to interfere really. Rob had gone through a traumatic accident and he had obviously

THE ULTIMATE BETRAYAL – Gráinne Farrell

never got over it. But it seemed he had now. Just in the nick of time. And that was all that mattered really.

'But how did you get here? Did you bring Sharon in? What happened?' Laura asked quietly as she did not want to wake her friend.

'Sharon gave the nurses my number as next of kin when she first visited the hospital months back. After Sharon notified the hospital that her waters had broken and contractions had started, she was ordered to come straight to the hospital. The nurse in charge knew that Sharon and I were apart, but she phoned me anyway. Said that my beautiful girlfriend had gone into labour and was currently in a taxi on the way to the hospital, alone. That she thought I should know. Then she hung up on me. It was like everything became clear in that minute. All the fog and trees and clouds that were stopping me seeing what was in front of me cleared. And I realised what an absolute plank I had been. The love of my life was having our baby. And I had deserted her. But more than anything, it was the fear I had that anything would happen to Sharon. I panicked. I suddenly realised, that I couldn't live without her. The last few months, being apart was so tough, but I knew she was OK. So, when the hospital phoned, I started to panic. She was alone, having my child. And that's when I knew, that if Sharon agreed, I wanted to come back. For her. And the baby. And hopefully a couple more kids to come. Please forgive me Laura,' Rob said taking the baby back from her.

'If I can forgive you, then so can she,' came Sharon's voice from the bed. Laura ran over to her and hugged her tight but being careful not to hurt her at the same time.

'Sharon, you have the most gorgeous little girl. I can't get over how beautiful she is,' exclaimed Laura. Sharon smiled and held out her arms, and Rob placed Sophia in her arms.

'Yes, she is a pretty little thing isn't she!' laughed Sharon.

For the next hour they chatted amicably about the baby and other things and Laura didn't mention Rob's dramatic reentrance in to Sharon's life. He was here now and Sharon seemed happy, so that was the main thing. Rob and Sharon laughed at the antics of Laura's new job. Laura told them she didn't think she would go back.

'Ah Laura, come on. You were never one to give up. Yes, so you have gotten off to a bad start. But it will come good. Once you have the office ready to go and know what work you must do, you'll be all sorted. It's just the first week or two are going to be hard as he has no time. I have a suggestion for you. Why don't you tell him you want to shadow him for a week? Wherever he goes, you go. To all the meetings he has and everything. That way you will learn a lot from the meetings, and at the same time, ask him questions in between.

'It does seem like he is fairly busy. I am sure he doesn't mean to put you off,' advised Sharon. Laura thought about it for a minute. She didn't know. She would see. She wasn't going in tomorrow anyway. If Rob hadn't have arrived, Laura would have spent the day with Sharon at the hospital but now she felt a bit like a third wheel.

'I'll think about it, but thanks for the advice. Right, I'm going to head off. How long are they keeping you?' Sharon looked at Rob.

'What did they tell you?'

'They will be keeping you in tonight obviously and probably tomorrow night, Rob said. As it's your first they just want to keep you in for observation. So, with any luck, we'll be home Saturday morning.'

Sharon felt a warm glow when Rob said, 'We'll be home.' The apartment had still not sold, although the agent thought a couple were going to put an offer on it this weekend. Even if it sold, they could have another month or two before they would have to move out.

When Sharon had seen Rob, she didn't think she had ever been more relieved in her life. They had both cried for a while before any words were spoken.

The nurses backed off, and let them alone, although they stayed nearby to keep an eye on her. Rob had told Sharon how stupid he had been. What a mess he had made of everything.

He was so sorry, and would she have him back? Sharon was so weak with relief that she just kissed him and told him of course she would take him back, but for now, could he just help her get through the delivery!

Another hour, and Sharon pushed their baby girl into the world, holding tightly to Rob's hand at the same time. They spent some time with their new baby and then the nurse took the little one to be washed.

Sharon was exhausted and slept for a short while. She was wheeled up to a ward and the baby along with her in her crib. When Sharon had woken up, Rob was sitting in the chair by her bed, with their daughter in his arms. He was looking down at her with such love in his eyes. It was then they had a long conversation. About everything. Sharon told him everything that had happened since he was gone and how she had felt most of the time. And Rob filled her in on how he couldn't cope, and the trip away didn't help. How everyone at work was sick of him and his bad humours. Sharon also told him about her plan to go to Gibraltar. Rob couldn't believe she had planned on starting a new life with the baby in another country. His cheeks burned with shame as he remembered what he had put her through.

Sharon told him that the only way they would make a success of the relationship is if he stopped beating himself up. Both about what happened to him in earlier years and what happened to their relationship. Sharon wanted to hold a special memorial for the little boy he lost and his ex-fiancée. She thought it would be a good way to put it to rest finally for Rob. Surprisingly, he agreed with her. Although Rob was back, Sharon still wanted to move to Gibraltar. He was a bit taken aback and didn't know what to think. But then if it made her happy, he would do it. He would look into it himself; maybe he could start up a branch of his company over there, or with technology the way it was today, he could work remotely, use Skype or one of the many other applications available. There was no need to sell the one over here. They could manage just fine without his physical presence. The idea began to grow on him. A fresh start

CHAPTER 24

Laura thought a lot about what Sharon had said. Maybe she would take her advice. She was sitting on one of the large rocks on the beach that she often frequented. She had been to the hospital again that morning and Rob, Sharon and baby Sophia were all on great form. Sharon told her they still planned on going to Gibraltar. Laura was glad for her, although saying that, she would miss Sharon like hell. She liked the other three girls but they weren't any way as close to her as Sharon was. She would never confide in them. Not that there was anything wrong with the girls. She loved them and knew she could trust them. But there were just some people you clicked with, and for her, it was Sharon. In saying that, she was looking forward to taking trips out to see her.

Sharon assured her that now Rob was in tow, and would also be working, that they were going to get a three, maybe four-bedroom house so there would be plenty of room for her. She was looking forward to it already. It was 6 o'clock in the evening and the sun was getting lower in the sky. It was still quite warm and there was a lovely cool breeze. As Laura watched the people out walking on the beach, she suddenly sat upright as she thought she recognised Michael. Yes, it was him alright. Only he wasn't alone. There was a beautiful looking black-haired woman with him.

They were walking hand in hand and were making their way over to the shore. Michael reached down and helped the woman take off her shoes.

She was giggling, and Michael began to tickle her. He then took off his own shoes and they walked in a bit, letting the water run over their feet.

They began to kiss, and that was enough for Laura. He had a girlfriend. She didn't know why but it really annoyed her. Not because she cared. But he hadn't time to sit down with her for more than ten minutes to explain the job to her, but yet here he was at 6 o'clock in the evening going for romantic strolls. Laura wondered was this woman the reason he was never available? No, surely, he wouldn't let that come between him and his work. Stop it Laura, she told herself. It has nothing to do with you. And with that she got up and made her way quickly back to the car before Michael could see her. Laura decided she wasn't going back to work for him, maybe the black-haired beauty could work for him instead!

When Laura got back from her walk, Ben asked if they could have a take-away. A Chinese. Apparently, all his friends had a Chinese every weekend and now he wanted to try it. Laura wasn't sure he had ever tasted Chinese food but she would pick out a few things like chicken balls, spare ribs, curry chips and a few other dishes that she knew he would like.

Laura didn't think ordering him a chicken chow mein he had asked for would be a good idea. Maybe she would order that for herself and let him taste it just to keep him happy. She knew he wouldn't like it. Jess and Ben were watching the Saturday night movie, well Ben was, and Jess was scrolling through her phone. Bill walked in and flopped down on the recliner chair.

'Ah, what a long week,' he exclaimed. 'So, honey, do you think you'll stick out the new job?' he enquired. Laura didn't really want to talk about it in front of the kids, and gave him a telling look,

'I'm sure I will, yes; just takes a bit of getting used to.' When the Chinese arrived, they all dug in hungrily, the spareribs proving the most popular.

And as Laura suspected, Ben made a disapproving face when he tasted her chow mein.

'Yuk! how do people like that,' he complained. Although he was happy enough tucking in to his curry chips. Later that night she received a text from Michael. Strange, him texting her so late. 9pm.

Well, OK, it wasn't that late, but for a boss to text a colleague at 9pm on a Friday night could be classed as inappropriate.

'Hope Sharon and Baby doing well. Are you coming back Monday? Let me know.' Laura was annoyed at the text. It made her feel guilty, as she hadn't called him today like she should have. Well, he could take a running jump. She would not reply tonight. Maybe tomorrow. Depending what humour she was in. What annoyed Laura most about the job, was that she could see that there really was so much to do. And that if she could get to grips with what's going on, she reckoned she would be really happy there.

There was a lot of potential. But it was trying to get her job up and running that annoyed her. Laura always hated being bored. She couldn't work in a job where she had little to do. She needed to keep busy.

Ahhh, she sighed to herself. She wasn't going to think about it anymore tonight. She'd sleep on it. Bill asked her if she wanted to go for a drink at the local pub. Jess was old enough now to keep an eye on Ben. But she declined. And told him to go on ahead without her. To be honest it would be a relief to not have his eyes on her constantly trying to work out what she was thinking.

Laura knew that Bill was aware that she wasn't herself with him anymore. He had asked her several times if there was something the matter, but she always said everything was fine. Laura felt guilty because she knew that Bill was starting to get a bit down himself. He wasn't happy either. Oh, it was such a mess.

Bill sat at the counter staring into his pint of Guinness. The pub was quiet enough for a Saturday. Just a few of the locals and a couple of tables full with young men and women getting a few drinks in before hitting the town. He let out a long sigh. Shirley, the landlady, smiled at him.

'That bad, is it?' Bill smiled back at her. Shirley had owned The Cozy Corner for the last five years. She and her husband had once owned a pub in the city centre.

But when her husband passed away, she sold up and moved out to Clontarf. She wanted to be near the sea. Her children, Bobby 20, and Linda, 18, helped in the bar every so often. Both were in college so this earned them some money to keep them going during the week. The pub had a house attached next door that came with it on the sale. So, it was convenient for them. Bill always got on well with Shirley, as did Laura. She kept herself to herself, but was always friendly and up for a laugh. Bill had got to know her a bit better over the last month.

He had taken to dropping in a couple of evenings a week for a few pints.

'Ah no, I'm grand Shirley. Just been a long week, that's all,' he told her. He took a drink of his pint and motioned for her to pour another one for him. Another customer came up to the bar and got chatting to Shirley.

Bill didn't know what to do. He loved Laura so much, but he wasn't stupid either. He knew in his heart that he had lost her. It was like she had no interest in him as a person anymore. She only ever discussed the children with him. She wasn't unpleasant or anything. But he knew. He had tried everything.

But Laura's love for him had died. And he had no one else to blame but himself. As much as he loved her, he wasn't prepared to stay with her if she was never going to come around. And Bill knew now she wouldn't. At the start, when she first took him back, he thought it would just take a week or two to go back to normal. But she had frozen him out since day one. And it wasn't going to change. What made him love Laura more was the fact that she let him stay and she tried to pretend everything was fine. He knew the last thing she wanted was another break-up.

It took so much out on her and the kids. And him. She probably didn't have the energy to do anything about it, with helping Sharon so much lately and with the new job. He decided he would give it another couple of months; his marriage was worth that. But if things didn't change, he would move out of his own accord this time. He knew Laura wouldn't protest. But he intended to rent somewhere local this time, not far from the house.

Bill had a nice amount of savings put away and he could easily afford to buy an apartment or small-town house. But then if he and Laura got divorced, they would have to halve everything. He hoped that Laura would be able to keep the house and wouldn't have to sell it. He spent ten minutes working out their assets in his head. He reckoned he might just be able to sign over the house to her, but then he would get the rest of the assets.

If Laura wanted to sell the house and split everything, that was fine too. He just wanted to know what the options were. He sighed again, except the sigh was inwards this time. Otherwise, Shirley would be back over wondering what was wrong with him.

The next day, around 12.30pm, Laura's mobile rang. When she saw who it was, she didn't answer it. She let it go to voicemail. He had left her a message.

'Laura look, I know things haven't got off to a good start, and it's my fault, I know that. But I really do need you. There is so much to be done. Please call me back so we can have a chat,' Michael's tired-sounding voice came over the line. Jess had gone to work and Ben was out the back bouncing on his trampoline. Bill was catching up with some work in his office upstairs. She made her decision.

Laura wasn't a quitter; however, if she was going back, things had to change, she thought to herself as she waited for the phone to be answered.

'Laura, thanks for calling back.' Michael came on sounding relieved. Laura could hear the hammering of the drills in the background. He was obviously down at the site.

'Hi Michael, sorry I haven't been in touch. With Sharon and the baby, which, by the way she had a girl, Sophia! I haven't really had time,' she lied. May as well come clean she thought or she would get nowhere.

'Well, that's not entirely true. I have been avoiding you.' He laughed at this.

'I thought as much.'

'But.' she continued, 'Michael, last week was a disaster. You couldn't even dedicate ten full minutes to me. It made me feel so unimportant, like you had much better things to do. There is so much I could do for you and I could have that office up and running in no time. I could also manage your schedule for you so you can take a pee without having the phone glued to your ear. I know I would be an asset to you. But I cannot do that with little or no contribution from you. I am not asking you to hold my hand. I am well able to get on with the job and manage projects myself. But it's a bit hard when I don't even know what those projects are!' Laura paused for a breath and then wondered if she had gone too far.

Was Michael even still there?

'Ehh, Michael?' she asked, lowering the tone of her voice immensely.

'Yes Laura, sorry, I had to hold the phone away from my ear, I think you burst one of my eardrums!' He laughed again and then said, 'I'm only joking. You're right. And I needed to hear that. Glad you got it off your chest. Please come back Monday. I promise you things will be different this time.

'And if you're not happy come Monday afternoon you can quit, and I'll even give you compensation for your troubles.'

'Michael, I don't want your money, unless it's money I have earned. But I will come back Monday for one last attempt,' Laura told him.

She felt relieved having got what she had to say off her chest. And the fact he still wanted her back. Michael's voice broke in on her thoughts.

'I have a few meetings Monday morning.'

Oh lord, here we go again, said Laura to herself. He just didn't learn. But then to her surprise he continued.

'How about coming along with me? We can go through the stuff I need done when we are going to and from the meeting venues and you can learn bits and pieces too. You can take my phone and call out each contact and I will tell you what ones you'll need and why. That way you can start calling them all and telling them to deal with you from now on,' Michael told her. That was exactly what Sharon had suggested. Laura became suspicious.

'Michael, have you by any chance been talking to Sharon recently?' asked Laura, a smile playing on her lips. He coughed loudly, obviously putting it on in good humour.

'You caught me. I had to visit a friend of mine in hospital this morning. I met Sharon on the way out, new baby and man in tow. The baby is such a cute little thing. Anyway, we had a quick chat and your name came up. She gave me some advice on what I needed to do. And what good advice it was! Although I didn't hold her up too long, not with the newborn making her first visit home,' he chuckled.

Laura felt much better now. Now that they had some form of plan in place for Monday. Please god, this time it would work out. Otherwise, she may find herself offering babysitting services to Sharon!

CHAPTER 25

When Laura arrived on Monday, the portacabin was no longer there. She looked around in surprise, trying to see where it was or what happened. Michael was on site as his jeep was there. Just then he came walking around the side of the building. He smiled when he saw her and made his way toward the car. Laura grabbed her bag and got out.

'Morning Laura, and how are we today?' he asked good-naturedly. Laura was pointing over to where the portacabin had been located and he laughed.

'Looking for the office? I thought you could do with some sunlight. It can be very dark and dreary in there what with the shade from the trees. I have had it moved to the other side of the building. I think you'll find it to your liking.' He grinned at her. Laura followed him around the side of the building and they made their way to the back.

Laura realised that when Michael had given her a tour of the building site the first day, she hadn't really taken in what was around her. She looked out at the views across the bay. It was beautiful.

'This area here will be a beer garden.' Michael said. 'We will serve food out there as well. Think it would make a fine setting.' He walked on a bit further, and there was the portacabin, over towards the sea wall. It looked so much more appealing from the outside when it was out of the shade. When they got inside Laura gasped in delight. It was like a different place. The walls had been painted a rich cream colour; the desks had been put together. All the computers were set up and in the right location. As was the photocopier, fax and printer.

A new wooden floor had been put down and there was a phone line and WiFi hub on a table in the corner. She couldn't believe it. The canteen had also received a makeover. It now had a proper kitchen counter, microwave, cupboards, and a new table and chairs. There was a full set of cutlery, plates, cups and saucers. Everything had been tidied away.

'Up to scratch?' he asked Laura. She had to sit down. She was so happy. He had so much done in such little time. Her respect for him was reinstated, and more. This was why he was successful. When he really needed things done, he got them done.

'It's brilliant, Michael. Much better. And if I claim this desk as my own, I can look right out over the harbour. Do you mind if I take this place?' she asked him.

'Of course not, sure I'm not going to be here much anyway. The new girl you take on can use the other desk there and I can use the one at the back if I need to for now.'

Laura looked over at the Wi-Fi device.

'How did you get the phone line and internet in? I thought they weren't coming until today? And even then, they said it could be a few days before it's connected? Assuming it is connected,'

Michael was looking out the window towards the site. He saw a couple of men he didn't recognise wandering around.

'Ehh, I called in a couple of special favours,' he smiled, 'and yes, it is all connected and ready to roll. The phone number and Wi-Fi passcode are there on the desk. Right, I am just going to run out here for five minutes. Then we will need to leave. Make sure you have your notepad and pen ready. We have a lot to go through,' he told her looking quite serious. Then he disappeared out the door.

Finally. She felt like she had a job to do now. She hugged herself with delight. What a beautiful setting. When the office inside the building was ready, she didn't think she would want to move. And with the lovely sunshine, the office was so much brighter. Didn't even need the lights. She just hoped her optimism lasted.

Laura lay on her bed and sighed contently. She had a good day today. She had made the right decision going back. The day had absolutely flown. The first meeting was with the interior designers. They were showing the different fabrics they had for the walls and seating areas. They also had curtain samples and floor textures. Michael was glad he brought Laura as she seemed to have a good eye and he was pleased with her feedback.

It was easy enough to contribute given they had large 3D plans in front of them with how the final venue would look. After that they had three more meetings. And good as his word, Michael went through his phone telling Laura the contacts she would need and what for.

He had also bought her a new work phone. Laura had noticed that Michael became much more serious when he was actually working. It reminded her a bit of when she had first met him. He could be quite direct, even abrupt at times. But then Laura supposed he needed to be to get things done. Laura had gained so much information after one day alone that she couldn't wait to get back in the office and spend the day at her desk getting the projects in place. However, he wanted her to go with him again tomorrow. He said Wednesday she could start in the office.

As the weeks passed, Laura was engrossed in her new role. She worked until 3pm most days, even though she didn't have to, and usually picked up Ben from school on the way home. She was much happier, and she and Bill even seemed to be getting on better. She wasn't pretending anymore. Laura genuinely enjoyed chatting to Bill again about stuff.

It was still a long way off from where she wanted their relationship to be, but at least it was a start. Michael's life was much more organised now. Yes, he still was very busy and had a lot of phone calls, but that hectic approach of trying to be everywhere at once had stopped. Laura managed his diary as much as she could, and it really helped them both. When Laura needed decisions on things, she would not phone him up about each one. She could collect about ten or maybe twenty items that needed decisions together over a day or two. Then she would make him sit down for ten minutes and she would get an answer all at once on everything.

This strategy was really working. Except of course if it was urgent.

Then she would phone him, but she did that as little as possible. Laura didn't want to be managing his diary as she had other projects she wanted to focus on and to be honest it was a part of the job she didn't enjoy. She had gotten approval from him last week to take on a receptionist/PA and she had been interviewing all week.

She had finally decided on a nice girl who seemed to have a lot of common sense. Laura knew from experience that common sense could go a lot further than education. And for this job, a good head was needed. Sandra had just finished college where she had done a two-year secretarial and admin course.

She had never had a full-time job, but she had worked part-time in different offices over the years. Laura set her a few tasks with Microsoft word and excel just to test her skills. Laura was happy that she would prove a good employee. Sandra was also very keen, and Laura warmed to her. But she didn't want to offer her the job until Michael had interviewed her.

Michael had told Laura that he was too busy to be interviewing admin staff, that it was her job, and if she was happy with the girl, then hire her. So, Laura did just that. And she was starting next Monday. Michael could be challenging at times to deal with. At the start Laura took it personally if he was a bit abrupt with her. His no bullshit attitude could be refreshing at times, but it could also be hurtful. He noticed one day that she was having trouble with how he spoke to her.

Laura was watering some flowerpots in the windowsill and Michael had walked into the office.

'Have you nothing better to do than water bloody flowers? I am still waiting on you to email me that proposal. I told you it was urgent,' he had barked at her. And to be honest, he was right. Laura was annoyed with herself. It wasn't like her to let something like that slip her mind, but she had been dying to go to the bathroom when he phoned and after the call she had run to the toilet.

A supplier rang her on the way back to her desk and Michael's request had gone completely out of her head. Hence, she was watering plants. But when Michael saw the look of hurt on Laura's face he sighed and sat down.

'Laura look. I know my humours can be all over the place. I am well up for a bit of banter and a joke, but when there really is work to be done or I need something, I don't have time to joke around. I know I am abrupt and even rude at times.

'For that I apologise. But please, I need you to do one thing for me, do not take it personally. It's just the way I am. You are doing a great job here, as I knew you would and I do appreciate you. But maybe keep a notepad beside your desk phone so you can write down tasks as they come in. Like a to-do list. I am not being patronising, so please don't take it that way. But someone once told me the same. To write down everything that had to be done. No matter how much you think you will remember it. Write it down. And cross everything off as it gets done. It proved to be great advice for me and I still do it to this day. Now, stop looking so sorry for yourself and send me that proposal!' He laughed and without giving her a chance to reply, had got up and walked out the door.

He was right though. When Laura had worked for Sports for Life, she had her own PA. So, she didn't need to write stuff down. Julia reminded her of everything and even wrote out her to-do list for her. But then it was Laura's choice to take a step back in her career, so she would suck it up and deal with it as Michael suggested. Laura had taken him at his word, and she now knew how to handle him. She didn't bat an eyelid at his response about the new girl. Laura was used to him now and knew he meant no harm.

But he made up for it in other ways. He would try and take her for lunch on Fridays, or even after work sometimes if she stayed late and joined him and the men from the building site for a few drinks. They were always pleasant to her but weren't afraid to tease her either. Laura knew she would need a thick skin in this industry and so she joked and teased back.

Michael always stayed close to her on such nights. Laura would ask him was he worried she was going to do a moonlight flit with the foreman! But he would just smile and say he was watching out for her as she was the only female in the group. That was until on the nights Michael's girlfriend showed up. Laura had met her twice now. And as much as Laura hated to admit it, she was lovely. Her name was Ellie, and she was a schoolteacher down in Cork, which was a good three hours down the south of the country.

That explained why Laura didn't see much of her.

She thought she might see her turn up at the site, or drop by the office, but this had not happened yet. Michael tried to go down to Cork every third weekend and Ellie came up every second. Michael spent one weekend a month just with his daughter Natalie. On the weekends he was with Ellie, Natalie would join them sometimes, but most often she would meet her friends. Laura had also met Natalie. But just once.

She had got the bus to the site and had to wait in the portacabin as her dad was taking her to lunch and then to do a bit of shopping. She was shy at first with Laura, but then when she was more comfortable, she chatted a good deal easier. Natalie was really enjoying Uni and was glad she had made the decision to come here.

Overall, Laura was happy enough with life.

She must call over to Sharon tomorrow. Sophia was one month old on Sunday. They had sold the apartment and were due to fly to Gibraltar in two weeks to check out some houses.

They were only going for two days and one night as they were leaving the baby with Rob's sister Chloe, and Sharon didn't want to be away from Sophia too long. She had taken to motherhood like a duck to water. Sharon and Rob seemed to have put their differences aside as whenever Laura went over, she could see how well they were getting on. And Rob thankfully seemed to be entirely over his set back.

He doted on Sophia just as much as Sharon. Yes, thought Laura, she

would go see her friend and godchild tomorrow.

CHAPTER 26

In early November the weather had turned very cold. It also rained every day, making walks on the beach less enjoyable. But Laura tried her best to get a few in every week as they helped clear her head. Sharon, Rob and the baby had moved to Gibraltar yesterday. When they went over a month ago, they had seen four or five places, one of which Sharon had fell in love with. It had been a bit over their budget, but they didn't care. It had a small front garden and a large back one. It looked right out over the sea, and you could walk down to the beach via a garden path in less than a minute.

Sharon had sent Laura pictures. It looked amazing. Laura was so happy for her friend. But she couldn't help feeling a bit miffed. She didn't know what was wrong with her, she just felt as though she was missing something in life. Laura wasn't unhappy. The job was going great; the new girl had worked out brilliant. Laura was now focusing on larger projects and really making progress. Michael was delighted with her work and was taken aback at how much she had achieved.

But then she had been Commercial Director of a large company; Laura knew what she was doing. Family life was fine. Jess and Ben seemed happy. Jess was either at school, working or hanging out with her friends. Sometimes the two of them, just she and Laura would go into town, go for dinner, do some shopping, or go the cinema. She really enjoyed those days. She thought Jess did too.

Laura was so glad that Jess didn't give her much trouble. Yes, there were the usual teenage arguments and tantrums, especially if she wouldn't put her phone away at dinner or such, but nothing that made Laura lose any sleep over. She just hoped it lasted.

Ben was thirteen now. Always full of energy. If he hadn't a rugby or football match scheduled, he would have training. He would zoom into the house after school, wolf down his dinner and go out and play with his friends for an hour or two. Then he was back in the door grabbing his gear, and either shouting goodbye or shouting at his mother to hurry up, if it was her turn to take him and his friends to training. But he seemed as happy as a thirteen-year-old boy could be. They went to see Laura's parents every Saturday morning, and sometimes they would stay overnight, depending on whether Ben had a sports game on or not. Honestly, his whole life had to be lived around his games. But Laura didn't mind. It was healthy. So, she was happy with work and happy that her kids were happy. That just left her marriage really.

She and Bill were still getting on, but she didn't fancy him anymore. She didn't find him sexually attractive, and to be totally honest with herself, although she loved him dearly, she did not think she was in love with him anymore. They got on great as friends. Laura felt that Bill had now accepted this also. Although they shared the same bed, it was to sleep only. Bill didn't even try to cuddle her anymore. He stayed on his side of the bed. It wasn't awkward or anything. They still had conversations in bed, sometimes laughing or joking. But that's as far as it went. Laura knew it was only a matter of time before Bill came to her for a chat about their relationship. She wasn't stupid.

While Bill had been trying his best for things to work out, he wouldn't wait forever. He had a lot of pride, and he also knew when he was beaten. Laura hoped that she had read the situation right, and that Bill was of the same opinion, that they were just friends, and it was never going to go any further. Otherwise, it would be so much harder to deal with.

Christmas was less than two months away. Laura would wait until the New Year, and then the inevitable would have to be done. She wasn't looking forward to it, and she knew Bill wouldn't be either, but it had to be done. They both deserved to be happy, to have a loving partner they wanted to be with. They had to move on. No point in hiding from it any longer.

The weeks rolled on, and the building site was beginning to look a lot more like a destination. All going well, the new office would be ready to move into after Christmas. Laura was looking forward to this. It was a lovely big space with large windows overlooking the bay. There was also a large meeting room and a proper fitted=out canteen.

Laura would have her own small office, as would Michael. Then there were open-plan desks for around five to six people.

Laura would have preferred to sit out with others on the floor, but Michael insisted she had her own space; after all, she needed privacy to get on with her work. She did agree with him there. Sometimes she found it very hard to get anything done, what with the phone ringing, people calling into the cabin, faxes coming through and the rest. So, she supposed it wasn't a bad idea. Plus, she was now helping with Michael's Property Portfolio, which was becoming very full.

Sharon had phoned last night from Gibraltar. She had Skyped her so Laura could see Sophia. She was such a beautiful little pet. Laura found she missed cuddling her, and the smell of her lovely baby skin. Rob was setting up a new branch of his business over there. He would start off working from home, and then hopefully, move in to an office space. Sharon hadn't looked yet for a job. She wanted to wait until Sophia was at least six months old before she went back to work. If she didn't have Rob with her, she would have had to go back sooner, but thankfully now she didn't. So, she had a bit of time before she started looking for something.

But Sharon told Laura she was confident enough. That she had several calls already from recruitment agents about jobs. Sharon wanted to know when Laura was going to come out and visit her. Laura had laughed, saying, 'Sharon, You're only there a few weeks. Give yourself a bit more time before you start inviting the likes of me over.'

But Sharon wasn't taking no for an answer.

'Ah, come on Laura. I want you to see it. There is still time left before Christmas. Surely you could take a Monday off. Fly over here on Friday evening and go back Monday? That would only be three nights, and you would only need one day off work. I am sure Michael wouldn't mind. And anyway, didn't you say he was back in Spain at the minute?' Laura thought to herself, maybe she should go over to Sharon. It only took a couple of hours on the plane. But then what about the kids, and Bill? Should she invite them? Or even just Bill? As if reading her thoughts, Sharon broke in. 'Sure, bring Bill. Your parents won't mind taking the kids. And it might do you both good to get away.'

Laura sighed. Maybe she should ask Bill. See how they got on.

'OK, look I will ask him. I'll give you a call tomorrow and let you know.'

So, Laura had asked Bill that evening, and to her surprise, he declined.

'Look Laura, you would enjoy it much better on your own. Sharon is your best friend and I would just be in the way. I know Rob would be there, but I just wouldn't feel comfortable. It would be different if the kids were going too. No, you go on, Laura. You deserve a bit of a break after how hard you have been working lately.' Laura didn't know how she felt about his response. Although deep down she didn't want Bill coming, she was a bit disappointed he rebuffed her. It felt like the old days when he made excuses about her not going with him on a work trip.

But Laura knew she was being selfish, she couldn't have it all her own way. Bill knew well she was only asking him because she felt she had to. He recognised the trip would be full of tension. Laura now knew for definite that Bill had given up on their marriage. If it had been a couple of months ago, he would have jumped at the opportunity to go with her. But Laura couldn't blame him. He had his pride, and it looked like he wasn't going to beg anymore. Laura let out a sigh as she stared at her computer screen. Although she was a hundred percent sure that her marriage to Bill was over, it still hurt at times. They had been together a long time.

Laura had texted Michael rather than ring him that morning. He was in Spain with his other daughter, so she didn't want to interrupt him. She had written, *Hoping to take next Monday as a day off. Is that OK? Laura.* He had come straight back saying *No problem.* So, Laura now clicked on to a flight's website, and after scrolling through all the options, booked a Friday evening flight over to Gibraltar and back late Monday afternoon. She was beginning to look forward to it now. She could also do some Christmas shopping, picking up some things for her parents and the kids. Bill? Mmmm… what on earth would she get him? She'd have to wait and see.

Bill, once again, sighed into his pint. This time Shirley wasn't working so he felt he could sigh freely. He now knew that his marriage was over. There was no way he was going to go to Gibraltar; the way Laura had looked at him with sympathy. When he said no, that she should go on her own, the relief seeped through her. It was evident now that Laura was never going to forgive Bill for his affair. He didn't blame her; he just couldn't help being a bit annoyed. He had thought he could make it work; he really did.

But Bill couldn't keep doing all the running. He had a pain in his face being the nice one, Laura always being the injured party. They had tried, and failed. And in fairness to Laura, he supposed, she didn't have to give him a second chance. But to be honest, Bill felt like she never really had given him that chance. Yes, he had moved back in alright. But that was it. Laura had never given herself to him, or opened up to him since the affair. The old Laura was gone. She had taken him back for the kids' sake, that much was clear. But she had certainly not wanted to give their relationship another go. She hadn't really even tried. It was all false.

Well, Bill had had enough. It was sad. The kids would be upset. But they would get over it. There was no point in people staying together for the children's sake. The parents had to have a life of their own too. In the long run the kids would be happier, as both Bill and Laura would be happier eventually.

He was sure Laura would have no problem meeting anyone. He just hoped it wasn't that Jack Downey. Bill didn't want to say anything to Laura at the time, but he knew Jack was a player. He had seen him over the years stringing several women along. He was rumored to be having several affairs with married women, including his best mate Sean Dawson's wife. But Bill knew if he had told Laura that at the time, she wouldn't have believed him. She would have thought he was just trying to put her off. Well, thankfully he was well out of the picture. It wasn't long until Christmas. Bill would wait until the New Year, and then he would have a chat with Laura about their future.

CHAPTER 27

Laura felt like a little girl on her first school tour as she landed on the runway. She was ridiculously excited. Was Laura's life getting that predictable that a short trip to Gibraltar was able to arise such excitement within her! It was 7.20pm and Sharon said she would get Rob to meet her at the airport. And there he was, as Laura strolled out of the arrival's hall pulling her small suitcase with her. He had a baseball hat on and a light denim jacket.

'Laura, great to see you.' He hugged her tightly. 'Sharon is so delighted that you decided to come.' And so was Laura.

'Ah, thanks Rob. I can't wait to see her, to see the baby, to see the house, to see everything really.' She laughed.

Rob had arranged for a friend of his to bring over Rob's jeep from Ireland. It was only two years old and Rob had not wanted to sell it. Sharon had sold her car though, and intended to buy a new one once she was back working again. They lived close enough to the centre that at the minute she could either walk (about ten minutes) or get a bus in. There wouldn't be much point in even taking a car to the centre. Not when it was so close. Rob informed Laura that the airport was also very close, and that they would be at the house in ten to fifteen minutes if the traffic was OK.

There were a few Friday evening commuters still on the road, but it wasn't bad. Fifteen minutes later Laura was hugging her friend. The house from what she could make out looked beautiful. As it was dark, it was hard to really appreciate the location. But the inside was so cozy and warm. Each room had big bay widows and although Laura could not see the ocean, she could make out the lights down on the harbour area.

The kitchen was a large open plan that opened onto a sitting room area, not unlike the villa in Spain they had spent a week in. Sophia was lying in a Moses basket over beside the stove. She was sleeping soundly and Laura gently took her little hand and stroked it lovingly.

'Ah, the little pet. How is she?' Sharon beamed.

'She's an angel. She is just so good. Always seems happy and only cries if she has a dirty nappy or is hungry'.

Sharon looked brilliant. She was breastfeeding Sophia, and the weight she had gained in pregnancy was dropping off her. She nearly had her figure back. It had taken Laura a year to get back in to shape after both her kids were born. And she still held an extra few pounds after each birth.

Laura knew she had lost a lot of weight herself in the past year, but that was down to the goings on in her life. Over the last couple of months, she had begun to put it back on again. Sharon showed Laura the rest of the house. The kitchen had double doors opening on to the back garden, which looked out over the ocean. The three bedrooms were very spacious. At the minute Rob was using one for his office. The room Laura would stay in was going to be the nursery once they moved Sophia into her own room. And the bathroom was large with an amazing looking bath by the window.

Laura fully intended trying this out before the weekend was over! It was such a beautiful house. But Laura knew she would only really know how much, when she had seen the views in the morning. Rob, Sharon and Laura had a lovely dinner and several glasses of wine. Well, Sharon only had half a glass as she was breastfeeding, but Rob and Laura made up for it. By 11pm Laura was wrecked, as was Sharon, who had fallen asleep on the couch, with Sophia sleeping soundly in her arms.

Laura laughed, thanked Rob for a lovely night and said she would go to bed. Rob told her to have a nice lie-in. That when she got up, they had a nice day planned. Laura quickly undressed and got into the large comfy bed. She looked around the room and thought what a pretty nursery it would make come the time. It wasn't too big, but in saying that, did not lack space. The white wardrobes had large mirrors on the front, and there was a nice chest of drawers over by the window, with a framed photo of Sharon's mother. Laura was sure that Sharon must miss her mother so much. Especially with what she had been through in the past year, and with the birth of her daughter. She thanked god that she still had hers. Laura turned and reached over to the small bedside lamp and switched it off. She had feared that she may not be able to sleep, with her mind being so occupied, but she had fallen in to a deep sleep within minutes of closing her eyes.

The sun on Laura's face woke her up. For a minute she wasn't sure where she was, but then she remembered she was at Sharon's. She jumped out of bed and ran to the curtains. The sun had been peeking through a creak. She pulled them back excitedly to see what the day looked like, but already knew it should be promising.

Laura had been expecting a nice view, but it really was breathtaking. It was like something from a postcard. The ocean, the sand, the harbour, and the ever-famous Rock of Gibraltar, which resembled a very large hill made of rock, or even a tiny mountain. But the view was beautiful. Laura opened the window and she could hear the waves from below. She looked at her watch, it was 9.30am. Delighted that she hadn't slept that late, Laura put on the new clothes she had bought at the airport especially for the occasion.

A nice pair of cotton combats and a white fitted t-shirt. She grabbed a light jacket too and put on her comfy trainers. Sharon was downstairs cleaning around the kitchen.

'Ah, you're up, great. I have opened the patio doors. It gets a bit nippy in the winter, but we can still have breakfast out there. Just take your jacket out. It's not windy today. I'll throw on some bacon and eggs. Won't take me long,' Laura walked over to the Moses basket and there was Sophia, lying asleep once again. She laughed. 'All she seems to do is sleep.'

And Sharon joined her.

'She does sleep a lot yes. But she'll wake in the next hour or two and you can play with her for a bit. But for now, let's enjoy our breakfast while we can.' Laura strolled out on to the patio area. It reminded her a little of Spain. The view was different, as Spain was more of a resort area whereas Gibraltar was more residential and commercial. But the view down on the harbour and shore was so peaceful. Laura understood why Sharon wanted to move somewhere like this. It really was refreshing.

In no time, they were both tucking into soft eggs, bacon & tomato on toast, Laura's favourite. They had been talking so much they managed to drink three pots of tea. Rob was up in his office working and had some breakfast earlier that morning. Sharon asked Laura if she would like to go down to the beach for a walk. The buggy was able to go on the sand without problems.

Then they could then walk into town and do a bit of shopping, and finish having an early dinner in a restaurant down on the ocean front. Rob wouldn't be with them; he was taking advantage of Laura's visit and was working most of the day.

However, that evening they had invited some new friends around, neighbours mainly. Sharon apologised but Rob thought it would be a nice idea and had organised it before Sharon could tell him not to. She wasn't sure if Laura would want to mingle with their neighbours the minute she got here. But Laura was fine.

'No problem. Would be nice to let my hair down and have a few drinks.'

The two women had a fantastic day. Sharon really enjoyed having her best friend here to experience her new home and surroundings. And Laura was so enjoying Gibraltar and was surprised at how much she had fallen for it. They had a beautiful stroll on the beach, followed by a few hours' shopping.

Laura had bought most of her Christmas presents. She tried to keep them small in size as she would have to bring them back on the plane. She could get anything else she needed back home. The dinner was amazing; fresh seafood, followed by a couple of glasses of Prosecco for Laura. Sophia was such a good baby. Laura had played with her a good bit today. When she was awake, she would take her in her arms and carry her for a bit. Just to feel her close. Laura always loved babies. By the time they got back, the sun was just setting and Rob was just putting the kettle on.

'Ahh, just in time for tea, Pass over my little princess to me, please.' He winked at Laura. 'Laura, the guests won't be arriving until 8pm, you have a couple of hours if you want to take a shower and chill out.' Laura thanked him and said she might try out the bath, and so Laura spent a blissful thirty-minute soaking in the big bathtub. She never took baths at home. There was always someone banging on the door the minute you got in so she didn't bother anymore, unless she had the house to herself. She might indulge in one the odd time. She then went to her room to lay down for a while before she put on a nice black cocktail dress and headed down for the party.

Laura awoke with a throbbing headache. She had drunk way too much last night. She had to think about events for a few minutes, but then she relaxed as she realised she hadn't made a show of herself to anyone. There had been about ten people there, not too many. Rob had put on a real tasty buffet. Laura had spent time chatting to the women and their partners or husbands. She did feel a bit of a tool, being the only singleton, but she drank a good bit of wine to ease her comfort. Hence, the hangover.

There were still a good few of them there when she went to bed. She looked at her watch. It was just 8.30am. Laura didn't think the others were up yet. She eased herself out of bed, got dressed and went downstairs quietly. She grabbed a warmer jacket than yesterday as it was cooler given the earlier hour and she slipped out the door. She walked down the garden path and went for a refreshing walk on the beach. It was so peaceful. She sat down after walking for twenty minutes. After a while she realised she better get back. If Sharon had got up, she would be wondering where she was. Just then her phone beeped. It was a text message form Michael.

'*I Hear You Are in Gibraltar. I am not far away. Would you and Sharon have dinner with me later? I can meet you at La Brocca near the harbour at 6.30pm. Let me know.*' Laura didn't know what to think. How did he know she was here? She hadn't told him. And why did he want to meet them for dinner? She knew that the resort they had stayed in and where Michael was texting from was less than an hour's drive, so she supposed it wasn't that far out of the way. But she thought it strange. When Laura had first spent time with Michael in Spain, she thought she felt a small connection with him. She had been attracted to him, although she wouldn't have admitted that to Sharon, or even to herself for that matter.

And then when he contacted her about the job, she felt it again. The first week, even though it was a disaster from a work perspective, Laura really felt drawn to him as a person. She knew she was sexually attracted to him. And deep down she thought he might have felt something for her. But then once she got settled into the job, Michael seemed to back off, and only really conducted a business relationship with her. And he also had a girlfriend.

He wasn't cold or anything, but Laura felt he wasn't interested in her romantically at all, and she had obviously got her wires crossed. But she had been fine with that. Laura had enough going on in her life without adding to it. She was happy in her job, and she got on well with Michael. He was good to her and paid her well, so she just got on with it. But now he wanted to drive to Gibraltar and take her and Sharon out for dinner. Laura didn't know why, but she felt a bit nervous at the prospect. She was an idiot. He was just being friendly, sure, he invited Sharon too. Get a hold of yourself Laura. It's only dinner, and it's the three of you. Not just you and him. You work with this guy every day, calm down, Laura continued to lecture herself.

Maybe it was because they were in a different country that she was behaving this way. She wasn't sure. Anyway, she wouldn't do anything until she got back and could see what Sharon wanted to do. She might have something else planned.

But Sharon hadn't anything else planned, she was just going to let Laura relax today and do whatever she fancied. Sharon thought it was a great idea, and told Laura to respond immediately and say yes. Laura looked quizzically at Sharon. 'What?'

Sharon replied: 'I just think it would be nice to meet him for dinner. After all, I haven't seen him since Sophia was born and you two are working together every day. Would be nice for me to catch up with him,' she said innocently. Laura wasn't sure why, but she felt there was more to Sharon's keenness than wanting to catch up with Michael. Laura and Sharon had plenty of chats over the last couple of days. Laura had told Sharon that she didn't think she and Bill had a future and that after Christmas, she would probably have to sit Bill down and talk to him about what they were going to do.

She also told Sharon that she didn't think it would come as a surprise to Bill; she felt he might be thinking the same. Once Laura had explained her reasoning, Sharon agreed. Bill was a smart man, and probably realised that it was no good. The marriage wasn't going to work. Sharon told her although it was sad, that at least they had both tried. And they would be able to part as friends. Which was important with having the two kids. And secretly Sharon felt like she always knew it wasn't going to work, but she had to let Laura work that out for herself.

And at least now Laura could move on with her life. She deserved some happiness. Sharon knew that Laura was not happy at all. Oh, she put on a good front, and said everything was great, but Sharon knew her friend. She was lost. And if Sharon had anything to do with it, she was going to try and help Laura move on. Starting with Michael Smith! Oh, she knew it had been a bad mistake, pushing Jack towards her, but she felt this time it would be different.

CHAPTER 28

Laura could have killed Sharon. Using her baby as an excuse! She was a horrible person. There was absolutely nothing wrong with Sophia! She looked perfectly fine to Laura and had been cooing and caaaing all afternoon. But just as Laura came down the stairs, all dressed and ready for dinner with Michael, Sharon turned to her, still in her day clothes and holding the baby.

'Oh Laura, please don't go mad, but I'm afraid I won't be able to go with you. Sophia has a bit of a temperature and I'm a bit worried about her. I know Rob would be fine with her, but I just wouldn't enjoy dinner just in case there really was something wrong with her,' Sharon guiltily lied. She hated using Sophia like this but she knew it was the only way.

Rob had his back to them, pretending to be busy at the sink.

'Sharon, don't do this to me. If you don't go, I'm not going,' Laura stated.

'But you have to go. It's 6pm and he will already be on his way or even here. Why can't you go alone? Sure, you see him most days; you have lunch together regularly, what's the problem with dinner? There is no difference,' Sharon innocently enquired.

'You are so full of shit,' Laura fumed. 'And it is different, I don't know why, but it is.' She flopped down on the couch. Rob turned around and gave Sharon a look, as if to say, enough now, you better go with her.

But Sharon wasn't giving in.

'Look Laura, you will have a much better time without me. I can't even have a drink with you. Go out and enjoy your meal with Michael and have a few drinks with him after. It is supposed to be your little holiday and I can't even have a proper night out with you while I'm breastfeeding. So please, just go and enjoy yourself,' Sharon pleaded.

Laura sighed. She supposed she could go on her own. She needed to snap out of this humour. What was wrong with her? Why had she such a problem with having dinner with Michael? Right, get yourself together. Pretend it's like any other lunch.

'OK, I'll forgive you this time Shaz, but only just!' Laura stood up from the couch and Rob went to grab his keys.

'Come on Laura, I'll drop you down to the restaurant.' Laura walked over to Sophia and kissed her on the cheek.

'Let's hope you don't turn out as devious as your Mammy!' and then she looked at Sharon who was feigning innocence. Laura smiled and said goodbye and Sharon felt better. Laura had smiled, she really was forgiven!

The dinner was going much better than she expected and Laura was enjoying herself. Michael seemed disappointed that Sharon couldn't join them but he said he could see her again. He was over in Spain at least once a month to see his youngest daughter. Michael was very relaxed, much more so than when he was at work. Even when Laura usually went for lunch his phone would ring the whole way through or he would have to make some calls. Laura always felt she never really had his attention. But tonight was different. It was Sunday evening and his phone was quiet. They had spent the last hour catching up on what Laura and Sharon had been doing and Michael filled her in on the time he spent with his daughter Isobel. Michael had booked into a hotel for the night so he could have a few drinks.

He enquired about Jess and Ben, and seemed enthusiastic as to how they were doing and laughed at some of the stories Laura told him. But he never mentioned Bill. Never asked how things were or mentioned his name. And so Laura did not mention Ellie's name either. After a beautiful dinner, which Michael insisted on paying for, he took her to a cocktail bar, further down toward the harbour.

It was quite busy and Laura realised this was because it was happy hour.

They both enjoyed a few cocktails each and Laura realised it was 10pm already.

'Oh Michael, look at the time. I better be getting back,' Laura said making a move for her bag. But Michael took her hand, stopping her, and dragged her out onto the dance floor.

'Come on, dance with me first. It's still very early. I'm sure Sharon won't be expecting you home!' He smiled. At first Laura enjoyed dancing with him as the music was quite upbeat and she was feeling more confident with all the alcohol she had.

But then it changed pace to a slow set and Laura made to go back to their seats. Michael pulled her back.

'Where are you going? Just when the songs get good!' And he pulled her close to him. Laura felt the hairs stand up on her back. Every time she felt his breath on her cheek, it was like a bolt of lightning running through her. There was no mistaking the sexual chemistry.

Well for her, anyway. Maybe it was all one-sided. She'd had a lot to drink. Suddenly Michael looked down at her and asked her

'Fancy finishing off the night with a drink at my hotel? It's quite nice, and I think they have music in the bar until midnight.' Laura just nodded and followed him, collecting her things on the way.

The hotel bar was not so busy. There was one guy playing a guitar. Michael informed her he wasn't able to drink any more cocktails or beer, he needed a whisky! He asked her what she wanted. Laura felt the same. She didn't know what she could manage.

'A Baileys please.' She thought that might freshen her up. Michael and Laura were both drunk now, talking about work and what they could do and what they needed to do. Suddenly the singer said goodnight and started packing up his things. It was midnight already.

Time was flying.

Then Michael took her hand and nodded towards the lobby area.

'Shall we?' Laura didn't really know what he meant. Did he mean shall we go? Call it a night? Or did he mean, shall we go upstairs and shag each other crazy? Because Laura knew she wanted to. Thankfully, Michael was of the same mind. He pulled her into the lift and as soon as the doors closed, he started kissing the face off her.

They weren't in the room two minutes when they were both in bed naked, bodies wrapped around each other. Both were very drunk however, and it wasn't the most romantic interlude. Fast, clumsy and very noisy! She reckoned they were on their third round – or maybe even their third attempt - when she'd finally passed out.

Laura opened her eyes suddenly and closed them again just as quickly. Her head was throbbing. It felt like a dead weight. Suddenly she realised what had woken her, the sound of a man snoring. It wasn't Bill; she was lucky, he had never snored. And then she remembered the night before. Oh, no.

How embarrassing. Laura forced herself to open her eyes once again. It was still dark, but light came through behind the curtains from a street lamp. Michael had his arm around her and mouth wide open. The noise of him. Good lord. She maneuvered her arm so as not to wake him to check the time. It was 5.30am. Fuck. What would Sharon think? Oh, she knew what Sharon would think! She had to get out of here and back to the house. Her head was splitting and she needed a couple more hours sleep before she got up for the day. Laura managed to quietly slip from Michael's clutches. He was out cold; his snores proof of that. She quickly dressed, grabbed her things and then wondered should she leave him a note. But what would she say? 'Thanks for a great night, see you in work tomorrow!' No, she would leave it. Laura slipped out the door and out of the hotel.

Thankfully her shoes were comfy and so she went back to the house via the beach to try and clear her headache. She really hoped that Sharon had left the door unlocked. The last thing she wanted was waking the house up and having to give an explanation. Luckily, though, when Laura tried the door, it opened quietly. Laura quickly locked it, tiptoed up to her room, and fell into bed in relief.

Laura slept until 10am and once again awoke not knowing where she was. But it wasn't long until the events of the night before came back to her. She checked her phone quickly. No message from Michael. Should she text him? She felt a bit bad. Maybe she shouldn't have just left without saying anything to him.

Laura packed all her things in to her bag to get it ready for her trip home. Her flight was at 2.30pm but she had already checked in online so didn't have to leave the house until 1.15pm. She made her way downstairs and Sharon was making some breakfast.

'Ahh, the dead arises,' smiled Sharon. 'I thought I was going to have to wake you. I wanted a couple of hours with you before you have to leave. So. SPILL. ALL. NOW. Rob's not here; he's gone into the centre but he will be back to take you to the airport,' Sharon said as she poured Laura a cup of tea along with handing her a glass of water and two aspirin.

Sophia cooed from her basket. Laura didn't have the energy to go over to say hello. She would after breakfast. 'It was a good night. I lost track of time. Went to a couple of bars. Didn't get home till around 1.30am. Sorry, if you waited up,' fibbed Laura. She knew Sharon would be in bed then. But Sharon chuckled.

'Liar, ha. You even believe it yourself!!! Rob was also out on the town last night. He didn't get home until 2.30am! He woke me, and so I checked on you, and alas, your bed was empty! So come on. Stop trying to con me! I know you better than that. What time did you really get home at and what happened? Is he good in bed??' Sharon threw a hundred questions at her. Laura could only smile. Sharon knew Laura so well.

How did she think she could keep it from her? And so, Laura complied. And told her everything. Sharon sat open-mouthed for the last bit before exclaiming, 'I was only joking when I said was he good in bed, I didn't actually think you did sleep with him!' laughed Sharon. 'And you didn't even say goodbye, leave a note or send him a text! Oh, god Laura. Talk about making things awkward at work!'. Laura sighed. She knew that.

She was dreading going into work tomorrow. Although Michael wasn't flying in till the afternoon, so there was a good chance she wouldn't actually see him until Wednesday. Laura shuddered. She was still quite hungover, not as bad as earlier, but she felt very tired. She did not look forward to the airport and the flight home.

Sharon, Laura and Sophia took a walk on the beach. Sharon laughed as Laura told her about her moonlight walk at 5.30am that morning. They took off their sandals, rolled up their trousers and leaving Sophia in the buggy, had a paddle in the sea. The water was freezing, but in a way it was refreshing to Laura. They came back in and dried off with the towel Sharon always brought with her for such purposes. They strolled on for a bit further and then sat outside a coffee shop and had some tea and a scone.

'So,' asked Sharon. 'What are you going to do now?' Laura had no idea. Did she really fancy Michael? Or was it just the drink. And did he like her? He never mentioned anything to her. Never told her he fancied or and never paid her any compliments unless it was to do with work. So, did he only see her as a convenient lay? Oh, lord.

Deep down, if she was honest with herself, she realised she did like him. Liked him a lot.

'I don't know Shaz. To be honest, I don't know how he feels about me,' she said. 'He never mentioned anything to make me think he liked me. OK, I know. We ended up in bed together. But he still never actually said anything about us. So, I don't know if it was just a one-night stand for him or not.'

She continued, 'Anyway, I don't need the distraction at the minute. Bill and myself aren't separated yet, so it wouldn't be fair to do anything until we have sorted out stuff our end. I'm just going to go back to work as if nothing happened and see what he does. If he wants to talk about it then I will happily. But I'm not bringing up the subject. And don't let's forget, he has a girlfriend!'

Sharon sighed. She knew Laura really liked Michael. She hoped that she hadn't made a mess of this the same as she had with Jack Downey. She had more or less set them up and look what he turned out to be like. Sharon really hoped Michael was different. But he did have a girlfriend, and he had just slept with Laura. It could be that they were having problems. Maybe he was on the verge of dumping Ellie. She didn't know. But she was afraid to encourage her friend too much just in case it had been a one-night stand for him.

'I think you're right. Go back and get on with things as if nothing happened. And you and Bill need to sort things out before you do make any decisions.' And with that, the two friends made their way back to the house with Sophia, and then Laura got ready to leave. She would not see Sharon again until March when they were due back to

Dublin for Rob's sister's 40th birthday party. She would miss seeing her friend, especially over Christmas.

Laura had wanted them to come and stay with her for the holidays, but Sharon said she and Rob wanted to make Gibraltar their home. And they would like to spend their first Christmas there. Laura understood. She hugged Sharon tightly and then cuddled little Sophia.

'Take care, Sharon, and make sure you Skype me on Christmas day!' she laughed, walking out the door to Rob's jeep where he was waiting patiently.

As Laura thought back to six months ago, when Sharon was alone and Rob nowhere in sight, she marveled at how life was so unexpected, and how things changed so quickly for her friend, and in most cases, for the better. She just hoped that in her case, it would be for the better, too.

CHAPTER 29

It was the Friday before Christmas and Laura was getting ready for her work Christmas party. Sandra had booked a restaurant in Howth and reserved an area in the pub next door afterwards. Partners had been invited, but Laura didn't mention this to Bill. To be honest, she didn't think he would go anyway. There were twenty people going including Laura, Sandra, the new admin person Barry, the foreman, Michael, and the rest were construction workers on the site.

Laura was looking forward to it as she got on well with them all, and she knew they would have a good laugh. She was nervous however, of seeing Michael. Or of speaking with him. But she would make sure they were never alone together so it would be OK. Ever since they had returned to work after their night in Gibraltar, things had been strained between them.

That was the last thing Laura wanted. She had gone back to work and tried to pretend nothing happened. But Michael seemed to regret their night together, and hadn't joked or smiled with Laura once since. He was very business-like towards her, but he still joked with the others in the office. When Laura tried to join in, he would walk off, or pretend he had to make a call. Sandra had noticed and asked if everything was OK. Laura told her, yes, absolutely, not to worry herself. The last thing she was going to do was get into a discussion with the PA about it. Laura found out that it was Sandra who had told Michael that Laura was visiting Sharon in Gibraltar. She didn't mind. Sandra hadn't meant any harm. Even though a lot of harm had been done! Laura made an extra effort at work, making sure everything was done on time and professionally. However, Michael seemed to have issues with everything she did.

He was constantly having a go at her, either by email or phone call. He said a lot less to her in person. He found it hard to look her in the eye. Laura was beginning to get rightly annoyed with him. It was like he blamed her for sleeping with him. And to her annoyance he was still with the lovely Ellie. Laura had secretly hoped that maybe they had broken up. But she had phoned the office several times for him in the past week or two. Laura's patience with him was running out, and if he didn't change his attitude, she was just going to leave. She'd get a job somewhere else; life was too short as she had once learned.

Bill dropped her off outside the restaurant and told her to have a good night. She thanked him and told him to have a few drinks in the local on the way home. Bill said he probably would, but not many. He was tired and wanted an early night. Laura got out and thought to herself that he spent a good bit of time in the Cozy Corner. She felt a bit sorry for Bill. She really did love him, and she wanted him to be happy. It just wouldn't be with her.

'Laura, over here,' called Sandra. She was standing over towards the bar, with some of the construction workers. Barry, the new admin guy, was also there, smiling happily up at Sandra. They had taken Barry on quite quickly after Sandra, as Laura's workload had trebled creating more paperwork than Sandra could handle on her own. He was a nice chap, a bit innocent and never said a word back. But he was efficient and good at his job and that was the main thing. Laura noticed Michael hadn't arrived yet.

Although partners had been invited, no one was bringing them as far as she knew. It was always better to go to work parties alone, Laura thought. You always knew everyone, but if you had your husband or partner with you, you couldn't let go. You had to make sure they were OK and having a good time. And you didn't want to keep talking about things that had happened at work as it wasn't fair. So, Laura thought it much better going alone to these things. It worked both ways.

She had stopped going to Bill's work parties for the same exact reason. One of the men handed Laura her gin and tonic and Sandra nudged her towards the table.

'Right, we better take our seats, the waiter said it's ready for us.' They were still missing about eight people so they just ordered drinks until everyone arrived.

Michael arrived last, and to her (and probably everyone else's surprise) he had brought Ellie with him. What a fucking asshole, thought Laura. If he was trying to make her feel bad, he was doing a good job of it.

Thankfully she and Sandra were sitting at the far end of the table. Laura wouldn't be forced to make small talk with a woman she hated, but who was actually really nice. Laura felt like a bitch. But she couldn't help it. She was furious at Michael. Talk about making her feel like a total idiot. Well, screw him. She wouldn't go as far as saying hello to him tonight. And she wasn't going to make an effort anymore. She would go in, do her job, and go home. On time from now on.

She wouldn't be putting in any extra hours of work. Fuck him. Laura downed her G&T and accepted a large glass of red wine from one of the waiters. There were several bottles on the table. She put Michael to the back of her mind and enjoyed herself with her work colleagues. The food was lovely, and she ate plenty, aware that she didn't want to be drinking on an empty stomach, as she hadn't eaten much that day knowing they were dining later. She had a coffee afterwards also, as she felt the wine going to her head. Once dinner was over, Sandra directed them all to the pub next door.

Laura sincerely hoped Michael would just go home now and not join them, but in he strolled with Ellie on his arm. Laura made sure to wait until he took a seat before she sat down. She wanted to be as far away from him as possible. The music was upbeat and Sandra had some of the men up dancing. Laura had to laugh at her. She was great fun. Laura was glad she had hired her as she was also good at her job. She was well able to handle the construction lads. As Laura headed to the bathroom, she bumped into someone nearly knocking their drink. She looked up apologising, and found herself staring at Jack Dawson!

'Jack, ha, no way, Jack, how are you?' Laura was genuinely glad to see him.

She would always have a soft spot for Jack. She knew he was a bit of a rogue with the ladies, but he had a good heart and was great company. Jack smiled in delight.

'Laura, good god, how the hell are you? You look amazing. Got a bit of meat back on your bones I see! It suits you.' He laughed and Laura laughed with him.

She knew he meant it as a compliment.

They chatted for a while and then Laura excused herself. She really did have to go to the bathroom. Jack promised to take her out for a dance later, and she agreed. Half hour later Laura was spinning around the floor with Jack. It felt good being back in his arms. She felt bad when she thought of how she had ended her relationship so abruptly with him. Jack had been good to her. And when she had been at such a low point in her life. He told her to sit down and brought her over a drink. Laura introduced him to the others (except Bill and his company, they were down the other end). They all chatted together, drank some shots and danced all night. Laura genuinely forgot all about Michael and really let her hair down. When Jack offered her a lift home, she raised her eyebrow ready to scold him about drink driving. But he put up his hands.

'I'm not driving, got a taxi waiting outside. We both live close by so we may as well share. I promise, I'll keep my hands to myself, even though I'd love to grope you!' he joked. Laura laughed too, said goodbye to the others, grabbed her jacket and bag and left with Jack's arm draped over her shoulder. If Laura had have looked around as she was passing Michael, she would have seen the murderous look on his face. He was not a happy man.

Laura came to work Monday on great form. She had really enjoyed herself at the Christmas party and they were only in for two days before breaking up for Christmas holidays. They would not be back in the office until the first Monday in January, which gave them nearly two weeks off. Jack had been as good as his word, and only kissed her hand when she was getting out. She did however agree to have dinner with him sometime in the New Year. But Laura knew it would just be as friends. She didn't feel that way about Jack anymore. To be honest, she didn't think she ever did fancy him. He was just in the right place at the right time. To her surprise, Michael was already in his office when she arrived. Normally she was first there. Well, she wasn't going to let him spoil her good mood.

She put her bag and jacket in her office and went to the canteen as she did every morning, sticking on the kettle. She walked over to the window looking out over the Bay. It was beautiful, even in December.

'You certainly had a good night Friday, you must have been in bed recovering all weekend,' came Michaels somewhat angry voice. Startled, she turned around. How dare he! And she wasn't even drunk on Friday night. OK, so she had a good few. Certainly tipsy. But she hadn't been drunk. Laura could have hit him. Facing him across the room as he stood in the doorway.

'And what's that supposed to mean? Yes, I enjoyed myself, had a great time in fact. But I wasn't hungover as I didn't get drunk,' she barked back. Laura walked over to the kettle and poured herself a cup of tea refusing to look over at him.

'Pity YOU didn't seem to enjoy it yourself,' she said without looking up.

'I did enjoy it,' Michael's voice bounded back. 'Myself and Ellie had a great time,' he said smugly. Laura turned around and picked up her cup.

'Well, it certainly didn't look that way from where I was sitting. You both looked like you'd rather be anywhere else. Ellie looked bored out of her mind, poor girl' Laura said feigning sympathy.

She could see she had angered Michael so she headed for the doorway with her tea. As she walked past him, he stood in front of her. He looked down at her and said, 'Well I'm surprised you noticed anything, hanging out of that fella with the leather jacket all night, and then even going home with him. And I thought you were back with your husband! Says a lot, don't it!' he smirked at her. Laura didn't think she had ever been so utterly furious in her life. But she didn't want to let him know that he had bothered her.

'Yes, myself and Jack had a great night together,' and she smiled sweetly as she side-stepped him and walked back to her office. She closed the door behind her and sat down at her desk with her head in her hands.

He had some cheek. Who the hell did he think he was? Well, Laura wasn't going to tell him that she and Bill would not be together much longer. It was not his business. But he made her out to be some sort of tramp. He thought she slept with Jack. Well, let him think that. That's why Laura responded the way she did. Fuck him. He had Ellie. She didn't care what he thought of her anymore. And she didn't want to leave the job just yet. She had her teeth in some new projects and she wanted to get them finished. They would look good on her CV, but only if she completed them and could show positive results.

Laura decided she would just keep her head down and get on with the job, and avoid Michael wherever possible. She only needed him for a few decisions here and there, and although he was being horrible to her, he would not let their relationship come between work decisions. He would make the right decisions for the right reasons. But he would be frosty about it. Laura didn't care; she wasn't going to let him win by handing in her notice. Not yet anyway.

CHAPTER 30

Thankfully, they had a peaceful Christmas although that had been threatened as Bill's mother, the poison dwarf, had tried to invite herself to dinner. Laura was having none of it. Not on Christmas Day. Bill knew there was no point in pushing it. But Laura agreed to have them over the next day. She was dreading it, but deep down, Laura knew this would be the last time she would have to entertain them, so she didn't mind too much. Laura had been up early preparing everything for the dinner.

She was doing more work and taking more care today than she had for their own Christmas dinner yesterday. But she knew why that was. Bill's mother made her nervous. Laura never felt she was good enough, and that no matter what she did, it would be wrong. Ah, well, thought Laura, you got your way in the end. Bill can find himself a more acceptable partner next time. Maybe he can bring her home to his mother before he actually made someone his new partner. Laura would like to see Pauline's face if he had brought Johnson home to his mother. Ha. Now that she would pay to see! Just thinking of Rita Johnson now made Laura realise she hadn't thought about the woman in a long time. And her heart didn't contract in pain anymore when she did think of her.

Laura was glad. She knew she was over the affair now. It didn't hurt her the way it used to. Yes, it had ruined her marriage. But Laura had to move on now. It had been over a year since it happened. She wondered vaguely what Johnson was up to these days. Not that she cared really. Deep down she didn't think Bill would ever go back near her. He got what he had coming to him by being with her for a year. He had finally realised what an insane vindictive bitch she really was.

Bill and the kids came back from walking Barney, and Bill started to help Laura in the kitchen. Although they didn't say much, there was no tension, and it was a companionable silence. Laura would miss him. She would miss his presence, the feeling of security of having him there. She felt sad now. Did they really have to go their own way?

Yes, she thought. Laura, and Bill for that matter, knew that they were at the end of the road. But she sincerely hoped they remained good friends. She knew a lot of couples who broke up intended to be friends but always ended up in bitter feuds. Laura really didn't want that to happen to them.

Bill's parents arrived fifteen minutes early, which was the norm and always irritated the hell out of Laura. She bit her tongue though, keeping in mind it was their last visit.

'Laura, how are you? You look great, the new job must suit you!' came Pauline's warm tone of voice, which was generally kept for the local priest and the well-to-do gentry. Laura was flabbergasted. She had never received a kind word from Bill's mother.

Even on Laura's wedding day, she had told Laura that it's a pity she didn't have her hair done like Elisa Reilly down the road had on her wedding day that Laura's looked a bit like an overgrown bush. But never mind. It would do.

'Here, let me help you,' she proceeded and went into the kitchen and started lifting plates and things and moving stuff around. Laura recovered and found her voice.

'Eh, no, no, it's OK Pauline, please, go into the dining room and sit down. Bill, get your parents a drink, will you please?' She gave Bill a desperate look. Bill got the message.

'Come on Mother, leave Laura be, she has everything in hand!' He steered her out of the kitchen.

'Jess, Ben, come on down and say hello to your grandparents,' he roared up the stairs. Bill's dad winked at Laura as he followed them out of the kitchen. Laura took a breath for a minute. Then she laughed out loud. She couldn't help it. After all these years, not a kind word, a compliment, a friendly smile, and now all of a sudden, the poison dwarf had turned in to Miss Can't be Friendly Enough.

Laura wondered what it was all about. After all, Pauline had phoned Laura when she and Bill first broke up, blaming it all on Laura and demanding she took Bill back. So, Laura knew she never had sympathy for her when she and Bill split. So, what was behind it now?

There had to be something. Pauline Murphy didn't give praise or offer to help without having a hidden agenda. She suddenly thought back to one Saturday when she and Bill were having dinner in the poisonous dwarf's house when her husband's mobile rang. He had been in the middle of spooning some vegetables on to his plate and the loud shrill of the phone caused him to spill the contents of the bowl everywhere. Laura waited, secretly delighted to hear what Pauline would have to say.

Her precious son could do no wrong, but Pauline wouldn't appreciate a mishap like this. So, Laura could not believe her ears when she heard the bitch blame her for the accident. The bossy old boots put down her knife and fork sharply, directed her gaze at Laura and said, 'If you had told him to switch off his phone before he sat down, this would never have happened'.

If Laura hadn't been so outrageously angry, she might have laughed, but the anger boiled up inside her. She could feel herself going beetroot red, and she had to swallow several times to try and keep her anger in check. Bill's father saved the battle commencing, he being his sweet-natured self, scolded his wife, saying, 'Don't be an eejit, Bill isn't ten anymore, this is nothing to do with Laura.' He then smiled at his daughter-in-law, which always had the same calming effect on her. She felt she could just about last another ten minutes.

That was it. Laura didn't even offer to do the washing up as she usually did. As soon as the cardboard meal was over, she and Bill were out of there. Of course, Bill had made excuses for his Mother.

'Oh, she hasn't been that well lately,' he'd sympathise. Laura had to bite her tongue to stop herself saying, 'I don't think she has ever been well and that's what's bloody wrong with her!' her quick wit near getting the better of her as it had so many times before.

Ah well, thought Laura, she really didn't care what the old bat thought anymore, she just found it amusing.

Dinner was a success, something Laura had rarely got to say when it involved Pauline Murphy. Her sweet antics were kept up throughout the dinner, and even Jess and Ben looked bewildered. They all retired to the sitting room and watched some TV after dinner, bellies all full and teas and coffees were dished out. As Laura was tidying up in the kitchen Pauline went in to help her. Laura didn't want any help. She wanted to be on her own. She had to decide the best time to have that chat with Bill. They needed to know what they were both doing and she wanted to sort it out before the New Year so they could both start afresh.

'Laura, I know I wasn't always the nicest mother-in-law, and I want to apologise. It's just when your little boy grows up, it's hard to let him go. You'll understand when Ben is older. But I want you to know that I have always admired you. You are a great mother and have always been a fantastic wife to Bill. I am so glad you sorted things out.'

She went over and held Laura's hand. Laura wanted to puke. One, because the vindictive woman was holding her hand, and secondly, because she knew that what she said was pure crap. What was this woman on? Laura just smiled, took her hand back, and kept herself busy tidying up.

'I'm glad I got that off my chest. I'll go back in here to the others. We'll probably head off soon,' she told Laura.

'No problem, take your time,' Laura smiled. And ten minutes later when his parents were leaving, Laura found out the reason for Pauline's assumed warmness. After bidding farewell to her and the kids, his parents went out to the front door with Bill. Laura happened to be hovering close by as she was looking for her slippers.

'I'm so glad you and Laura are OK again. Now keep it that way. I never want to hear again about your antics with that, with that TART. I have never been so embarrassed. The whole neighbourhood was talking about it. That woman was nothing short of a whore and you were sleeping with her! UHH, disgusting! I know I never had much time for Laura, but she's a hundred times better than that piece of filth!' spat Pauline.

Laura snook back into the kitchen. Ah ha, thought Laura. That was it. She knew there was something. Pauline had found out about Rita Johnson. And yes, it would have been a social embarrassment for her, considering the circles she hung around in! Laura should have been annoyed, but all she could really do was laugh. Some people would never change.

The next day they all bundled into Bill's car, including the dog, and went to the beach for a walk. They had planned on getting chips as well from the chippy van that tended to be there at weekends. It was a cool enough day and they were all wrapped up warm. Ben ran on ahead with Barney, and Jess wasn't far behind him, listening to her iPod, which left Bill and Laura walking together alone.

Was now the time? They were trying to work out how to approach the subject. Neither really knew how the other was going to react. Not being able to stand the silence any longer, Bill broke first.

'It's not working Laura, is it?' he said quietly. Laura looked at him and smiled sadly. She was right. He had been on the same wavelength as her. Laura sighed.

'No, it's not Bill. And I know it's not fair on you. You have bent over backwards to make our marriage work. But the problem is me. Unfortunately, I just can't see past the affair. It just did too much damage. I'm sorry Bill. I did try.' Bill was somewhat glad that Laura recognised the effort he had put in. At least she knew that he had done everything he could to try and make up for it.

He hadn't thought Laura had noticed.

'I sort of realised that. What I did was wrong Laura. And I know you were willing to try and forget it. But it's not that easy, is it? You have changed Laura. And not for the worse. The better. You are much more confident now. It suits you.' Laura wasn't sure what to make of this. She supposed she had changed. With the year she had, how would she not have changed?

Bill continued.

'And please don't take this the wrong way, but I know I am never going to win your love back. We both know that. Our marriage is over, which I take full responsibility for. But it's time to move on now. The last year has been hectic. It feels like someone else took over my body and I have been watching from the outside. I'm fed up not knowing where I am in life, or where I am going. And I am sure you are too.' Bills words were sharp, but Laura knew it was more out of frustration than anything else. Laura didn't want to talk about the past anymore either.

'You're right Bill. What's done is done. Let's move on. The main thing is, I want us all to be happy. I know that sounds like a cliché, but I really want me and you to remain friends if possible. It will be much easier for Ben and Jess's sake.' Bill was happy with Laura's response. He had hoped for the same.

'Absolutely, and Laura, I want you to keep the house. I have looked into it, and with our joint assets, I should be able to sign it over to you, and still have enough to buy myself a nice place,' he told her. Laura was astounded at his generosity. Their house was worth quite a lot; especially being in its location.

But Laura had already decided on living arrangements.

'Bill, that is more than generous of you. Thank you so much. It really means so much to me that you have gave me this option. However, thanks but no thanks. I have been doing a lot of thinking myself. And I want a fresh start. The house is you and me Bill. It's our memories together. Our first married years together, then Jess as a baby, Ben as a baby. Even Barney coming along. The house is the past. I want to buy somewhere new. Not far. But my walks on the beach are becoming more frequent lately and I love the sea air. I know our own house isn't exactly far away, but I would like to buy a house right by the beach, so I can see the ocean from my windows, and hear the waves if I open them. Ben and Jess would have to get used to it but it's not like we're moving neighbourhoods really.

'It will just be a smaller house. I'm sure Ben will prefer it actually as he can go swimming every day in the summer.' Bill was saddened in one way. He wouldn't like to see their house up for sale. But on the other hand, he knew what Laura meant. And she was probably right.

'I think that's probably a very good idea. I was thinking of buying something further out of the city in Portmarnock, on the beach too, which won't be too bad for the kids.'

Laura thought that was a great idea. It was only about a twenty-minute drive. And it was a real summer haven. The kids would love it.

'So, where do we go from here then? When do we start the process? When do we tell the kids?' Laura asked, as she could see both Ben and Jess had turned and were walking back towards them.

'Let's have another chat ourselves tonight and put a plan together,' Bill said. But if you are OK with it, I think the sooner I move out the better. I would like to start the New Year afresh'.

And with that, Laura nodded her head and smiled at him. In ways they were so alike. She had been thinking the exact same thing. As she looked at her two kids, now trying to push each other into the sea, and Barney barking like mad around them, she felt very sad. This would most likely be the last time the whole family would be together. She was sure they would be together again in the future, at birthdays, graduations and things. But it was the last time they would really be together as a family. And not a broken one. It was sad alright. But then, life could be sad.

CHAPTER 31

The kids were understandably upset. They told Jess first rather than both together, as they knew Jess could help when they told her brother. Ben wouldn't accept it at first. Screamed and cried and told them he hated them. But Jess calmed him down by telling him that both Mam and Dad were going to buy new houses right on the beach and he would have to help them search for good places. He was slightly mollified by this. Ben loved the beach; he loved swimming and even had a body board that he tried to surf with.

It also helped that both Bill and Laura were still getting on so well. Bill didn't move out right away. He waited until a few days after telling the kids. He moved out on New Year's Eve. Laura was taking the kids to her parents' house for the night to bring in the New Year. Bill was going to his mother's (god help him) for a few nights but was hoping to rent a place nearby until they sold the house and had enough to buy new ones. Laura spent two nights at her parents as her brother Shane, his wife and kids were home for a few days. She got to see so little of them she wanted to spend some time with them when she could.

Shane thought she was doing the right thing, and he praised her for being so strong. He told her that it might be hard now, but that it would work out all right in the end. Laura had told Jess that her dad was gone to stay with his parents, but he would be getting his own place. Jess seemed to take it well, but then she was older and understood more than Ben. Jess had told her she was glad that her parents were getting on so well, that some of her friends' folks hated each other and were always arguing.

And some of them even still lived together. Jess told her she would prefer them to be living apart and good friends and living together and not being happy. Laura was extremely proud of her daughter. She was turning into a young woman. It was her last year in school too and in fairness to her, she had been studying hard. Jess had decided she wanted to study veterinary.

But the university she was applying to was in Edinburgh, Scotland. Apparently two of her best friends were also applying to Edinburgh, not for the same course, though. Laura and Bill, while pleased she had chosen veterinary, asked Jess if she was sure that's what she wanted. And that it wasn't just the university itself that attracted her. But she said no that they had a visit from a vet last year in school who gave a speech about his profession. She found it really interesting and he had gone to Edinburgh.

And that's where she wanted to go. So, Bill and Laura supported her. Jess knew she might not get a place there, so she had applied to some other universities, including one in Dublin. Laura knew she was being selfish but she secretly hoped that Jess took a place in Dublin. The thought of Jess going to a new country on her own scared her. But Laura knew that Jess was getting older. Laura would have to allow her to spread her wings. She had always encouraged her to take a couple of years out after college or Uni and travel the world. But thinking about it now scared her. Anyway, she would put that out of her mind for now. Focus on Jessica getting good results and getting to uni. They would take each step as it came.

The next few weeks were crazy. Laura was glad they had the Christmas break to relax beforehand. Laura had arranged for an estate agent to come to view the house, and everything had moved so fast since then. She had put it on the internet and within days had shown the house to three interested parties. One of them seemed very keen. Laura was very surprised as with the price of the house she thought it could take months, maybe even a year to sell. But the way things were going, it looked like it would be much sooner.

Apparently, some man who had moved to America twenty years ago had decided to move back home. He had made a nice few dollars over there and was coming back with his family.

Laura was expecting a call any day now to say whether or not he had put in an offer. So, she had been frantically looking through the internet for places to rent. Just for a couple of months until they had the money secure from the sale. That's if it even went through. She had asked Sandra and Barry if they knew anywhere that would allow a short-term rental but unfortunately, they didn't. Her relationship with Michael was a little better.

They were both civil to each other, and all the tension had gone. Laura didn't have time to think about him really as she was also trying to look at houses to purchase. So, between trying to get her job done on top of the rest, she didn't have a minute. She hadn't even called Sharon back. They had spoken at length on Christmas day, but not since. Sharon had called yesterday morning but she'd missed it and she had meant to call her back but didn't find the time.

However, the office seemed quiet now.

Sandra and Barry had gone for an early lunch and there was no sign of Michael or his new financial manager, so Laura gave Sharon a call. She filled her in on what happened with Bill and what happened at the dinner with his folks. Sharon got a good laugh out of that. Laura was just explaining how now they might be homeless if she didn't get somewhere when she heard a knock at the door.

She looked up and Michael was standing there.

'Sorry Shaz, I have to go, I'll call you later,' and she hung up.

'Sorry Laura, I didn't mean for you to end your call, I just wanted to know if the post had arrived.'

'Yes, it has.' She said. 'Anything that needs your attention will be on your desk,' Laura told him. He thanked her and was about to walk off but stopped and turned back.

'Sorry Laura, I wasn't eavesdropping, but I heard you saying you might be homeless. Is everything OK?' Laura was surprised to hear the concern in his voice. He was obviously over their whole drama.

So, Laura filled him in about the decision to sell the house and how it looked like it would sell a lot sooner than they thought. She didn't however, tell him that she and Bill had separated. It was none of his business.

'I might have a solution for you,' he said. 'You know the apartment I'm having built at the back of the building? Well, it will have two bedrooms and will have... OK, sorry, you know what it will have as you helped lay it out… Anyway.... it will be ready in a couple of weeks if you and your family would like to use it. It would be a bit of a squeeze, but it will be free, so it's yours if you want it.'

Laura was astounded.

'Michael, I couldn't allow you to do that. Anyway, were you not building that for yourself?' she asked him.

'I was originally. But Ellie got a job up here in Dublin and so we are getting our own place together. The apartment would be too small, so I was going to rent it out. Maybe see first if some of the staff wants to rent it. But you can have it for as long as you need it. And I don't want a penny in rent. Just pay the bills. That's it.' Michael smiled.

'Anyway, I have to take this call. The apartment is yours if you want it,' he said again and with that, he took the call and went into his office closing the door behind him. Laura sat back in her chair.

He had offered her the apartment rent-free for her and her family. She assumed he thought Bill would be with her. He still thought they were together. And it didn't seem to bother him. He was moving in with Ellie. And, of course, the apartment wouldn't be suitable for them. Ridiculous. Laura remembered being involved when the apartment was first being built. From what she could remember, the plans were quite spacious. And it had a huge bay window looking out over the harbour. It would be perfect. Jess and Ben could share a room. It wouldn't kill them for a few months. It wasn't ideal, but at least it was an option. No point in making any decisions yet. She'd have to wait and see.

As it happened though, that man put in an offer, and for the asking price, which both Laura and Bill accepted with delight. As all parties were keen to move this project on, the estate agent said the quickest possible time the deal could be done, given paperwork and legalities would be six weeks. Bill groaned. He was hoping to rent a place for himself but no one would take him on such a short-term basis. And his mother was driving him mad. Laura had an idea.

'Look Bill. Why don't you move back into the house until it's officially sold? I'll move out. I have been offered the loan of an apartment at work for a few months. It has two bedrooms but me and the kids would manage. We could move in there in the next two weeks.' Laura filled him in some more on the offer she had got from Michael. Bill thought about it.

'Thinking about it Laura, that would be great. But I don't want to put you out.' Laura reassured him.

'Honestly Bill, it's an ideal situation.' He looked thoughtful again and then said 'Well, maybe I could take the kids half of the week and you take them the other half, just until we both get sorted out with new houses. I am a bit slack at work at the moment and have nothing major coming up so I could work around it. And the kids wouldn't feel as cramped if they weren't in the apartment seven days a week. What do you think? It's just a suggestion?' Bill worriedly hoped he hadn't gone too far.

But Laura was thinking.

'You know Bill; I think that would be great. It would give me time to look online for houses and go to viewings. Offer accepted,' she laughed and shook his hand. Michael had no problem with it. He was more like his old self and even helped Laura bring some of her stuff up. He had got some of the lads on the site to do the rest. The apartment was really impressive. It was large and very bright. The sun came right into the kitchen, which was a decent size, with a seat in the bay window area. It had a table and four chairs, and state of the art kitchen units. There was also a skylight window which really brightened up the whole place.

The sitting room also had a large window. There were two comfy looking couches which were brand new by the looks of them, and a flat screen TV on the table nestled in the corner. There were no pictures on the wall, and they seemed a bit bare. Laura would have to fix that. The hallway was a wide, open space, but not very long. There were two good sized bedrooms, one when you came in the door on the left and one down further on the same side. The bathroom was at the bottom end of the hall. Even if their stay was temporary, she wanted to make it as homely as she could. Although she knew she could never live here long-term, Laura looked forward to spending the next few months here. Plus, it was very convenient for work! Maybe too convenient! She laughed to herself. Ben was all excited, jumping up and down on the couch, pointing out the different boats in the harbour.

Michael had met Bill when Bill had come over with the kids once all the stuff was in. They shook hands and Bill thanked him for the apartment. Michael caught up with the kids for a while and then disappeared back to work. Laura realised that she was misleading Michael even further. Michael definitely seemed to think Bill was moving in with them. Ah, well. Not her fault, she thought.

On their first night there, Bill actually stayed for dinner with them. They had ordered pizza and pasta from the restaurant over the road. They enjoyed the evening, but Bill said he better get going as poor Barney was on his own at home. They had decided that Barney would go to her parents during the week and Bill would have him at the house on weekends. Laura planned on taking him for walks as well. Unfortunately, she couldn't have him in the apartment. It wouldn't be fair. He needed some sort of garden. Hopefully it wouldn't be long until Laura had her new house and Barney could come back and join them again.

CHAPTER 32

The weeks passed in a whiz. Life, although somewhat hectic, was enjoyable. Laura and the kids loved the apartment, as it was a novelty from what they were used to. And the views were just so amazing. The sale of the house had gone through and all going well, in two weeks they would have the money from the house in the bank. Laura had riskily put a deposit on a house between Clontarf and Portmarnock.

It was exactly what she had been looking for. It had three big bedrooms, an office, a large kitchen and a sitting room. The views from the floor to ceiling windows were beautiful. Similar to Sharon's place in Gibraltar, it had a little fence at the bottom of the garden, which led to a path down to the beach. It had set Laura back a bit more than she had budgeted for, but she didn't care. She would certainly have to keep working as although she would be able to buy it outright, with the sale of the house in Clontarf and other assets split between her and Bill, she would not have much change left over for bills and everyday life.

The only downside to it was it was not in a town. It was between towns. Although there were still a couple of shops and restaurants nearby within walking distance, she would have to get used to being out of town rather than in it. But she could live with that.

And the public transport was great so the kids would manage. Bill, likewise, was keen to get a house sorted, and had also put a deposit on a house in Portmarnock. Laura had gone to see it with him and the kids. It was a three-bedroom bungalow with a small garden. It wasn't right on the beach, but about a five-minute walk away.

You could still see the ocean from the front windows. It was an older house than Laura had bought, but it was quite modern inside. Laura thought it was quite cozy too. Ben had already picked his bedroom out in both houses. So, Laura and Bill were crossing their fingers that everything would go alright with the sale. Or they could both lose a lot of money on deposits.

Thankfully three weeks later, the deal was done and dusted. And both Laura and Bill followed swiftly through with their plans to get their own houses purchased. As they would both be cash deals, they would be able to move in much quicker. It was usually the mortgage that held things up. So, Laura was told that she would be able to move in about three weeks' time after she had all the papers signed. Laura could live with that. She went out for lunch that day with Sandra and Barry to celebrate.

'We should have a few drinks later Laura, what do you think? We haven't had a night out since our Christmas party and that was nearly two months ago.' Laura thought about it. The kids were staying with Bill tonight. Maybe she would, sure, why not.

'Yes, actually, why don't we. See if any of the lads want to join us. It's Thursday, nearly the weekend, so we might have a few thirsty fellows,' laughed Laura.

Later that evening, Laura was really enjoying herself. She felt a great relief that her life was finally going in the right direction. She was doing well at work and the venue was progressing on time. It was due to open mid/end of July and was all on schedule thanks to her close eye and attention to detail. Selling the house in Clontarf had been the right move. It felt like a massive weight off her shoulders. It had too many memories. The drink was going to Laura's head a bit as she hadn't eaten much that day. She started doing impressions of Michael and had all her colleagues laughing their heads off.

She was in the middle of doing a Michael when he was angry when the circle around her went quiet, and a couple of the men sniggered into their pints. Laura knew before she looked around that he was standing there.

'Having fun Laura?' he said quietly, making it difficult to see if he was annoyed or not. Laura was mortified.

'Sorry Michael, we were only having a laugh, I didn't mean any harm,' she stuttered. Thankfully, Michael started laughing out loud, and it seemed everyone else had also been holding their breath as loud sighs were heard all round and then they were all laughing. Michael stayed, had a few drinks with them and seemed in good spirits.

He cornered Laura on her own at one stage and Laura was terrified he was going to sack her. Before he even said anything Laura spoke.

'Michael, I am so sorry, you have been so good to me and I... ' Michael interrupted her.

'Stop it Laura, you were only having a laugh. You might be surprised, but I actually have a sense of humour, you know.' He smiled at her. He looked a bit anxious.

'Laura, look, I've been meaning to say this to you for a while. But it's been a bit awkward. About Gibraltar, I'm sorry the way I treated you when we got back. But I was a bit miffed that you walked out on me,' he told a flabbergasted Laura. Whatever she expected him to say, it wasn't this.

'Michael, I'm sorry, I just didn't know what to say,' started Laura.

'No, it's OK, you're married, I understand. I acted like a spoilt brat. But I just wanted to clear the air between us. I just want you to know though, I still don't regret that night,' and he looked at her meaningfully. He carried on.

'But you're with Bill and I'm with Ellie, so, friends?' He smiled at her, holding out his hand. Laura was speechless. She was trying to digest what he was saying. Did he mean that he actually had liked her? That he hadn't just used her? Why didn't he tell her? But then he thought she was happily married.

Laura shook his hand and smiled .

'Friends,' as warmly as she could. She wanted to tell him that she and Bill weren't together anymore but then he had said he was with Ellie now, so Laura didn't want to look stupid. Oh god, why did this have to happen this way. Miscommunications, that's all it was. And men being pig-headed. Why did she just leave that night? She should have left a note, or even texted him. He was hurt that she hadn't. And thought she wasn't interested. Laura decided not to say anything tonight. She would need to think about this and maybe talk to him tomorrow or Monday. Yes, Monday sounded better. Give her the weekend to think and work it out. Sure, what could happen in one weekend? She did feel very strongly for him.

She was able to lock it down when she had to, and not think about it. But there was no point in lying to herself. She wanted to be with Michael. She wanted to relive that night in Gibraltar once again. Well, maybe sober this time. But she hadn't wanted someone like this since she first met Bill. Maybe they could actually work it out after all.

Laura went for many walks that weekend. She also spoke to Sharon at length, filling her in on what happened. Sharon said she felt all along that Michael had feelings for her and told her to go and have a chat with him. And tell him the truth.

'I mean for fuck sake,' Sharon had scolded her. 'You let him think you are still with Bill!' Sharon was only telling Laura what she already knew. She had handled the whole thing badly. But it had been a difficult time in her life. Her future was clearer now, and she wanted Michael to be part of it. Michael usually was in the office first thing Monday mornings. She would take the bull by the horns and tackle him then.

Only when Laura arrived Monday there was no sign of Michael. She hid her disappointment and got on with her morning's work. At

11am she had to nip out to the bank to make lodgments for the business and it was an hour before she was back. She saw Michael's jeep and her heart hammered. When she walked into the office a group had assembled outside his office. They were holding glasses of champagne, yet it was a Monday and only 12 o'clock in the day.

'What's this?' said Laura nervously. 'What are we celebrating?' although Laura had a horrible feeling she knew what was coming. The realisation hit her out of nowhere. That was probably why he wanted to clear the air. Talk to her beforehand…

'Oh Laura, Guess what, our Boss here had just gone and popped the question to the lovely Ellie,' Sandra squealed. Laura's heart fell like a heavy boulder. Although she felt it coming, to hear it made her feel sick. She was too late. She wondered if he had hoped she would say something Thursday night. About them. But she would never know now. It was too late. And she wasn't going to ruin this for him. She managed to plaster a smile on her face and took the glass that Sandra handed to her. 'Congratulations Michael, I hope you'll both be very happy/' She raised her glass in his direction and everyone gave a cheer. She did not imagine, however, the look he gave her, and the fact he had held her eye a lot longer than necessary.

When she got home that evening, she phoned Sharon. But she got only her voicemail. She'd forgotten that Sharon had a job interview today for a role with a company only a five-minute walk away. The company also had an on-site crèche, which meant Sharon would be sorted with Sophia. It was her second interview with them and Sharon told her the package was very attractive. She had got to the last round of interviews for a different role which also seemed like an excellent position only few weeks ago, but unfortunately, she had not got it. Sharon had been so disappointed. But Laura assured her that something else would come along. Laura was right, as here she was at her second interview for an even better job. She just hoped Sharon got this one, or her friend would be so disappointed once again.

Although Sharon loved Gibraltar and was glad they had moved, she said it could be lonely at times. She was looking forward to going back to work and setting a routine for herself and the family. They were due home in four weeks for the birthday of Rob's sister, Chloe.

Sharon wanted Laura to go to it, but Laura wasn't sure. She had only met Chloe once and although she seemed very nice, Laura didn't want to be intruding, especially as the family would all want to spend time with Rob, Sharon and the baby.

Her phone suddenly rang in her hand and gave her a fright. It was Sharon.

'Hey, hun , how did the interview go?' Laura enquired. Sharon sounded so excited .

'Laura, how are you? Oh, it went great, really well. I so, *so* want this job, Laura. It would be just perfect. The good news is there is no third interview. They are just going to make their decision now. It's down to three people; one of them me. So, fingers crossed!' she squealed. Laura hated when her friend got this worked up about something that hadn't happened yet. Sharon had phoned her after the third interview with the last place sounding exactly the same and saying the exact same things. Please god she has got this one.

Laura hated to think of her friend being disappointed when she wasn't there to comfort her.

'I have my fingers crossed for you, hun,' she told Sharon. Then Sharon squealed again.

'Oh my god, how did it go? Did you declare your undying love for each other?' Laura smiled sadly to herself.

'No, well I didn't. Michael did alright, but not for me unfortunately. He announced this morning that he and Ellie had gotten engaged at the weekend.' Sharon was silent at the other end of the phone. What a mess.

'Laura, this is so frustrating. It is only a matter of miscommunication. And now he is going to go and marry someone he doesn't even want. Because he thinks you're taken. Please tell mc you at least told him that you and Bill aren't together?'

Laura sighed.

'No, I didn't. I couldn't really just blurt it out after him announcing his engagement. But look, it doesn't matter now. If it was meant to be, it would. Just leave it, Sharon. I have decided to forget about men for a while. Concentrate on the new house. I'm moving in, in less than three weeks. I cannot wait. So that will occupy me. I'm so looking forward to you seeing it. And you definitely have to stay with me, even for one night?' Sharon told her that she would stay with her on the Sunday night. The party was on the Saturday and they were flying back the Monday, as it was a bank holiday. 'Well let's hope by the time I come over you have set Michael straight, otherwise I might have to intervene! Again!' Sharon laughed and hung up the phone.

CHAPTER 33

Laura moved into her house with little hassle or problems. Ben and Jess were on hand to help, along with some of the guys on the site. Michael allowed her to use some of them, although he couldn't understand why Bill wasn't around to help more. Michael felt under a lot of pressure lately. They were only a few months away from opening and there was still so much to do. Also, Ellie kept pestering him about the wedding, and what month they should go for, and if he wanted a church wedding or a garden wedding.

He loved Ellie, as a person. She was beautiful, kind and fun to be with. But Michael knew he wasn't in love with her. She had kept hinting about getting married as she was getting on in life. She wanted to start trying for kids right after the wedding. Michael didn't mind so much about more kids, he loved having his own two. A couple more would keep him young. He had proposed to her as he felt if he didn't, she would leave him and meet someone else. Michael didn't really fancy being on his own for the rest of his life. He had been on his own for the past ten years. He had had many brief encounters, but nothing serious. Ellie was the first woman he had a steady relationship with since his marriage. Paloma had been the love of his life. He loved her so much. But she had hurt him badly. He swore he would never give his heart to another woman after that. He didn't want to feel that emotional pain again.

That's why Ellie suited him. He thought about Laura and their night together in Gibraltar. It had been amazing. He had been a little hurt that she had left him so abruptly without so much as a note or a text message. But he really liked Laura. He felt a strong bond with her. But he was also afraid to get too close. She had that same vulnerability that made him fall for his wife. And Michael was staying clear of love. But he thought about Laura a lot. He knew at times he treated her badly, as in the way he spoke to her, but he couldn't help it. He just liked her so damn much. She drove him mad too, with all her ideas and challenging him on everything. She was great at her job; maybe too good.

But Michael was finding it harder and harder to be around her each day. Firstly, he didn't think he and Laura should get together as he knew there was potential for him to get hurt again, and secondly, she was still with her husband Bill. And he wasn't going to break them up. That wouldn't be fair. No, he would just have to stay out of the office more which wouldn't be a bad thing. And once the venue was open, Laura could stay on running the office and his property portfolio, and he would be off on his next project, which would mean he would never really see her. Feeling better, Michael put Laura to the back of his mind.

Laura was settling in nicely. It was now the middle of March and Sharon was due to stay that Sunday. She had gotten the job thankfully and was starting in a week's time.

It was a Friday evening and Sandra and the two new admin girls were going out for drinks later. Laura said she would think about meeting them. She wasn't sure yet. She found it hard to come home from work, and then drive back there again. She'd usually just curl up on the couch if the kids weren't there and read a book, watch TV or look out at the ocean thinking about the future.

She definitely felt more content in her new life. Barney had moved in with them and although it took him a while to settle in to his new surroundings, he seemed happy now. Especially as his evening or morning walks were always on the beach. Her phone beeped with a text message.

'Going to the new cocktail bar. It's not that far from you. Meet you there at 7.' It was now 6, and Laura realised that they would already be in the pub, having gone straight there after work at 5.

They would have a few there, and then probably get a taxi to Tequila Sunrise, which in fairness was only a ten-minute walk up the road. But Laura decided she would drive there. After her last experience with cocktails, she didn't think it was a good idea, not that Michael would be there anyway, but still.

However, when she got there, they already had a cocktail ordered for her. Laura told them she was only having one. But she may as well be talking to the wall. Some of the usual suspects from the site were with the girls. They had a good few drinks on them and started dancing to the music.

Laura just laughed and sat back, enjoying watching them.

'I seem to remember you are fond of the cocktails.' Laura jumped and turned around to see Michael grinning at her. She slapped him playfully.

'This is the one and only for tonight,' she said pointing at her drink.

'We'll see,' he said and went to the bar. Laura was very surprised to see him there. She hadn't realised he was coming. Would she have come if she had known? Just put it out of your mind and stop fretting about it she told herself. Five minutes later a waiter arrived over with about eight or nine cocktails. One for everyone. She looked at the large glass that was handed to her and studied it suspiciously. It was a greeny-blue colour, with different types of fruit on top of the glass. Mmmm... Laura had never heard the name of it before but was told it was top quality.

She groaned, as she knew no number of protests would work. She would just have to leave the car here, and get a taxi back. It tasted surprisingly good. Maybe too good. They had several more cocktails before moving on to a disco bar.

They had to get more than one taxi to take them. Laura would never normally do this, but she was enjoying herself. She even danced with several of the men from the site. When the music slowed down, Michael grabbed her arms and pulled her to him.

'Come on,' he said, 'Just the one.' She danced with him fully aware of every breath he was taking, and she was sure he could feel the pounding of her heart. Their faces were very close together and Michael looked down into her eyes.

'Let's get out of here,' and with that, he dragged Laura out the back door, where the others were too drunk to notice, or so she hoped anyway.

The next morning Laura woke up not knowing where she was. She looked around the familiar bedroom and realised that she was back in the apartment at work. She looked to her side and saw Michael was gone. Had he left entirely? Or was he up in the kitchen? Laura quickly dressed and went up to check if he was there. But there was no sign of him. And no note. Now she knew how he felt in Gibraltar when she had left without so much as a goodbye. It wasn't nice. Laura walked over to the window and opened it wide.

She sat down letting the fresh air blow the cobwebs away. Laura tried to remember their antics the night before. But to be honest, she couldn't really recall much. She had had way too much to drink. Oh god. What had she done? It had happened again. They had come back here and had wild romping sessions! Oh god. Putting her head in her hands, her feet resting on another chair, Laura tried to remember more. She didn't think there had been much conversation between them. Just a lot of groping and drunken sex. She did remember Michael helping her into a taxi and giving the driver instructions to the apartment. Then they were inside tearing each other's clothes off.

They had gone straight to the bedroom. And then she had woken up. They hadn't actually even had a conversation. How strange.

Suddenly Laura felt used. At least in Gibraltar they had spent the evening together having dinner and drinks. But now she felt like a quick lay. She started to get angry. As soon as this launch was out of the way, Laura was changing jobs. Enough was enough. She was tired of being taken for a mug. If he liked her, all he had to do was tell her. Rather than just sleep with her. No. That was it. Men. Laura could do without them.

'You two are as bad as each other,' Sharon exclaimed when Laura filled her in.

'First you walk out on him, and then he walks out on you. The absolute worst is the fact that you slept with him again and DIDN'T tell him that you and Bill were separated!!! Come on Laura. Why the hell not?' Sharon demanded angrily.

Laura didn't know what to say. She was tired. She had told Sharon several times that she hadn't a chance to tell him. That they didn't even have a conversation. Laura thought that she had probably intended to tell him the next morning, but alas, he had done a disappearing act. Sharon looked at Laura and then felt guilty.

'I'm sorry, hun. I just think the two of you would be great together. And the two of you are being so stubborn.' Laura didn't agree with Sharon.

As Michael was still engaged to the lovely Ellie. Surely if he was interested in Laura, he would have called things off by now, whether she was with Bill or not. You wouldn't marry someone when you liked someone else, would you?

Bill was nervous as hell. His new home wasn't ready as quickly as Laura's had been so he had been staying in a B&B until he could finally move in. He hoped to be in within the month. He had asked Shirley from the Cozy Corner out for a drink, obviously not in the same pub. But one just up the road. He liked Shirley and they had developed a close friendship over the last year. Bill hadn't been sure whether he should run it by Laura first, but then she wasn't his mother.

They were separated now and lived separate lives. Anyway, he didn't think Laura would mind, at least he hoped not.

Shirley arrived on time, and Bill bought them both a drink. After his initial first few minutes of nervousness, Shirley put him at ease. Bill relaxed then and they enjoyed their few drinks together. He did not see Michael walk in and look over at him. Bill was too busy chatting to Shirley.

Michael had been fuming with himself. He did it again. Slept with Laura and cheated on Ellie. What was he doing? And what was Laura doing? She was still with Bill. It would be different if Laura was single, he might approach his future differently, but they were after buying a new house together. He could understand one slip-up, but twice. And likewise, with him. Maybe he shouldn't marry Ellie. It wasn't fair on her. With or without Laura, he shouldn't be marrying someone he was capable of cheating on.

Ellie deserved better. He had fully intended on breaking up with her the next day after sleeping with Laura with nothing else in mind only that he didn't love Ellie enough to marry her. But when he got back to the house they were renting, she had a surprise for him. Both his daughters were sitting in the garden with a large buffet lunch spread out in front of them. Ellie's family were also there, along with Michael's own parents and siblings.

'I thought I would surprise you. We never did get to have a proper engagement party, so I thought I would plan a surprise one for you,' Ellie told him in front of everyone. Michael was delighted to see his daughters and his family.

He didn't get to see enough of them. But his heart was heavy and he felt trapped. How could he break up with her now? He'd have to try and put the wedding off a bit further. Michael had refused to set a date until the launch of the venue had taken place, as he used the excuse of being too busy. But Michael knew once that came and went, he would be under pressure. Still, he had a few months. He would just have to put up with it until then.

Now, on entering the pub, and seeing Bill with another woman, he didn't know what to think. At first, he was angry and felt protective of Laura. But then he thought himself a hypocrite, as that was what both he and Laura had done. Except he didn't know if Bill had slept with the woman, not like he had with Bill's wife. Michael's feelings turned to guilt as he hurried further inside the bar. He had stopped off for a drink on the way home from work. But he didn't want Bill to see him.

He wondered idly if Bill and Laura had an open relationship. I mean, here was Bill, in a local enough pub, having a cozy drink with another woman. It was either perfectly innocent, or else Bill had a lot of balls. Ah, well, it was none of his business. He wasn't going to get involved; he had enough problems of his own to worry about.

CHAPTER 34

Laura was so busy she didn't have time to go to the bathroom. With the launch scheduled for mid-July, a Friday, she had just three weeks to ensure everything was finished. And she was worried. The lounge area and bar didn't look half-ready, and it had taken them nearly six months to get done what they had. The kitchen still had a long way to go, and they still needed it to be passed by health and safety. Only two of the ten rooms that were being developed even resembled bedrooms. She also had to get the B&B officials to approve them as an operator. She and Michael had been civil with each other since their night together.

They had both recognised that the work on the venue needed to take priority and so they both threw themselves into getting things signed off and done. Michael had to calm Laura down only last week. He told her he had been in this situation many times. That buildings always look like they won't be finished in the weeks prior to opening. It was only ever in days before the opening that things began to take shape.

Laura wasn't so sure she believed that, and certainly didn't share his confidence. Plus, it didn't help that the lovely Ellie kept dropping by and distracting all the workers. It drove Laura mad. Laura was hardly ever in the office these days. She was always on site, inside or out, ordering someone to do something. But as much of a headache as it was, she still loved it. Her phone shrilled and it was Sandra.

'Laura, do you know when the wash basins are arriving?' she asked. Laura thought for a minute.

'Yes, I think they are due in this week,' she said.

'Are you sure? Sandra said. 'Because I have in my diary that they should have been here last Wednesday?'

Mmmm… thought Laura, Sandra was rarely wrong.

'Gimme two minutes and I'll come back upstairs,' and she clicked off. Laura went into her office and sat down. Sandra brought her in a cup of tea.

'Here, looks like you could do with this. You don't look so good,' she said.

'Thanks for the compliment,' Laura laughed. But she knew what Sandra meant. Laura had not been well a few weeks back. She had needed to take a few days off work.

She hadn't really fully recovered, but as there was so much to do, she came back to work anyway.

'You're doing too much Laura. Slow down. We'll have the place looking tops for the opening. I can assure you!' Sandra promised her.

'I know Sandra. Maybe I'll go home early. I'm feeling a bit ropey.

'Yes, do that, Sandra said, 'and get some sleep. You'll feel much better then.' Laura had been putting in eight-hour days instead of five. Sometimes it could be ten or eleven, depending on what had to be done.

As she made her way to the car, she saw Michael in the distance. She raised her hand to wave at him, but the sudden movement made her head spin. Laura put her hand up to her head and felt her legs give way. Then everything went blank.

When Laura woke up, she was once again back in a hospital bed with Bill sitting beside her.

'Welcome back. How are you feeling?' he asked when she started to move. Laura was confused. Last thing she remembered seeing was Michael. She looked around the room.

'How did I get here?' she asked.

'Michael rushed you here. He waited till the doctors checked you out. Once he knew you were OK, and that it was because you've probably been just overdoing it, he called me. He left about ten minutes ago. Nice chap that fellow.' Laura thought that was strange. Why would he run out on her like that? And not wait until she had at least woken up?

But then he still thought she and Bill were together. Oh, god. She would have to tell him soon. For convenience sake if anything.

'How are you feeling?' Bill repeated. Laura felt very tired. And worn out. She was also hooked up to a drip.

'I'm OK. Thanks for coming Bill. You didn't have to.' Laura thanked him. Of course he was going to come, Bill thought to himself. They might not be together anymore, but he still cared for her.

Bill had planned to talk to Laura that weekend about his progressing relationship with Shirley. They were seeing each other regularly now and Bill really liked her. They got on very well and made each other laugh. It was refreshing after all the tension and stress he had been through. But then he better put off saying anything about it for another week or two. Let her recover first. Bill stayed for another hour and then headed back to the office. He had told her that Michael said the doctors were going to keep her in overnight but would most likely let her out tomorrow. Bill had not spoken to the doctors himself directly, although he had tried. But there were none around. Not long after Bill left, the nurse came in to check on her.

'Ah, how's the patient. Are you feeling better?' she asked. Laura smiled and said she was.

And what the nurse said next left her in total shock.

'You need to look after yourself, especially now there are two of you,' she laughed. Laura thought she misheard her.

'What do you mean, 'two of you'?' Laura asked, her voice shaking and her heart hammering.

'Oh,' said the nurse. She sat in the chair beside Laura and took her hand.

'Well, I don't know if it's what you were hoping for, or not, but you're ten weeks pregnant.' Laura nearly passed out again.

'OK, obviously this has come as a shock. That explains why you were working so hard. You didn't realise you were pregnant.'

A hundred thoughts went through Laura's head. Pregnant. She was thirty-nine. Nearly forty. Oh, good god. It was Michael's. She hadn't slept with Bill in about six months, maybe more. She couldn't think straight. Did Michael know? Did the doctors tell him? She wondered to herself. No, they wouldn't have. Patient confidentiality and all that. She dropped herself heavily back down on the bed, putting a hand to her forehead. Oh, Good god - what was she going to do?

A week later, after getting plenty of rest, Laura went back to work. Michael and everyone in the office were very good to her. They seemed to have gotten a lot of the work done that past week, which helped Laura relax a bit. She had decided that she would take each day as it came. Yes, she was a bit on the older side to be having a baby, with Jess and Ben near grown up, but such was life. Laura believed everything happened for a reason, and although she was dreading telling the kids and especially Bill, who no doubt would be shocked, she had begun to feel a little bit excited about it. She couldn't help herself. After all, Jess would be gone to Uni next year and Ben didn't have long left at school.

Laura had no man to come home to each day, to talk about what had happened at work, or to watch the latest box set series with. The baby would fill that gap. She didn't need a man. Though when it came to Michael, she didn't know what to do. Should she tell him? But then he was due to get married soon. Laura would ruin it all for him and Ellie. She couldn't imagine Ellie would forgive him. She could pretend to Michael that it was Bill's baby. But Laura wasn't stupid, she knew he would find out sooner or later that she and Bill had separated months ago. Laura decided to put it to the back of her mind for now.

She would deal with that after the launch, which was in two weeks' time. Although she still had a lot of work to do, she wouldn't push herself too much. She didn't want to end up back in hospital. Sharon was coming over for the launch and she and Rob were staying with her. Chloe was taking the baby for the night. Laura wanted to tell Sharon her news so badly, but she said she would wait until she saw her. Laura couldn't help laughing to herself. It was a mad world.

Michael didn't know what to do.

He knew Laura was pregnant. The doctor had assumed Michael was her husband when he brought her in. After being in the waiting room for half an hour, the doctor came out and told him that Laura would be fine, that she was just overdoing it. And that she really should take it easier considering her condition. The doctor told him he had hooked Laura up to a drip to ensure she had enough fluid for the baby and that they would most likely release her the next day. And with that, the doctor smiled and walked off having no idea the bombshell he had just dropped on Michael.

At first, he thought it could be his. But then he realised that he had slept with Laura nearly three months ago. And she probably was only a few weeks' pregnant. Otherwise, she wouldn't have been doing so much at work.

Michael couldn't help but feeling a tiny bit disappointed that it wasn't his baby. He shocked himself. Here he was due to get married in the next year, and he was hoping the woman he had a one-night stand with a few months back was carrying his baby. Right, enough was enough. Michael knew he had to do one thing now, no matter. He couldn't marry Ellie. It wasn't fair. He knew he had no future with Laura, not now with she and Bill expecting a baby. But he couldn't live a lie either. He would have to break it off. And soon. There was something else bothering Michael. A lot. He had seen Bill several more times with that same woman, and he knew without a doubt that they were having an affair. He had seen them kissing in a restaurant just last week when he walked by. Should he tell Laura? Or should he confront Bill? He had to do something. He couldn't let that scoundrel get away with this, not when his wife was pregnant. Michael sighed. He really didn't need this right now.

The day after Laura had been hospitalised, Michael broke the news to Ellie that he wanted to call off the engagement. And the relationship. She did not take it well, nor did he expect her too. He was a coward. Leading her on all this time, when deep down he had strong feelings for someone else. He didn't tell Ellie this. He just told her that he didn't want to get married again. Or to start another family, which was a lie, but Michael couldn't think of what else to say. Ellie had begged him not to break up with her, that she would settle for them just being a couple. She could live without kids and a family. But Michael said No. He wasn't going to stop her having a family, it wasn't fair. She needed to move on and eventually she would find another bloke, more worthy of her than Michael. And Michael meant it. Ellie was great. She was beautiful, kind. Loving. Extremely thoughtful. But Michael just didn't feel what he should in order to marry her. He had been playing it safe. Which wasn't fair. He had moved out straight away and into the apartment at the venue.

Luckily, he hadn't rented it out yet; he had wanted to keep it free until the business was up and running. He would have to let his own family know, including his daughters. They were very fond of Ellie. She had accompanied him to Spain several times to see his other daughter Isabella. Why does everything have to happen at the one time, he thought to himself.

With her first week back in work over with, Laura was flaking out on the couch with Barney tucked up beside her. Bill was on his way over which was strange. He called and asked if he could drop by for a short visit to check how she was doing, but Laura felt there was more to it. Jess and Ben were gone to the cinema with Laura's dad. When Bill arrived, he seemed nervous. He kept rambling on about her health, the weather, work. He obviously had something he wanted to say that he wasn't comfortable with.

At first Laura found it amusing, but then she began to lose patience.

'Right enough Bill, just spit it out,' she said to him. Bill looked taken aback and was about to protest, but then he knew there was no point. Laura knew him too well.

'OK, Laura. Sorry. I'm just a bit nervous. It's just that... mmm... I had been going to the Cozy Corner pub a lot in the past year and I built up a friendship...' He didn't get any further. Laura decided to relieve him of his agony.

'It's OK Bill, I know you're dating Shirley, the owner. We do live in a small enough area you know! I'm happy for you, honestly. Although I did wonder if you were ever going to tell me,' Laura laughed. She had heard about Bill being out and about with another woman and eventually found out it was Shirley.

Laura didn't mind. She was surprised to find that she was genuinely happy for him which told her they had made the right decision. The feelings they had once just weren't there anymore. And thankfully she liked Shirley. Laura was just glad it wasn't that bitch, Johnson. That, she didn't think she could handle. Laura wondered should she tell Bill about the pregnancy?? But then she dismissed the idea. She couldn't tell him yet. She still hadn't worked out what she was going to tell Michael. Plus, she didn't think Bill would take it as well as she did about his new relationship.

The relief on Bill's face was obvious.

'Ah Laura, why did you put me through that when you knew well what was I was trying to tell you? Or why haven't you said anything before?' he demanded, but he was smiling.

'Bill, we are separated, and let's face it, divorce is imminent. What you do is your business. As long as the kids are happy and you are not doing anything to upset them, then what you do now is your business. But I do understand you coming to me and I appreciate you respecting me enough to tell me yourself. But really, I wish you and Shirley all the best. At least you'll have free beer on tap from now on!' Laura smiled and winked at him.

CHAPTER 35

It was the week of the opening and as much as Laura was trying to take it easy, she was still running around like a mad woman. She wasn't showing yet, thankfully, so no one knew she was pregnant. She still hadn't told Sharon who was arriving tomorrow evening, the night before the launch party, but was staying with Rob's family. She would see Laura at the opening. All the important things were finished and ready. It was just now a matter of getting everything sorted for the party. Invites, food, drink, entertainment, the list went on.

The opening was scheduled for 5pm that Friday. It would tie in nicely with people finishing up work for the weekend and after all, they hoped to draw a lot of this crowd as regulars.

All her friends and family were coming. Jess, Ben, her Mam and Dad, even Shane and Emma were flying in for it. Which made her even more nervous. Laura knew once she got the first three hours over with at the party, she would be happy. Once 8pm came she intended to have a well-deserved glass of champagne. (Just one, a small one). She wondered what her parents would think when they realised they were going to become grandparents again. She laughed at the thought. They would take it in their stride like they did with everything and give her their full support. The fact she wouldn't see Sharon before the opening meant Laura wasn't sure when she would get the chance to speak with her privately. She would have to try and nab her for a minute at some stage.

But maybe at the party was not the best time to tell her. Ah, she would see what way it went. She wasn't too worried about it. If she knew her friend at all, she knew Sharon would be delighted, although no doubt somewhat amused.

Bill had phoned her earlier to see if she would mind if he brought Shirley to the party. Laura told him not to be silly. Didn't the invite she sent him have Shirley's name on it? Bill said he just wanted to be sure. Laura hadn't thought about her parents coming across Bill at the party. After all, they weren't as forgiving as her. They wouldn't be too happy with him having another woman in tow. Laura would have to talk to them beforehand. She felt lucky that she wasn't in love with Bill anymore. It meant that she genuinely wasn't hurt that he was with someone else. It was great that they were remaining such good friends. Laura patted her stomach and sincerely hoped their friendship would last.

Everything was in place and there was nothing more Laura or the team could do. She nipped up to one of the bedrooms that all the staff were using as a dressing room. Most people had dressed by now so thankfully there were was no one in the room when Laura got there. She had chosen a black knee length dress with a large gold shawl and gold sandals. The dress had a flowy style, just so Laura could be sure no one would see the tiny bump beginning to show. She had a quick shower and blow-dried her hair, using a styler to add some curls. She had planned on going to the hairdressers to get it done that morning but as usual, she didn't have time.

Once she had her dress, make up and jewelry on, she looked at herself in the mirror. Not bad, she thought. She was pleased with her appearance. She had made sure to wear her new shoes regularly at home over the past couple of weeks so she could break them in. The last thing she wanted was her feet killing her while she ran around checking everything was running smoothly.

And she was glad that they seemed to be now comfortable to walk in. Laura made her way down to the restaurant where the main event would begin. After some canapés and drinks, they would all head into the bar for the main entertainment. Laura bumped into several staff on the way, stopping to go through some final things each time. She was happy that they were all sticking to the running schedule she had prepared for everyone.

Laura was coming down the stairs and she raised her head to see Michael staring up at her. He gave her a shy smile. She descended the stairs and walked over to him to have a quick chat.

'Well, nothing more can be done. It's now or never!' She smiled at him. Michael kept looking at her and then spoke.

'You look amazing Laura.' She was taken aback by the change of topic, and giving him a head-to-toe appraisal said, 'And you scrub up well yourself. That's a top dollar suit,' she laughed. Michael continued.

'Honestly though, Laura, before the madness starts, I just want to thank you. For all you have done. This wouldn't be happening if it wasn't for you. OK. OK. It would. But not to this extravagance. You certainly know what you're doing. And I would have been lost without you the past year. You have proved an irreplaceable employee. I don't know what I'll do when… or, I mean, *if* you leave.' Laura was a bit stunned with the compliments flowing from Michael. But also, by the last statement.

Did he think she was leaving? She had no plans to. Yes, she would be going on maternity leave alright, but that wouldn't be for another five or six months. Laura didn't manage to reply as they were interrupted by the bar manager, wanting a decision on something. Michael winked at her and made his way to the bar with the manager. Men! thought Laura.

The event was going smoothly. All Laura's family and friends had arrived, including Bill and a somewhat nervous Shirley. Laura had welcomed Shirley and took her aside for a word. She told her that she was happy for her and Bill, and that Laura genuinely hoped their relationship worked out. Shirley seemed delighted with her words, and had relaxed visibly. Gabby, Carol and Becky had also arrived. Laura was glad. She felt guilty that she had spent such little time with them over the past year. But life events had taken over. Maybe now, once the launch was over, they could start meeting up again regularly. Laura did miss their company and the laughs they had. Laura's concerns that people wouldn't show up, or would come late, proved to be unfounded. By 5.30pm the place was heaving. People mingled, complimented the food and the interior décor of the restaurant. Before they had moved into the bar area, Michael had made a lovely speech, and had specifically mentioned Laura and how hard she had worked.

Sharon had caught her eye at the time and gave her a cheeky wink. God, thought Laura, if she only knew. The music started, and after speaking to all the people she needed to, she made her way over to her family. Sharon and Rob were with them. Ben was showing her father something on his phone and Sharon was chatting to her mother and Shane.

Rob and Jess were laughing about something, and everyone seemed to be enjoying themselves. Laura sat back and checked her watch. 7.45pm. Ah, what's fifteen minutes she thought? And with that she picked up a glass of champagne and made her way outside for some fresh air.

Unfortunately, things weren't going all well for Michael. Although he was happy with the event and how it was going, he was absolutely fuming. He couldn't believe Bill had the cheek to bring his mistress with him. Well, enough was enough. No more.

Michael had seen Bill break away to go to what he could only assume was the bathroom. Michael followed him. Before Bill got to the bathroom door, Michael grabbed him by the arm and pulled him into a quiet corner. Bill looked up, shocked at Michael's aggressiveness.

'What the… ' he started.

'Shut up. And listen to me. You are going to tell Laura. This has been going on long enough. You're making a fool out of her. It was bad enough as it was, but then to think you actually brought your bit on the side here, to the opening. I can't believe your cheek,' Michael fumed at him. Bill's face took a look of confusion, and he then relaxed a bit, realising Michael's mistake.

'Let go of me Michael. And I suggest you get your facts straight before going around firing accusations at people. I have the utmost respect for Laura. She knows about Shirley. Sure, she sent us both the invite,' Bill told him, angry at having to explain himself.

If Bill had been confused, then Michael was much worse.

'Invited you both. What are you taking about? Do you two have some type of open relationship? You just bought a new house together,' Michael replied, shakily. Bill didn't know what to say. Laura hadn't obviously told Michael about her private business, which was fine. And Bill wasn't going to start discussing her business with him either. But at the same time, he didn't want Michael thinking he was a total scumbag.

'Look Michael, I don't know what Laura has told you, or not told you. But she and I separated after Christmas. In fact, we really separated over a year ago as our relationship never recovered. Not that that's your business. But Laura bought that house on her own, as I bought a new house of my own too. Laura is happy for Shirley and me; if she wasn't, I never would have brought her here. Now, if you'll excuse me. I have to go to the bathroom.' And Bill stormed off. Michael's legs felt shaky, and he made his way over to a window-seat. He sat down. What the hell?

But they moved into his apartment after Christmas?? He had seen Bill there himself. But maybe he had just been helping Laura move. Was it true? But they seemed on such good terms, it was all so strange. Why hadn't she told him? Just then, a new realisation dawned on Michael. The baby.

It had to be his. Unless Laura had slept with someone else, but knowing her as he did, he doubted that very much. He suddenly felt a rush of excitement. Did this mean they could be together? Did Laura want to be with him? But no, she mustn't. She hadn't even told him about Bill, or the baby.

If she wanted them to get together, surely, she would have told him. As he looked out the window, he saw her. She was standing under a streetlight, looking out over the harbour at the late evening sky. She had her shawl pulled down around her arms and he could see a slight shiver run through her. Suddenly he had to get to her. To speak to her. He felt a massive pull towards toward her, and began to make his way outside.

Laura was beginning to feel the cold. She pulled the shawl tighter around her shoulders. It was so calm and peaceful. Laura felt happy. She knew things weren't perfect, but she was content enough. And was really looking forward to her new baby. Laura had a good support network; she would manage on her own. Suddenly a voice from behind startled her, and she turned around.

'Should you be drinking that?' Michael was saying as he walked towards her. He looked relaxed. Really relaxed and relieved. Laura laughed.

'Ha. I have to say, you look like a man with the weight of the world off your shoulders. You must be delighted it's all over and went without a hitch!' She was teasing him. But Michael only smiled at her. Suddenly it hit Laura what he had said to her. Should she be drinking that? What? Did he know? But how?

'Laura,' he said softly as he approached her. 'Why didn't you tell me it was mine?' Laura didn't know what to say. How did he even know?

'What. How do you... ' she started, but Michael interrupted her.

'At the hospital, the doctors mistook me for your husband. He scolded me for letting you do so much, given your condition!'. Despite herself Laura laughed. She could imagine poor Michael's faces when the doctor said that to him.

And she was glad it was out in the open now. And she could try and deal with it.

'Ah Michael, I'm sorry. It's just you are with Ellie and getting married. I didn't want to break that up. Look, I am not going to hold you to anything. If you don't want to be… '

Michael took her hands and bent down to silence her with a kiss. Although Laura was enjoying the kiss, it still wasn't right. Laura broke off the embrace. 'Michael, Ellie… ' Again, he silenced her.

He took her hand and they started a slow walk further along towards the pier. After five minutes of silence, both lost in thought, a hundred questions going through each one's head, Michael broke it by saying, 'Laura, the day you were hospitalised I realised how much I loved you. I felt disappointment when I thought the baby was Bill's. I wanted it to be mine. That made me wake up and realise I couldn't marry Ellie. It wouldn't be fair. Don't get me wrong, she's a great girl. And I am very fond of her. But there was always something missing. And that day at the hospital, I realised what it was. Laura, she wasn't you.'

He stopped and looked at her. He then continued.

'I broke up with her the next day, and figured that once the launch was over, I would busy myself with new projects and wouldn't have to see you anymore. I convinced myself I could forget you once I wasn't seeing you every day. But I don't think that would have worked.'

Laura couldn't believe it. She felt ecstatic. He really loved her. And he wanted this baby as much as she did. Laura had wondered earlier where Ellie was.

She hadn't seen her and thought it was strange for her not to be at the opening. Well, now she knew.

'Look,' Michael continued, pointing across the harbour at the calm waters. 'There is something beautiful about the ocean, don't you think?' and then took Laura by total surprise.

'Laura, I know you are not even divorced yet, and that this is very, very soon. But once all that is sorted out, down the road a bit, when our little one is running around trying to catch butterflies and doing other crazy things, would you do the honour of becoming my wife?'

Laura didn't know what made the tears flow. Had it been his marriage proposal, the fact she was pregnant, or had it been his reference to their child catching butterflies? She didn't know, and she didn't care. Laura hadn't been this happy in a long, long time.

'Yes Michael, I will.' And as her mother had told her many times, in order to survive life, you needed to have faith and hope. And lots of it. And Laura quoted her mother's favourite saying to herself, which she had heard so much in the last year.

'It will be alright in the end. If it's not alright, it's not the end.'

The End.

Author

Gráinne Farrell is a Marketing Consultant with nearly twenty years' experience in the Marketing Industry. She has a diverse portfolio at global and national level including gaming, software, energy, insurance & recycling.

Gráinne also lectures in Digital Marketing at City Colleges Dublin. In 2020, she wrote her first novel "The Ultimate Betrayal" which was released in June 2021. Prior to this, she wrote a non-fiction business book called "Power Marketing", and has recently completed her latest novel, which is also in the Women's Fiction genre and has yet to be released. You can find out more at www.grainnefarrellbooks.com.

www.grainnefarrellbooks.com

.

Printed in Great Britain
by Amazon

69362857R00293